Stiff Lizard

A Spy Shop Mystery

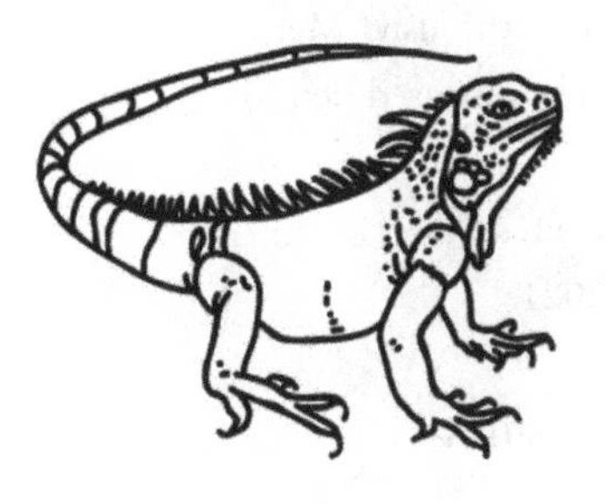

Lisa Haneberg

This is a work of fiction. All the names and characters are either invented or used fictitiously. Many of the restaurants mentioned in the book are real but used fictitiously.

Printed in the United States of America
First Printing, 2021

ISBN 978-0-9987801-8-4

Written Pursuits Publishing
838 High Street #269
Lexington, KY 40502
www.writtenpursuits.com

Cover design by Stuart Bache, Books Covered, Ltd.
Book design by Polgarus Studio
Editing by Jim Spivey and Jennifer Barricklow

For Monica

Stiff Lizard

"Dealing with people is probably the biggest problem you face." Dale Carnegie, *How to Win Friends and Influence People*

"Rogue rats, predatory jellyfish, suffocating super-weeds, wild boar, snake-head fish wriggling across the land – alien species are taking over. Nature's vagabonds, ruffians, and carpetbaggers are headed for an ecosystem near you." Fred Pearce, *The New Wild*

Chapter 1

Day 1, Wednesday, February 28
10:00 a.m.

My stomach tensed as fifteen retirees aimed tasers at me. We'd had a few trigger-happy participants last month, and I'd gotten zapped four times—three more than intended. We used a rubber dummy named Celeste to help customers improve taser and pepper spray accuracy but started each class by allowing one lucky participant to discharge their weapon at me.

Had you been there, you might've thought I was off-my-rocker crazy for letting drugged-up seniors with twitchy muscle control point loaded weapons at me, but hear me out. I'd asked for this mistreatment so I could practice fighting through the weapons' effects. I was a fast runner and could usually outmaneuver opponents using parkour or common sense, but bad guys sometimes lucked out and managed to spray or buzz me while in full stride or mid-vault.

How do you think cops train? They get tased and sprayed, and then have to complete an obstacle course of defensive and offensive tasks. I underwent a similar training sequence while Dora, my researcher and spy shop manager, narrated and kept time. My tech and surveillance guru, Sparky, videotaped each session so I could watch and learn from my efforts. I accepted this challenge every month because I loved being a private investigator and was committed to improving my skills. This training and preparation was especially important because I don't generally carry a gun.

Yes, I own a gun, and I'm a terrific shot. I know you were wondering. I prefer to use more creative and unexpected methods when taking down the scumbag du jour.

For workshop participants, the taser and pepper spray practice helps them build the confidence they'll need to save themselves if a jerk tries to mug them. In addition, seeing a stand-in for the jerk—me—get tased and then recover shows them how much time they'll have to escape. It's shorter than many imagine and reinforces the importance of a good getaway plan. We recommend using multiple self-defense measures for this reason.

We drew names to determine which workshop participant would get the honor of zapping and spraying me. This morning's winner was eighty-five-year-old Gertie Grimes. Gertie used a walker that we'd outfitted with our signature Seniors Self-Defense System Ditty Bag. The "Triple S," as it was known at the Island Cove Active Living retirement community, included a taser, a UV dye-marking pepper spray canister, a personal alarm, a sling shot, zip ties, a tactical pen, aspirin (in case of heart attack), and an Ensure High Protein shake.

Gertie's hands were shaking as she slowly lifted and then pointed the black plastic taser gun in my direction.

"Aim at my torso or legs," I said.

"Tasers work best when you hit large muscle groups." Dora walked up to Gertie and pointed at my stomach. "While the electrical charge causes pain, your primary goal is neuromuscular incapacitation."

I saw that we didn't have time to lollygag because Gertie's arms wouldn't hold up for long. "Gertie, you ready? Dora will count to three."

"One…"

Gertie either couldn't wait or count. I heard the snap and then felt a sharp pain ripple through my body. I tensed up and fell to the ground. My hands clenched and shook. It felt as though I'd been turned into stone against my will. I could see Gertie wheeling toward me and prepared for round two.

Dora followed behind Gertie. "Spray left to right, just like we demonstrated during the mock session."

Gertie rested her arm on the front top rail of her walker while pointing the spray at my head. "I'll try."

Even with my eyes closed tight, I couldn't escape the burning sensation of capsicum powder. It was the pepper spray, not the taser, that made me question my sanity every time I agreed to play the attacker during our monthly workshops.

DON'T TRY THIS AT HOME, readers. Tasers are safe, nonlethal defense tools but are dangerous when not used properly, especially if your attacker has an underlying heart problem. I practice being shocked and sprayed because I've had suspects get away while I struggled to get up from their attack.

Of the two products, it's the pepper spray that'll have the longest-lasting effect on your attacker. If you can carry only one thing for self-protection, make it pepper spray. One with a UV marking dye that'll help police identify your assailant. It goes without saying that we didn't use that kind during our workshops.

Gertie scooted closer to me. "Xena, I'm sorry, did I do it wrong?" She sounded like a grandmother who'd burned the cookies.

Dora took the pepper spray out of Gertie's hand. "Nicely done. Now in a real attack, you'd need to roll as fast as you can to get away before the attacker recovers. We use these tools to give ourselves time to escape."

"They'll be mad at me." Gertie turned and started scooting away at a sloth's pace.

"Really pissed, but that's why we practice," Sparky said from behind the video camera. "Xena, you OK to run the course?"

My face felt like it was on fire and my muscles were still aching and stiff. I extended and contracted my arms a few times, a technique I'd tried with success during the last workshop.

Sparky circled around me. "She's coming out of it."

"Could be a new record," Dora said. "Go, Gertie, go."

Still wobbly, I stood and tried to look for the orange cones we'd set up. My eyes were dry and didn't want to open. I forced a squint and ran like a drunk zombie through the cones, and then tackled the rubber dummy who was a stand-in for Gertie.

I stood up. "Drunbbed finwsher Rikeb." I sounded like I'd eaten a bull frog.

Dora clicked off the timer. "Thirty-five seconds. A personal best. Let's all give Xena a round of applause."

The workshop participants clapped and a few hooted.

"That's not much time to get away," Gertie whined. She was still making her way across the parking lot.

Dora looped her arm around mine to help me get steady. "You're right, Gertie, and while Xena recovered more quickly than most creeps will, you'll need to escape to a safe place as fast as you can. Use the items in your Triple S together—the taser, the pepper spray, your personal alarm, even the tactical pen if you need to. And be prepared to spray twice, which should not be a problem if you replace your canister after every encounter."

Sparky put down the video camera and walked over to the rubber dummy. He picked it up, brought it over to the middle of the parking lot, and put his arm around its shoulder. "Everyone, take five. When you come back, line up here to practice using the taser and pepper spray on Celeste." The real Celeste had apparently shattered Sparky's sixteen-year-old heart by agreeing to go to junior prom with his primary rival, Didget.

I'm Xena Cali, owner of the Paradise Lost Spy Shop and Private Investigations on ~~lovely~~ ~~gritty~~ ~~tropical~~ ~~corrupt~~ ~~enchanting~~ the always fascinating Galveston Island, Texas. Pour yourself a Darjeeling tea or smooth highland Scotch and relax in your favorite chair while I tell you about an investigation we've been working on. It has been a drama-drenched doozy for many reasons, including that it coincided with a dreaded birthday milestone—me turning forty. Don't tell anyone; I'm not ready. To ensure I kept looking "in my thirties," I got a new hairdo. Same dark brown bob and thick bangs but shorter, sexier (I hope), and much more rock and roll. And I got another tattoo, but I'll tell you about my tats later.

Chapter 2

1:00 p.m.

"Did you call Rodent Roger?" Sparky was standing in the retail section of the spy shop looking out the front window. The now-dangerous graduates from the seniors' self-defense class had left. "Because he just pulled up in his van."

"No." I limped out of my office, still stiff from being tased and pepper sprayed. "God, I hate that van."

The extra-tall, extended length van was completely wrapped in repulsive pictures of pests. A fat rat's body spanned the entire side of the vehicle, and its sniveling expression looked three feet wide. A surfboard-sized standing cockroach graced the back. Snakes and centipedes rounded out the four-color graphics. The words RODENT ROGER PEST CONTROL, BEST ON GALVESTON ISLAND 12 YEARS RUNNING left no doubt about who'd arrived.

I sighed. "Did I ever tell you and Dora about the first time Rodent parked in that very spot with that very van? It was before the shop was open."

"A few times," Sparky said. "Big infestation."

"Epic." I raised both arms like I remembered he had when describing the number of creatures living in my newly purchased retail store. "Rodent was excited about using my case to get a keynote speech at some conference for exterminators."

You might remember Rodent Roger from an earlier story about how he helped liberate my soon-to-be spy shop from a Noah's Ark for vermin. The building I'd bought hadn't been used by people in over thirty years, so extended families of snakes, raccoons, geckos, rats, mice, spiders, roaches, and cats had moved in. One ghost rat, too. But I don't have time to explain the ghost rat. I gave Rodent loads of money and more time than I had to spare to get the critters out of my shop so I could fill it with spy gadgets and then open for business.

"There aren't many like him," Sparky said.

"True." I rubbed the hip that I'd fallen onto during the taser demo because it was starting to ache.

Rodent Roger—born Rodney Roger, but he had his name legally changed to better embody his role as rat-whisperer/killer—was a lovely and strange man. He seemed completely obsessed with his work and energized by every creepy creature he encountered and then eradicated.

Rodent bounced into the store. "Look at this place… It's gorgeous!" He walked over to me, wearing his trademark coveralls, and gave me a hug. It had been two or three months since our paths had crossed.

My nose crunched into his chest, which smelled like basil and turpentine for some reason. "Hey, Rodent. You remember Sparky?" I mumbled, hoping the distraction would make him release his grip on me. It worked.

"Yep. Looking good, man."

Sparky waved.

Rodent bounded up to him, slapped his hand, and bumped his shoulder with his fist.

I walked behind the sales counter for my protection. Personal space is very important, don't you agree? Twenty-four inches, minimum. "To what do we owe the honor of your company?"

Rodent walked around the shop and looked up and down each row. "You've got some interesting stuff. How's the ghost rat doing?"

I raised my shoulders and tilted my head. "We think he's still living in the shop —"

"He's not living, Xena, he's a ghost. But he's most certainly still here. You might not be earning his company on a regular basis. Like every relationship, it takes some work. Do you talk to the ghost rat?"

"No…but he seems happy with the raisins I leave for him. Organic, of course."

"Those were for a ghost rat?" Sparky looked up toward the ceiling and put a hand on his mouth.

Rodent's crazy gray hair—which was longer now—danced as he bobbed his head in agreement. "Organic's best, fewer toxic chemicals."

This coming from a man who spent most of his hours applying toxic chemicals for a living.

Rodent walked up to me at the counter, brought his

hands together in front of his chest as if he was about to pray, and stepped closer to me. "I've got a situation and could use your help."

I paused and looked at him. "Oh? Come on in and take a load off." Rodent and I went into my office. I left the door open so Sparky could weigh in on our conversation, and because Rodent smelled more pungent in confined quarters.

Rodent sat up straight in my guest chair and leaned forward across my desk. He opened his eyes wide. "I'm getting iguana calls. Something's up."

I considered Rodent's surprising information and wondered what it had to do with me. "Iguanas."

"Green iguanas, to be precise," Rodent said.

"And this is unusual?" I asked.

"Astronomically unusual! I've been the island's top choice for pest control for over twelve years —"

"Just like your van says."

"Yes!" He punched a finger toward the sky. "And was the number two guy behind my father before that. In all that time, we averaged one or two iguana calls per year."

"And now?"

"Three in the last week."

I wondered if I was on *Prank Encounters* or *Punk'd* or maybe hallucinating from inhaling too much pepper spray. "That's quite an increase. Might it be a onetime blip versus a trend? Maybe a new Disney movie came out that increased the number of impulsive and ill-conceived pet iguana purchases?"

"Two things. First, Rodent Roger knows his reptiles. I

was the keynote speaker at last year's exterminator conference in Las Vegas." Rodent stood, twirled around, and pointed to my white board. "I need a marker. Never mind." He sat again and once more leaned toward me. "These iguanas were one or two generations away from the wild, not pet shop grade."

"Iguanas are graded?" I made eye contact with Sparky and thought, *Get me out of here.*

"Yes, and the lizards that gullible parents buy little Timmy come from vermin factories in California, where they breed them to be small and short-lived. More repeat business that way. These iguanas looked different. Their spikes were longer and more like what you'd see running down the streets in Jamaica or Mexico. And they're just as fast and mean as their wild cousins. I think these iguanas were bred from recent captures and then placed on our island."

I stared at Rodent as I tried to determine if he was full of shit or a savant.

"Don't doubt Rodent's expertise," he urged. "Skeeter agrees." Rodent showed us pictures of iguanas in cages he'd captured.

"Skeeter?" I asked.

"Guy I know." Rodent snapped his fingers. "Besides, there's more."

I was jolted out of my thoughts and swallowed. I was having a flashback to when Rodent told me my precious new spy shop was severely infested and the walls and ceiling would have to be ripped out. Seems he never did anything on a small scale. "More?"

Rodent handed me a flyer he'd had rolled up in his back pocket and then turned and handed one to Sparky, who was leaning on the doorjamb.

On the top it said: GOT IGUANAS? DON'T TOUCH THEM. LET LIZARD LIQUIDATORS DISPOSE OF THESE NASTY, BITING PESTS FOR YOU. WE USE HUMANE TRAPPING METHODS AND WILL REDISPOSITION CAUGHT LIZARDS SO THEY'RE OUT OF YOUR WAY.

"Cool name," Sparky said. "Wonder what they mean by 'redisposition'?"

I had the same question, but decided not to rabbit-hole the conversation by chiming in. "I'm not sure I follow. You think the iguanas are wild —"

"Near wild."

"Near wild…and this company is moving in on your territory? What would you like us to do? I hope you're not going to ask me to spy on your new competition."

Rodent placed his callused hands on my desk. "Yes, but not because of the competition. Rodent can handle any amount of that."

"Then why?"

Rodent stood up and walked over to the map of Galveston hanging on my office wall and thumped his fingers on several locations. "The iguana calls came from different parts of the island. And all three clients had received these flyers. Seems fishy and awfully convenient."

I joined him at the map and placed small sticky notes near the places he'd indicated. "You think they planted the iguanas and left the flyer hoping to make a few bucks redispositioning them?" I couldn't resist.

Rodent adjusted the notes and wrote a street address on each. "Don't know. Maybe it's the start of something worse. A whole other can of worms. Will you apply your investigative prowess and help me figure it out? I've got a few more leads to check out today, but I could use your vast spy resources to speed up my progress. Time is the enemy when dealing with unwelcomed pests, and green iguanas don't belong on this island." He raised his arm like a symphony conductor, then pointed at me and stared.

All of which I translated as his way of communicating that he meant business. Great. I'd been tased, sprayed, and now Rodent Roger-ed. What would the afternoon hold?

Chapter 3

6:00 p.m.

Homework. Although my head was spinning with thoughts of mean, near-wild iguanas, I kept my promise to myself to begin a self-study course in human relations. This, at the same time I was training for my first triathlon. Had to do it; cross off a few unmet goals before crossing over into middle age. Tick tock!

When I wasn't biking, running, or swimming outside (I wouldn't get in the Gulf when it was more than eighty degrees due to the higher risk of flesh-eating bacteria), I worked out in my big-ass garage in my small, two-story, concrete-and-steel home on Twenty-Ninth Street. The builder, an engineer who had worked on oil rigs during the 1950s, created the unlikely island home with its enormous garage and long sliding door so he could build an airplane in it. I loved it! My indoor triathlon training circuit included my punching bag named Betty 2 (after my former therapist Betty 1), a stationary bike, thick ropes, and a WaterRower. Five minutes each, full-out, three times through.

I decided to kill two birds with one stone by studying during my workouts. I drank some water and stretched out my still-stiff muscles. I huffed, clapped, and circled around my garage a few times to get my head into it and then put on my boxing gloves.

"Alexa, read the audiobook *How to Win Friends and Influence People.*"

You surprised? Even though it was first written in 1936, Dale Carnegie's classic remained one of the best books on the topic of human relations. And while you likely think I'm already a caring and lovable person, I'm not. Not enough, anyway. I'd come to the realization that I sucked at peopling after my boyfriend, Ari, broke up with me the day after my mother asked me why I don't have any friends.

I listened to the audiobook as I beat the crap out of Betty 2. It felt oddly satisfying to think productive thoughts while venting my inner rage. I repeated the most memorable lessons while moving through my circuit.

You can make more friends in two months by becoming interested in other people than you can in two years by trying to get other people interested in you.

You can make more friends in two months by becoming interested in other people than you can in two years by trying to get other people interested in you.

You can make more friends in two months by becoming interested in other people than you can in two years by trying to get other people interested in you.

I got onto my bike and pedaled as fast as I could for two minutes. Then I doubled the resistance and stood while pushing through the final three minutes like I was climbing a steep hill.

Ask people about themselves and use their name.

Ask people about themselves and use their name.

Ask people about themselves and use their name.

It was hard to speak Carnegie's truth the further I got into my workout because everything including breathing was difficult. I decided to stop listening after the first lesson and that I'd focus on putting Principle #1 into practice over the next couple of days.

"Alexa, stop. Alexa, play the Foals. Alexa, volume six."

The volume helped distract my mind from my on-fire biceps and triceps as I finished the final round of jumping power slams with ropes. As painful as it was, the ropes were good for building the upper body endurance I needed when doing parkour or escaping dangerous situations. Hanging from buildings, pulling myself up onto roofs, and stuff like that.

I sat on my WaterRower for the final five minutes of my workout. I loved how the water sloshed around the tank as I rowed. I isolated my back muscles with each pull because I'd need them to power me through the swimming portion of the triathlon—my weakest sport. With just two months of training to go, every workout was important.

"Alexa, stop. Alexa, play Enya. Alexa, volume four."

I stretched on a thick foam mat for several minutes and imagined how I would rock my new Dale Carnegie techniques the next day. A warm sensation moved throughout my body because I knew people would find me irresistible. That, or I had just peed my pants.

Chapter 4

Day 2, Thursday, March 1
9:30 a.m.

I'm usually moderately interested in the people I meet. But some people are just boring, right? Dale Carnegie suggested that the key to Principle #1 is to have an honest curiosity about people so you listen more deeply and well. He recommended we learn more about people's backgrounds, ask about their interests, and give them our uninterrupted attention. He stressed it was also important we greet people in a friendly manner. Show some enthusiasm! We needed to make it obvious to the other person that we were pleased to be with them. I knew this was going to be hard for me, but was ready to give it a try, beginning with my visit to Steve Heart's office.

If you've been to Galveston Island, you've likely read our local paper, *The Galveston Post Intelligencer*. Its reporters and editors offered readers a unique mix of local color, regional news, and investigative pieces about issues important to the island. Like the impact of climate change on persistent flooding challenges, the ebb and flow of full-time residents (read: tax base), and the expansion of our cruise ship terminals and whether cruising really benefits the island overall. Regular columns presented diverse opinions on matters such as sea wall parking (a perennial Galveston ache) and local politics. The GPI was a paper where fishing—Galvestonians' favorite sport—got front-page coverage and the police blotter could inspire Hollywood sitcom screen writers. Like the report about a pelican eating a newborn infant found in a trash can. Upon investigation, officers discovered the "infant" was an oyster po'boy sandwich. "From The Spot Restaurant," the officer said, "judging by the color of the sauce."

I walked into the lobby of the GPI and up to the reception desk. "Hello. I'm here to see Steve Heart. He's expecting me." The receptionist was a young woman in a black turtleneck with large round glasses and her blonde hair up in a tussled bun. I guessed she was a University of Texas Medical Branch (UTMB) communications or journalism major.

She made a call then looked up to me and her eyes got wide. "Hey, I know you. You work at the spy shop on Twenty-Fifth, right?"

Show an interest in her.

"Yes, I'm the owner. You know it?" I stepped closer to the desk.

She bent down in her chair, picked up her purse, pulled out a pepper spray canister, and showed it to me.

It was our best seller, mainly because it came in bright

colors. The canister, not the spray. Hers was kelly green, which I found to be an interesting choice.

"I remember seeing you. Cool store. Sparky's a trip." She smiled.

"Indeed. Sparky's also wickedly smart when it comes to technology."

"You're the owner? That's amazing. You dress so one-of-the-gang. I love your hairstyle. Very poet meets mobster."

I wasn't sure, but I think she was being complimentary. I usually wore jeans and a polo shirt. Hiking boots, or maybe runners. "I come from hairy roots. Scottish on my mother's side, Greek on my dad's." *Make this about her, not you.* "How about you. Born around here?"

She sat up straight and leaned forward. "Yes! Well, not BOI, but I grew up in Houston."

BOI. Born on the island. Sparky was ten generations BOI. There were BOI and then there were other residents, like me. Transplants. Welcome for the money we bring to this cash-strapped city, but not yet considered a local. Many BOIs felt you had to be born here to fathom what the island is really about.

I was about to tell the woman I had lived in Houston but stopped myself. "Are you a student at UTMB?"

"Yes, ma'am, I am," she replied in a sing-songy voice. "Graduate this spring. Trying to decide between becoming a reporter or a professional podcaster."

"A sign of our times! How wonderful. Maybe you can do both? The world needs great journalists." I stood up straight and saw the receptionist's name was Sasha. "I wish you luck,

Sasha, with whatever you decide, and be sure to replace your pepper spray every two years, even if you don't use it. Loses its potency."

Sasha nodded and gave me a thumbs-up.

"Was Steve available?" Steve and I had worked together on several cases going back to when we both lived in Houston. We had a win-win professional relationship. I got scoops from him about what was going on, and he got first dibs on reporting the breaking stories related to cases I was working.

Sasha bounced in her desk chair. "Oh! Sorry. Seeing you made me a bit starstruck. I've never met a spy shop owner before. He said to go on back, that you know the way. Steve's mentoring me on investigative reporting techniques."

I bet he is. This pretty little lady was definitely his type. Wide-eyed and eager to please. "He's the best the island's got."

"That's what he told me, too. See you later, ah…"

"Xena. I'm Xena, and I bet I'll be starstruck to see you again someday when you become an award-winning reporter or podcaster, Sasha." I smiled and started walking back toward the office area. I felt really good about the interest I showed in Sasha; a bit like Mother Teresa, or maybe Oprah.

I walked up to Steve's desk and stared. I almost said, *What's the story on the new facial hair?* but stopped myself, remembering today's lesson: show a genuine interest in others. "Wow, you've been working on that beard!"

Steve Heart had what celebrity magazines liked to call a metrosexual style. Bleached blond short hair, shiny, tanned skin, and dark rectangular glasses. He wore all black with turquoise-dyed boots. And what had been a short, nickel-sized soul patch was now a longer, wider, *S*-shaped goatee.

Steve stood up, grabbed his laptop, and started moving toward the conference room. He caressed and twisted his beard. "You like it? I've been growing and training it for a couple of months. It needs to grow another inch longer to form the shape I'm going for."

"Training? You mean sit, stay, look like a giant letter *S*?" I chuckled and followed him into the room.

"Very funny." Steve turned and stuck out his chin. "You ladies have no idea the work that goes into the proper styling and maintenance of facial hair."

"Obviously." I possessed the sarcasm to go much darker with my comment—perhaps something about menstrual cycles and childbirth being no walk in the park—but decided to take the high road because I wanted to practice showing an interest. While we'd never been lovers—that would've been a disaster for all involved—Steve and I were what I liked to think of as quasi-friends. Not best pals, but *sorta* pals.

We sat down next to each other at the table and powered up our laptops. I gave him a once-over look. "Nice boots. I don't remember seeing these. How many pairs do you have now?"

Steve cocked his head. "Thanks. They're lizard. Custom-made. Twelve." Steve answered slowly and in a measured tone.

I nodded. "Do you have someone local make them for

you or go to that guy on Westheimer in Houston?"

"Houston. He's the best."

I turned in my chair to face him. "Tell me how you're doing. It's been a while since we've seen each other. Are you dating anyone new? I met Sasha out front. Lovely girl. She said you're mentoring her." I raised one of my eyebrows and smiled.

"No, not dating anyone." He logged onto his computer and then turned his torso toward me. "Sasha's a good little reporter. What's with the questions? You're not trying to play HR department on me now, are you?"

Steve was referring to my stint as an employee relations attorney and human resources executive for several large organizations. That was before I owned a spy shop.

"No way, man. I'm done doing that gig. Bang whoever you want. I'm just interested in how you're doing."

"OK...well...thanks. And I'm not boffing Sasha, for the record. I think she swings the other direction."

I patted his hand and grinned. "Never stopped you from trying before."

"Touché and one point goes to Xena, but you're only partially accurate. The one you're referencing swung both ways, which is cool with me except that it doubles the competition." Steve pulled out the pen he kept in the wire coil of his notepad. "Dear Miss Cali, I appreciate your interest in my life and all, but your uncharacteristic sudden charm makes me wonder if you've been eating too many of Sparky's magic brownies."

I needed to work on my subtlety. "OK, that's all true

except I've not touched the yummy brownies lately. I'm working on my peopling skills because I suck at them. Trying to be a better human. It's a self-study Dale Carnegie program."

"The *How to Win Friends and Influence People* guy? I read that many moons ago." Steve nodded and started playing with his soon-to-be *S* beard again. "Why? I mean, I acknowledge you suck at…what did you call it…'peopling'? I guess I'm surprised you want to change."

Steve knew me well, so I decided to pull no punches with him. "Some people have hinted that I'm aloof and cold, Steve, and they could be right. I have very few friends and my boyfriends don't last long. I'm worried that my conscious detachment makes some people question my trustworthiness. Which would be bunk, because I'm very trustworthy and reliable. I'm just not a hugger."

"That's some self-awareness."

"Therapist. Paid good money for it."

"Even so, never thought I'd hear this from you. Wanna know what I really believe about trust?"

I didn't. "I do."

"Imposters come in many forms. Some wear explicit costumes and lead double lives. Others are imposters because they never open up, even to those who're closest to them. You have to let people get to know who you really are before you can feel true partnership, friendship, or love."

I stared at Steve, surprised at his extemporaneous eloquence. "Do you think I'm an imposter?"

He shook his head. "No, I don't. But then we've been

through some stuff together. This thing you called *peopling* is more art than science. It's something you have to shape and hone as you build relationships with people. Sometimes bad people do good things, and vice versa. But the more you let others get to know you, the better. So, go forth and conquer; but do it in your own way so you don't freak people out."

"I get what you're saying. What was it that tipped you off? My interest in your beard or in your boots?" I scooted my chair out a little so I could get another look at the boots.

Steve sat back up and readied his hands at his keyboard. "Both. How about we talk about why you're here? You almost never come to my office, and I'm sure it's not to get caught up on the boring details of my fashion or love life."

"I want to talk to you about lizards. Iguanas, to be more precise. Rodent Roger asked me to investigate an uptick in iguana complaints on the island."

"Didn't see that one coming, but OK. You want me to run a report with a list of the stories we've done about iguanas?"

"Not exactly. We didn't find any articles when we searched online, but I'm wondering if you can search tips you've received from residents."

Steven started typing and clicking. "These are iguana skin boots, by the way. Maybe if I supplied my own, Marcos wouldn't charge so much for my next pair. It's highway robbery, but they're the best in town."

"You have tremendous taste, Steve."

I caught him scrunching his eyes at me.

"I'll stop." I moved closer to see his screen. "Anyway, I'm more interested in live iguanas showing up in people's yards, boats, and houses."

"What timeframe should I search? I'll select call-in tips, and postings from our Facebook and Twitter pages."

"Last two months."

"Recent. Hmm." Steve was nodding as he was typing as if I might've piqued his curiosity.

"This is an emerging issue, if it's an issue," I said. "I told Rodent we should consider whether these sightings might be a coincidence. The local Walmart had a sale on pet iguanas, kids fed them too much —"

"As kids do."

"Right. Then they got big and were let go. Seems plausible."

He finished entering the search criteria and then looked at me. "Those things can get up to six feet long, right?"

I nodded. "And they're mean when pissed off, not that I've sparred with any myself. Rodent believes the iguanas he's caught don't come from the pet trade, though. That they were bred from wild stock, something he called *near-wild.* I'm not sure that's a thing."

Steve let out a click from the back of his throat. "I recall that Mr. Rodent Roger is known to exaggerate."

"That's an understatement, and one reason I'm here. I'm looking for validation or refutation of his theory that there's a problem brewing."

"Let's see what comes up. I've not heard anything myself, but near-wild iguanas aren't my usual beat." Steve's computer screen changed. He clicked a few more times, and then an hourglass graphic pulsated on the screen for a few seconds. A long list of items from the tip line filled the screen. The word *iguana* was displayed in bold font where it was mentioned.

"My, my, my, my, my," Steve said. "We've got lots of iguana inquiries, mostly on the west side of the island. How come a reporter hasn't been assigned to check this out? Looks like more than a dozen tips from just the last two weeks."

I read over his shoulder as he brought up each tip. I put my hand on my mouth. "Oh. My. Goodness. Rodent was right."

Chapter 5

1:00 p.m.

“Have you been eating Sparky’s magic brownies?” Dora looked at me and then my hands on the steering wheel and back at me again, as if she was debating whether to be concerned for her safety while I was driving.

Here we go again. I told Dora I was interested in what had been going on in her life. Recent fascinations, how her family was doing, whatever she might want to share. Instead of a response, she suspected I was high. Changing the perceptions people had about me was turning out to be harder than adopting new behaviors.

I smiled and shook my head. “No, why would you ask that?”

Dora gave me a motherly glance. “You seem loopy, or maybe just happier than usual. Different.”

I found it interesting she equated my showing an interest with happiness. “Sorry for the confusing signals, I’m no happier than usual.” I debated whether to tell Dora about my Dale Carnegie lessons, but then reminded myself doing so would focus the conversation on me when I was supposed to be listening to her. "We haven't talked for a while, and I'm interested in how you're doing."

Dora smiled and bounced in the passenger seat like my response surprised her. "Well..." The narrative floodgates opened, and for the next twenty minutes Dora told me about her childhood, her attempts at indoor gardening, crocheting parking meter sweaters, and a disastrous blind date with a man who'd lied about having good hygiene on his online dating profile.

After showing what I believed was a satisfying amount of genuine interest, I shifted the conversation back to our task at hand, which was to talk to one of Rodent's clients who'd had iguana problems. I parked in front of the lovely brick house with red shutters, one of the few homes on the island that hadn't been elevated.

Denny Wormington answered the door and welcomed us in. He was a well-known resident of Galveston who owned a store on Strand Street called Naughty or Knot, where he sold weird stationery, cards, and books with nautical and naughty themes. Things like pirate blow-up dolls, knot-tying kits for sailing or sex (or both), and ocean breeze-scented antibacterial soaps on ropes for mariners and pleasure boaters. The packaging touted benefits like *Smell like the ocean, not a rotting dock* and *Clean crotches save lives.*

I was curious whether Denny's house would mirror the strange vibe of his store and pleased when it didn't. Aside from the oil painting of the mermaid screwing a dolphin that hung over the *L*-shaped couch with throw pillows that said

I'M REELY INTO YOU, it was tidy and tasteful.

Denny looked comfortable but put together in his navy-blue velour suit and slicked-back hair. "I hope you don't think I'm a sissy for not taking care of the iguanas myself, all six-foot three and two hundred strong pounds of me." Denny winked.

Two hundred pounds my ass. Denny looked two fifty, minimum.

"Not at all," I said as I thought exactly that.

"Iguanas are carriers of over ten diseases," Dora said. "It's good to be careful and leave it to the professionals. I read one story about a woman who lost her arm after one bit her. Super-bad bacteria."

I looked at Dora and cocked my head. Sometimes I wondered about her information sources. She was an amazing researcher and I trusted her completely, but she had a habit of, and apparent curiosity for, finding articles about obtuse and oddball situations that had gone way wrong. The kinds of things most of us would miss and/or dismiss. Not to diminish the power of bacteria, which will get us all in the end.

Denny nodded and showed us to the back of his house and through the living room, kitchen, and into the pool area. It wasn't screened-in but had an iron fence around the patio and barbeque pit. He pointed into the pool. "Right there. That's where we found the two iguanas and all their shit." He lowered his head and looked at us over the top of his square glasses. "There was poop everywhere. Little drops, big plops, and some long stringy stuff." He walked closer to the pool's edge and looked into it. "Do you know how hard it is to clean pool water once it's been pooped in? How do parents handle this situation? Because you know their kids and all their little friends are peeing and pooping in pools. It took us three days and a few hundred dollars to our maintenance company to feel comfortable swimming in it."

I noticed Dora googling iguana poop on her phone.

Denny walked around the pool's edge and looked into the water again. Perhaps looking for more shit. "They were big, too, the lizards, and had long orange spikes on their back. Rodent called them green iguanas, but they weren't green. They were muddy brown and gray with bluish cheeks and snouts." He looked at us and cackled. "Butt ugly is what I'd call them."

Dora took notes. "Rodent caught and took them away? Did he trap or kill them?"

"I don't like to witness my sausage being made but love to eat it, if you know what I mean." Denny snorted. "I didn't see or ask, but it only took about a half hour. No blood splatter. He cleaned up everything except the pool water. Not his territory, he said. Don't blame him; that stuff is nasty. Rodent's a principled man."

"Have you seen any more iguanas since then?" I asked.

"A few around the house but they didn't get into the pool because we installed an electronic zapper on the fence." Denny grinned and tapped his belly. "Got that sucker turned up to cow rating, and it's working real good. Big lizard hit it just this morning and flew twenty feet in the air. Landed in the canal. Not sure if he made it. It's been quite entertaining."

Strange that he chose not to watch Rodent catch the iguanas but enjoyed electrocuting them. Takes all kinds, right? I looked at the canal and made a mental note to walk around Denny's zapper fence to search for carnage. "Has anyone else come around asking about iguanas?"

Dora pulled out the flyer that Rodent had given us. "How about these people…the Lizard Liquidators?"

"Yeah, I got one of those. Gave it to Rodent. My neighbor had that guy come out. I told him to call Rodent, but these guys called back first. Damn iguanas had gotten into his garage, climbed into his clothes dryer and crapped all over the place. No way to make that right. The dryer will have to go in the landfill. George said the guys did an outstanding job and had special pole snares and tricks they used to catch the iguanas."

I looked at the house next door that Denny had pointed to. "You keep saying iguanas? How many are we talking about?"

Denny removed his phone from his pocket and pulled up a picture. It showed multiple iguanas in a long rectangular metal trap. "He said they caught three. One was just a little thing, a baby, but the other two were big. George observed everything they did and took pictures. He hunts deer, so…you know…" Denny winked again. "Not sure what's going on, but it seems like our neighborhood has become the home of choice for these shit factories. You think they're good eating?"

I stared at Dora. *Don't take his bait.*

Dora shrugged her shoulders.

I smiled and nodded. "Let us know! Do you mind if we walk around your yard and take a look?"

"Help yourself. George is up in Austin for a few days, I'm sure he'd be OK if you checked out his yard. Is there anything in particular you're looking for?"

Dora looked up from her notes. "Yes —"

"Boring stuff," I blurted before Dora told him too much. "Dora and I want to get a feel for the environment."

"Be damned careful where you step." He cackled once more, then waved as we walked out his patio gate.

We moved to the side of Denny's yard. Dora stopped and turned to me. "Sorry, was there something you didn't want me to say?"

"No. He just seems like someone who'd turn whatever information we shared into juicy, exaggerated gossip. Would rather not cause an island-wide stir just yet."

"That HR radar of yours is in tip-top shape." Dora smiled.

Our work required deliberate management of information coming in and going out. I'd seen well-disseminated gossip turn non-issues into serious situations in just a couple of days. I pointed to a damaged yellow hibiscus flower. "Do iguanas like flowers?"

"Love them," Dora said. "I did some research last night. Green iguanas are mostly herbivores, although they'll occasionally eat insects, eggs, and small animals."

I took pictures of the mangled flower, a few snapped branches, and the gap in George's garage door through which they likely got in. I paused and shook my head, because I didn't know why I was doing this and felt unsure how to use our investigative skills to help Rodent. Or the type of assistance he needed.

Just check it out, he'd pleaded.

Whole other can of worms, he'd warned.

Dora looked around with her binoculars and then sighed. "I don't see any. Could be the Lizard Liquidator and Rodent got them all."

"Perhaps." I walked back to my car. "But that seems unlikely based on the number of inquiries Steve found."

Dora followed. "And to answer Denny's earlier question, iguanas are apparently an excellent source of protein and make for tasty burritos." She then came up beside me and pointed. "A friend is waiting for us."

An iguana was sitting on the hood of my car. It looked three or four feet long and had dark green and brown skin. I got out my phone to snap some pics, but the beast ran off as soon as we got close.

"Crap!" I said.

"Yes." Dora took a picture. "A load of crap."

The iguana had pooped on my car. I looked around for the offender but didn't see where it had run off to. I opened my door. "Yuck, that's stuff's gross! My poor car… Did you notice the long spikes on that one? And striped tail."

She got in the car and showed me the picture of the black-green-beige mound. "It was a fast bugger, too."

Near wild. I remembered how Rodent had described the behavior of the iguanas he caught. As I pulled out of Denny's driveway, he waved from his front window.

"Bizarre..." I looked around, hoping to see the iguana as we headed down the street. Maybe run it over for leaving its mess on my car. "I know this isn't an official, or paying, case, but this influx of iguanas on our little island is fascinating. Is Mother Nature trying to teach us something? I don't know, but I'd like more information."

"Want me to find a reptile expert on the island or in Houston we can talk to?"

"You read my mind, Dora."

Chapter 6

7:00 p.m.

After a day focused on iguanas and their poop, I was glad to get home and enjoy a glass of Edradour. The smooth, Highland single malt warmed my throat, then all of me, as I sat out on my second-story porch. The large, screened-in seating area was my favorite room in the house because it gave me a bird-in-a-tree view of people walking up and down Twenty-Ninth Street. And we're all voyeurs, whether we're comfortable admitting it or not, right? How else can we explain the success of reality TV?

While on the porch, I could hear the surf as it rolled onto the beach three blocks away and the music playing at the Pleasure Pier farther down the waterfront. I'd been putting off calling Gregory all day. Gregory Jackson owned a spy shop and was a private investigator up in Houston. We first met when I hired him to help me with a tricky corporate corruption case when I was the vice president of human resources for Granny's Home, Inc.

You might remember me telling you about the *glorious*

incident that changed everything in previous tales. It was a bizarre undercover operation (me in a bear suit) that seemed more like something you'd read about in the *National Enquirer*, except that it was true. Drugs, hookers, bagpipes, and traumatized macaws dive-bombing for sopapillas came together in a penthouse condo that had been owned by a former Enron executive. We busted and exposed several disgusting, corrupt business leaders who were anything but leaders. And I mean I literally…exposed them.

All this happened a few years ago. Then after my big severance check from Granny's cleared the bank, I got to work reinventing my career. I'd always loved Gregory's spy shop and opened my own in Galveston (with his blessing, of course). I took the private investigator exam and everything! I…was…legit and eager to be an entrepreneur. He helped me set up my store and has been a dear friend and mentor ever since.

I hadn't responded to the text Gregory had sent more than twelve hours ago because I knew it had to do with unfinished business from the Houston sting. It was something I wanted to avoid and forget. Problem was, I couldn't forget and believed doing nothing would make matters worse. Someone could get hurt again or killed. Last time that someone was me.

At 8:00 p.m., I put on my headset, dialed Gregory's number, and rocked back and forth in my chair. I watched the old oak's gnarly branches rustle in the wind.

"Hey, Xena." Gregory sounded tired. *"I was wondering if you were ignoring me."*

"Never." I shifted in my seat. "Just a weird and busy day."

"The usual...I get it. How's business? I've seen a nice spike in purchases ever since Houston PD caught our latest home-grown serial killer. Everyone wants security cameras now."

"No recent change here, but island property owners know they need exterior cameras. Security systems account for 22 percent of my sales."

Galveston was a wonderful and gritty place with lots of extremes. Filth and fine dining. Beautiful beaches and back-alley drug deals. Every street had well-kept homes next to junky houses that hadn't been repaired from the last big storm or two. We were a city of haves and have-nots with caring neighbors and criminals in both groups.

"This creep has hit a nerve with Houstonians," Gregory said.

"What was his MO?"

"They called him the Caffeinated Killer because he brewed and drank a pot of coffee while dismembering each of his victims. Except at one house. The police think he couldn't figure out how to use their fancy espresso machine. In Montrose, you might've guessed."

Montrose was the neighborhood of choice for creatives and solopreneurs and was also where I once had a townhome. "Nespresso to the rescue," I said.

"He still killed the entire family."

"Oh."

"I wonder what this guy's parents are thinking about themselves, knowing their precious kid turned out to be a

despicable human being," Gregory said.

"That's some heavy shit you're contemplating. Is that why you texted me at seven this morning? You know I love philosophy..." I rocked in my chair and smiled. "I might need to pour more Scotch into my glass if you get all deep on me, though."

Gregory laughed. *"Nah, I called because I have splendid news. Or rather I did what you asked; not sure whether you'll think it's good. I found and contacted your friend, Agatha Reacher."*

It's important for you to know, readers, that miss fake-name Agatha Reacher was not my friend. She was a private investigator hired, we believed, by one or more of the executives arrested during the Houston sting operation. The scumwhats were apparently still pissed at me. I'd received and ignored threatening letters we assumed were from them.

Why'd they hold a grudge? I wondered that, too. How about that scumwhats are scumwhats! Maybe they couldn't get over losing their ill-gotten fortunes and trophy wives. Perhaps getting kicked out of their swanky country clubs pushed them over their tender mental health edges. I didn't know or care except that this nastiness was mucking with my well-planned and -orchestrated charmed life on the island.

The letters seemed fairly benign, but then things escalated. A few months ago, Agatha Reacher drove to Galveston to deliver a personalized message. She told me that her client wanted me out of Texas, and before I could respond she punched me so hard I dropped to the ground on the side of the street. This happened three blocks from my house.

No, no one rushed out to help me. I know you were wondering. It happened fast and during the middle of the afternoon when residents and visitors were drunk, sleeping, or both. And while I admired Agatha's physical abilities—she was tall, muscular, and confident—I hated that I'd failed to see her blow coming, because I almost never lose hand-to-hand battles. After smarting from my bruised body and ego for a few weeks, I'd asked Gregory to track her down and relay that I wanted to meet with her. I wanted to cut a deal with the undeserving scumwhats and declare a truce. To turn the page on the *glorious incident that changed everything* once and for all.

I took a deep breath while swirling and sniffing my drink. "How is my quote-unquote friend Agatha Reacher doing?"

"Seems well. And impressive, no offense..."

Gregory used to tell me how impressed he was with my investigative instincts, and I didn't dare reveal my emerging jealous thoughts. But I'll tell you, readers, getting punched by that woman knocked my confidence down a notch, and I wondered if I was losing my touch. That's one reason I was training for a triathlon—to regain my power. The realization I'd soon be turning forty messed with my mind, too.

"Impressed *you*?" I asked. "Well, that's something. How so?"

"After I told her who I was, she rattled off the name of my spy shop and knew that we'd worked together on the sting. She'd done her homework, I'm sure, before she came down there and beat you up."

Ouch. "You were never her target —"

"I know. She was pleasant, calm, and sounded interested to meet with you."

I sat up and put my drink on the side table. "You don't say?"

"Umm-hmm."

My brain froze. Maybe you've heard the saying, *Be careful what you ask for, you might just get it.* Yeah…well…I was wondering if this face-to-face would be the smart tactic I'd imagined. "I'm glad but surprised. How did you manage that?"

"No management required. She seemed eager to meet with you and asked me to let you know she never wanted to hurt you. Mentioned that it was something her client needed proof of—she took your picture, apparently—and she said something about needing money for a new gun and laser scope."

I cringed. My new adversary possessed muscles, bullets, and a laser scope. "Not sure I believe she regrets assaulting me. She seemed in total control of her words and movements that night…and she had a devilish smile. That's the only reason I didn't see it coming."

"Fair point. Safest to assume the worst for now. I'll send you her number. She wants you to text her when you're ready to meet. She'll respond with a location and time."

"I'd like to determine the place." Rule number one in PI work is to control the setting.

"I know. She said that wasn't negotiable."

"Hmm. What do you think?"

"She seemed truthful. I'd do it. Get Sparky to watch as backup."

Gregory didn't know that I'd not told Sparky or Dora about the attack. I hid the bruises with makeup for two weeks.

"I suppose," I said. "Did she say anything else?"

Gregory paused for a moment. *"She offered to do contract work for me at a friends-and-family rate."*

"That's ballsy." Hearing this had awakened the control freak inside of me. How dare she move in on my friend's business like that!

"Girl's got to make a living," he said. "If all goes well with you guys, I might use her."

I slugged the rest of my Scotch, which made my entire body shake for a second. "Can I switch topics? How are you doing?"

"I've got in some new gadgets you might like. Come up for a visit and I'll show them to you."

"Deal. But throw me a conversational bone. How are you and Lynn? Doing anything fun this fall? Vacation plans?" I was hoping to practice some of my Dale Carnegie techniques. Show an interest, be an excellent listener, and such.

"All good. Nothing special. Lynn would love to see you."

He didn't seem in the mood to talk, which was fine with me. At least I tried. Besides, my head was churning over the news about Agatha. I'd double up on my workouts, just in case. "Me, too, Gregory." *Use their name, Carnegie reminded.* "Hey, you wouldn't happen to know anything about iguanas or know someone who does?"

"No and no. Do I want to ask?"

"Not yet, might be nothing. Thanks for everything, Gregory."

"A pleasure. Being your occasional wingman is a source of entertainment. Your world is way more eventful than mine. Sometimes in ways I'm grateful for."

I laughed because he was correct. After we hung up, my phone dinged with an incoming text from Gregory. Agatha's number. I stared at it for a few minutes, then googled her like I had right after we determined who she was. Nothing came up then or this time. She was too smart for that. I wondered who Agatha Reacher really was, how she got into this business, and what she did to get so damn strong. CrossFit? Maybe Pilates and weights.

Hello, "Agatha." It's Xena. GJ said you're willing to discuss a potential win-win resolution to this situation with your client. I'm working a case, but could we meet at the Mosquito Grill next Thursday for lunch? I look forward to a cordial discussion.

My finger hovered over the message, then pressed the green button to send the text.

To ensure I didn't stare at the screen for the next however long waiting for her response, I turned over my phone and set it on the side table. Time for another Edradour. I let a generous sip float around my mouth for a while. The spirit penetrated and stung my tongue, then left a satisfying sweetness. A sensation I loved.

Investigators make a lot of enemies. It comes with the territory but can be more of a problem when perps face costly and humiliating losses. I was learning the hard way that it didn't take much to trigger their well-funded wounded egos into action.

Chapter 7

Day 3, Friday, March 2
8:00 a.m.

I got out of my car on Post Office Street and tiptoed past a small green iguana sitting on a pink-and-blue turtle. There were nineteen hand-painted Kemp's ridley sea turtle statues throughout downtown Galveston. The Turtles About Town project sought to heighten awareness about this endangered sea turtle and ways to protect coastal environments. The iguana didn't likely know all this, nor did it move as I shuffled past it. I wondered if it was dead and snapped a few photos of the poor thing. Cold stunned, not dead, Dora would tell me later, because we were heading into a chilly spell of weather, and iguanas were cold-blooded. They slowed way down once temperatures drop into the forties.

After purchasing the coffees and scones I bought from the Mod anytime we had an early meeting, I headed to the shop. I was eager to tell Sparky and Dora about this latest reptile sighting, but then set that idea aside until the iguana portion of our agenda.

The world doesn't revolve around you, Xena.

I walked into the meeting room and smiled. "Hello Sparky! How are you?" I handed Sparky his usual vanilla latte and toffee walnut scone. "Tell me a good story about what's been shaking in your life." I plopped down in a chair and widened my eyes in anticipation. Sparky was a very good storyteller.

Sparky gave me a look that turned into an odd stare. His eyes intense, as if he was thinking.

I drummed on the table a few times to wake him up because he looked stunned or frozen, like the little iguana. "Do anything fun over the weekend? Got any interesting plans this week?"

Sparky tilted his head and scrunched his eyebrows. "Did you eat some of my brownies?"

Dora joined us at the conference table and laughed. "I think our boss has been surfing the Internet late at night and is trying some new techniques on us. Yesterday she surprised me with a similar request." Dora patted me on the shoulder and sat at the table. "Isn't that right?"

This was a moment of truth. Should I tell my staff I'm trying to be a better person? Doing so would reveal that I perhaps *needed* to be a better person. When I was in the corporate world, I used to preach that leadership was a social act. It occurred in conversations and was therefore visible. And I'd made the persuasive case that because it was visible, there was no downside to being upfront about weaknesses. If I believed this rock-solid coaching advice, my team already knew that I was socialization-challenged and telling them this wouldn't come as a shock or change their impressions of me.

I took in a deep breath and then let it out in a big puff. "All right, enough talk about the brownies. Can't I show an interest in your lives? I'll be the first to admit that I'm sometimes dismissive of the normal day-to-day conversations that most people have."

They both nodded, which I should've expected but didn't.

"I'm trying to be more attentive and interested." I shifted in my seat. "Actually, that's not what I mean. I've always been interested. What I'm attempting to do is better show my interest." I turned in my chair and looked at Sparky. "Let's try my question again, Sparky. Do you have anything fun planned for this weekend?" I grinned inside and out, pleased with how my confession came out.

Sparky slurped the foam from his latte for what seemed like five minutes. "Well…as a matter fact, I do. I'm going to referee drone races in Freeport."

"Sounds…enchanting?" Dora looked over her glasses at Sparky and grinned. She seemed fearful of drones and had been outspoken about her concerns over their potential misuse.

"Perfect and right up your alley," I said. "I hope you have fun." I opened my laptop to indicate that we'd reached the conclusion of the chitchat portion of our meeting. "How about we talk about Rodent's iguana issue? Something weird is happening. There was an iguana outside the Mod this morning. In the middle of the Strand, sitting on one of those painted turtles! This is new and different."

"I dig those turtles," Sparky said.

"I've been on the Dawn Patrol for turtle hatchlings and have helped babies get to the water. It's a life-changing experience," Dora added as she turned to a fresh page in her notebook.

"We all love turtles; my favorite is the chocolate variety." I turned my head back and forth between them and smiled. "Minds on iguanas now, please. Let's begin with what we've learned in the last two days since Rodent visited us." I tapped Dora on her hand. "Your turn to scribe."

She stood up and grabbed a whiteboard marker. "One: several of Rodent's customers have called him to remove unwanted iguanas from their property."

"And your visit to Steve revealed that the paper has received a lot of tips about iguanas," Sparky said. "Have you heard from Rodent since he was here?"

I shook my head and looked at my phone to ensure he hadn't contacted me this morning. "No, and I'm surprised because I figured he'd be hounding us like a pest—no pun intended—to get him some answers."

Sparky shot a finger gun at me. "Touché. How did it go with Rodent's customer yesterday?"

Dora and I filled in Sparky about our visit with Denny Wormington—what we found as we looked around the neighborhood, and the surprise we had waiting for us back at my car. Dora showed him her picture of the poopy present it'd left for me.

"I suggest you get that, umm—what is iguana poop

called anyway, iguana guano?—cleaned off your car. He-he-he." Sparky's head bopped. He was a big and fluffy dude who laughed with his whole body.

"Use of the term 'guano' is limited to describing the excrement of seabirds and bats, I think." Dora not only knew about such things but remembered things better than most people. At sixty-seven! She had a gift.

Sparky tapped his keyboard. "According to Google, you're correct. Iguanas leave behind pellets or urate—that's runny stuff. And the overall volume of their manure approaches that of a small dog. Iguanas are known to poop quite copiously."

I sighed and shook my head. "Relax about the poop already. I went through the car wash right after dropping off Dora. They charged me extra to extricate the excrement." I snickered and then looked in my notes at the list of assignments I'd given them with hopes of getting our discussion back on track. "We have some evidence and seem to agree there's been an increase in iguana sightings. This uptick doesn't mean there's a problem, and even if it's an unwelcomed development, it might be Mother Nature at work. But Rodent believes that the changes aren't natural, so let's focus on this angle for a few minutes."

I shook my head because I couldn't believe we were investigating why iguanas were turning up on the island. "The only lead we have in this regard is the Lizard Liquidators. How did they know to put flyers in residents' mailboxes?" I sipped my double cortado and pointed the cup in Sparky's direction. "Were you able to learn anything about these guys?"

"A few things," Sparky said. "Lizard Liquidators registered the business in Galveston County in February. It lists the owner as Zorin Montaña."

Dora wrote the name on the white board. "Interesting name."

"And quite puzzling," Sparky said. "Because I couldn't find any information about him. I searched several databases. Still working on it, but at this point Zorin's a bit of a mystery man."

"I'll ask Steve or maybe Ethan to look him up." Captain Ethan Slaughter was the head of the major crimes team for the Galveston Police Department, or GPD. He'd taken over for BJ Rawlins after he retired last year. Although I'd not yet gotten to know Ethan well, I was optimistic we'd develop a mutually beneficial professional relationship based on our initial interactions. The GPD had a small team of investigators, and we crossed paths with them often.

"I have an address because Galveston County requires all businesses to list a physical address, no PO boxes allowed." Sparky typed on his keyboard and projected his screen onto the large monitor mounted on the meeting room wall. "Here's where the Lizard Liquidators HQ is located. It's just past Pirate's Beach and the Kettle House on the bay side of San Luis Pass."

The Kettle House was a small home that started off as an oil tank that looked like a tea kettle, wide on top and curved and skinny on the bottom. This well-known oddity was built in the 1960s. Its metal structure rusted, and it was an eyesore until its investors renovated it. Now adorable and weird, it's listed as a vacation rental if you're interested in a unique place to stay when you visit the island.

Sparky zoomed in on the map to show the Lizard Liquidator's building.

"Not too far from Lake Como and the Country Club," Dora said. "Isn't that pricy real estate?"

I stood and walked up to the map. "I worked a cheater case out this way and remember seeing a mix of houses. Mansions and shacks. Sparky, will Google let you show us the street view?"

"Sure."

The property listed on the Lizard Liquidators' business license turned out to be a small, single-story cottage sitting on stilts. Medium brown paint with an off-white trim. It had a screened enclosure along the front. There was a carport and storage or workshop on the ground floor and a staircase that led to the home. Looked to be about a thousand square feet. The house sat on a grass-covered lot that had no trees except a few toward the rear property line. According to Google's last drive down that street, three empty homesites surrounded the house.

"Pretty small," I said. "I bet this is his house; the picture is two years old. Maybe we should have a look-see." I glanced at Sparky and Dora for reactions. "Unless either of you has a more interesting idea?"

"I doubt they're moving iguanas in and out of that tiny place," Dora said.

"We should go there," Sparky said. "I'd love to observe the Lizard Liquidators in action. You want me to get the van ready to do surveillance?"

"Yes, but let's do the surveillance tomorrow," I said. "I've got a full day planned. Do we know anything more about the Lizard Liquidators?"

I returned to the table and was about to sit, but then something caught my eye. I looked up at the security camera monitors, which we had mounted on the wall of the meeting room. "Someone's at the front door. It's still an hour before we open. Does she look familiar to either of you?"

"Not to me," Dora said. "I think I'd remember her. Very tall and extremely blonde."

The woman had her hands cupped on our front window and was looking inside.

Sparky stood and moved toward the meeting room door. "I'll go see who it is."

We heard him open the door and speak to the woman. The bell attached to the front door clanged, and we watched her enter the spy shop from the monitor. I got up to check it out.

Sparky stuck his head into the meeting room, and we nearly collided. "You'll never guess who's here to see you."

I opened my eyes wide and shrugged my shoulders. "The Avon Lady?"

"It's Rodent's wife."

Chapter 8

9:00 a.m.

Ultima Roger lived up to her glamorous name. She wore ironed straight-legged jeans, a cropped black leather jacket, and high-heeled boots. Her long, platinum blonde hair and generous boobs bounced as her hips swayed wide left and right when she walked. Her slow steps seemed deliberate, as if she was a beauty pageant contestant walking up to the microphone. Her outlined cherry-colored lips gave me a half smile as she came forward. She had a wrinkled brow and tired looking eyes. "You must be Xena."

I nodded but wasn't sure what to say. Rodent wore a simple wedding ring, but I knew nothing about his personal life or that his wife was such an uptown-looking creature. He seemed more the Birkenstock type, but perhaps I'd read him all wrong.

She stopped in front of me and touched my forearm with her hand. "I'm Ultima. Ro has told me about you, including that you're helping him with this unseemly lizard mess."

"Ro." I was a little slow to realize what she was saying.

"You call my husband Rodent, no doubt. I've never been able to stomach using that word for the man who shares my bed." Her eyes scanned the shop.

I nodded. "That would be odd. It's nice to meet you." My stomach tensed and I could feel my face get warm. Ultima didn't look the type to be in the market for spy gadgets. "Is something wrong?"

Ultima paused and her eyes got teary. "Have you seen my husband? Please tell me you have him working some secret spy mission."

Sparky's eyes got big and he cocked his head.

I hadn't seen that coming. "He was here two days ago, but we've not seen him since then. He's not helping us with any of our cases."

Ultima lifted and dropped her arms. "Shit, then he's missing. My Ro is in trouble."

We locked the spy shop and invited Ultima to sit with us in our meeting room. Dora cleaned away our Mod drinks and pastries while Sparky made a pot of coffee. I sat next to Ultima. "When did you last see him?" I lifted the box of tissues toward her because I could see she was about to cry.

Ultima pulled several tissues from the top of the box. "Yesterday morning; earlier than he usually gets up. I asked him why he needed to leave before breakfast. He told me he had some appointments and would be home by dinner. Then he texted, saying he'd not be home for dinner. He's still not home, and I'm worried sick."

Wives hated the question, but I had to ask. "Has he ever not come home before?"

Ultima wiped her tears and black makeup that was dripping down from her eyelids. "No. And he usually calls me several times during the day. I work from home. I'm a writer."

Huh. I'd gotten caught making wrong assumptions again. "I've always wanted to write a book."

"You should try it," Ultima said. "I've written thirty-seven romance novels."

"Wait," Dora said. "Are you U.P. Roger?"

She nodded. "My middle name is Penelope."

Dora was about to say something, but I gave her a *not now* look. "We'd love to learn more about your work, but you were saying that Rodent called you several times each day?"

Ultima turned to me. "We're very close; always have been. If he had car trouble or was working late at a client's site, he would've texted me. He knew I was making a lasagna; it's his favorite."

"Did he leave in his pest control van or some other vehicle?" I asked.

"The van."

"It can't be too hard to find an oversized van with a giant rat on the side of it." I nodded for Sparky to take over the conversation so I could text Rodent.

I have some information I think you'll find helpful. Please call me ASAP.

The text delivered. I excused myself, stepped out of the meeting room, and tried calling Rodent. His mailbox was full. I assumed Ultima had already called multiple times. I returned to the meeting room.

"Have you filed a missing person's report with the police?" Sparky asked.

"I called right before I came here. They didn't seem concerned or interested in helping me. Told me to give it another day before coming to the station. I know what people think. Husband's got side action and is in some sleazy hotel room sleeping off his hangover. Hell, I've written that storyline a million times." Ultima watched me as I sat back down. "That's not my Ro. We've been married several years, and I know my husband."

I looked at my phone. No response to my text. "Mrs. Roger —"

"Ultima, please."

"Ultima," I said. "Do you and your husband use the Find My Friends app?"

She shrugged her shoulders. "I don't know what that is."

I held up my phone. "It's an app on your phone that friends and family members can use to share their location."

"I don't think so. He's never mentioned it."

"Would you mind if Sparky looked at your phone to see if Rodent might've set it up? It could help you find him if it's active."

Ultima pulled her phone out of her purse, input her screen PIN, and handed it to Sparky. "We just got new phones last month and I'm still figuring out how everything works."

Sparky's fingers moved with lightning speed as he evaluated her phone. "The app is sitting in the cloud. I'll download it, but it doesn't look like they ever used it." After a couple of minutes, he handed the phone back to Rodent's wife. "Nope. Not set up."

"Darn," Ultima said. "I didn't know such a thing existed. I'm going to tell Ro we should use that app when he comes home." She began crying and grabbed a few more tissues.

We all sat in silence a moment.

I looked down at my home screen. No text from Rodent. "How many times did you try calling and texting him last night? Did you get any response?"

She pulled up a picture of Rodent Roger in a tropical print shirt and showed it to us.

"He looks very happy," Dora said.

"From our vacation in Mexico last year," Ultima said. "I took this picture the night he had a few too many strawberry daquiris and insisted on showing the bar owner signs he had a rat problem."

That fit the Rodent Roger we knew.

She put her phone on the table. "I didn't call until this morning because I fell asleep on the couch and didn't realize that he'd not come home until I woke up. Went right to voicemail. Left him a message to call me ASAP. My lasagna sat out on the kitchen counter all night. It's ruined."

"What time did you call?" I asked.

Ultima gazed up toward the ceiling. "Uh…a couple of hours ago…about six? Did I do something wrong?"

"No," I said, but then wondered who filled up Rodent's voicemail box in the last two hours if not Ultima. "I'm sorry we don't know where he is. I hope you hear from your husband soon."

Ultima put her hand on the table and straightened her back. "I'd like to hire you to find him."

Another unexpected plot twist. I crumpled my brow and wiped my mouth with my hand. "You mean open a case to find him? You're sure we shouldn't wait a bit longer?"

She shook her head. "Ro would never leave me to worry if he were able to reach me. I assume he can't reach me, and that has me terrified."

Truth be told, I shared Ultima's concern about Rodent's disappearance, given how sure he'd been that something wasn't right with this iguana situation. I hoped he hadn't gotten bitten by one, or worse yet, a roaming gator. As careful as he was when dealing with bugs and raccoons, I wasn't sure he had the same competence when dealing with wild iguanas on the open west side of the island.

"Please, Xena," Ultima said. "I'm happy to pay additional so that you and your team will drop everything else you're doing and look for my husband."

I looked at both Sparky and Dora and nodded. "We'd love to help and are able to prioritize this case. But I hope you call us later to say never mind because he's back."

I asked Dora to share our standard client engagement information and rates and to do an intake interview to gather some basic information. I stepped out and tried calling Rodent again.

When they finished, I walked Ultima out of the spy shop. "Is there anything else you can think of that might help us find Rodent?"

She thought for a moment and shook her head.

"Does he keep any weapons in this truck?"

"He has a loaded gun…some tranquilizers and traps." She broke down and hugged me. "Please find him. I need him back."

"We'll do everything we can," I said.

We watched Ultima get back into her Audi sedan and then returned to the meeting room.

Dora handed me the signed contract. "I've read every book in her *Tender Vixen* series. She writes very imaginative and extremely detailed love scenes." She paused and noticed my puzzled expression. "I know, focus on the case. Do you think something happened to Rodent?"

I looked at my phone again. "I'm worried about it. There's something hinky about this situation. And as lovely and intelligent as Mrs. Roger seems, I'm not sure whether to believe everything she's shared. We need to check her out."

Sparky showed me a few numbers he'd jotted down on his notepad. "When I was downloading the Find My Friends app, I looked at her call log. She started calling Rodent at 8:00 p.m. yesterday and kept calling throughout the night."

I gave Sparky a high five. "I thought you gave me that *keep her distracted* look. That's interesting for two reasons. Because she obviously lied to us and that she called so many times.

"Suggests she was really worried," Dora said.

"Or wanting to seem worried," Sparky said.

I moaned and spun around in the task chair a few times. I felt a bit dizzy. "Maybe Rodent's alleged disappearance has nothing to do with iguanas. In fact, that might make more sense. Who'd kidnap a pest control guy over lizards?"

"People sometimes do irrational things," Sparky said.

I chuckled. "Truer words have not been spoken."

"A woman from Kemah killed her husband after he attacked her because she wouldn't make him a fried bologna sandwich," Dora said. "She claimed it was self-defense. The jury agreed and acquitted her."

Sparky shook his head and played with his long stringy hair. "Don't mess with a man's meat."

"Or a woman's power over it," Dora said.

I put my hands on my ears. "Enough about death and bologna. I want to know if Ultima Roger hired us in an act of true love or if she's feeding us baloney."

Dora raised an eyebrow. "Fiction is her forte."

Chapter 9

3:00 p.m.

My stomach hurt, and I felt guilty. I hadn't seen Rodent for several months before he came to my shop and asked for help. And while we'd started looking into his concerns, our efforts were…honestly, half-assed. I'd assumed Rodent was being his eccentric self, obsessed with having complete dominance over the pest control industry on the island. But now that he was missing, I wondered if I should've or could've done more and sooner.

Sparky was putting out feelers with local drone hobbyists who loved to have an additional reason to use their expensive toys. Their mission? Find the rat mobile. Dora seemed thrilled with her assignment to work up a background sketch on the Rogers, especially Ultima Penelope Roger. I wanted to know more about her past, notable achievements or setbacks, finances (hers and theirs), and the health of the Roger marriage. Dora was also trying to find a local reptile expert I could talk with about iguana migration and habits. Maybe someone at Moody Gardens or perhaps the folks at the

Biological and Aquatic Research Labs would know someone.

I decided to search in person—analog, boots on the ground, the old-fashioned way. I drove around the island and visited the client sites Rodent had marked on my map, hoping that he'd gotten sidetracked trapping or catching iguanas. Maybe he accidentally shot himself with his tranquilizer gun intended for an iguana. Maybe he got drunk with the Lizard Liquidator guys and was passed out in his van somewhere. I needed to reduce the number of maybes swirling in my head.

I stopped at places where local business owners went to fuel up commercial vehicles, mail packages, or get supplies. The island didn't have a lot of any one thing except vape shops, so it was easy to ask around and determine if anyone had seen Rodent. Most islanders knew him, and many had been his clients. It helped that both he and his van were hard to miss.

But I felt uneasy because no one I talked with had seen Rodent or his van in the last two days. Remembering that Rodent said he was researching how the iguanas ended up on the island, I drove by Xorin Montaño's house but didn't see any signs that Rodent had been there.

I got another knot in my stomach when I imagined Rodent trying to do what my team and I did for a living: surveillance, interviews, and other investigative methods. The man didn't possess one subtle, incognito-proficient bone in his body. Imagine the lovechild of *Seinfeld*'s Kramer and Doc from *Back to the Future*. Rodent entered every room with a bang and a pop.

I should've made him promise he wouldn't do anything

stupid. But would that've worked? Not likely. Rodent was headstrong, determined, and committed to whatever problem he set out to fix. Even imaginary ones.

Where was he?

After driving the length of the island—twenty-seven miles—west to east two times, I drove into the Galveston Island State Park and then a small gravel lot between the Caracara Trail and Jenkins Trail. It was a quiet place I'd visited many times when I needed to walk and think. This part of the park was on the bay side, not the busier section along the gulf. I pulled my car under one of the few trees in the area.

I kept my windows up because I didn't want to get swarmed by early spring flying bugs. After reclining in my seat, I stared up at the shimmering shards of light through the glass sunroof and the tree above.

Where would you go if you were a jacked-up pest control expert possessed with owning the extermination business market share in Galveston County? Or where would you go to find the access point or source of these new iguanas? And why hasn't Agatha Reacher texted me back? Is she watching me now?

I must've fallen asleep because a noise startled me awake. Then I heard something scrape across my sunroof and saw it was a large iguana. It stayed there for a couple of minutes a then walked down my windshield. I held still and followed it with only my eyes, hoping it wouldn't notice me inside the car.

This iguana was gray and khaki colored with dark green here and there. It had two- or three-inch irregular spikes all the way down its spine and a long, striped tail. A large flap or pouch of skin hung down from its snout, throat, and head area.

The iguana turned around on the hood of my car and flattened.

"I bet you like my warm hood," I whispered to myself.

The iguana didn't seem to hear me, or notice I was looking at it.

"Maybe you've seen my friend Rodent? I bet you were quick enough to get away from him; you look like a speedy iguana."

The iguana didn't move, but its head turned toward me.

"Where are you and your iguana friends living and hiding?" Without moving my head, I looked up through my sunroof at the tree above and guessed that was where it had been and wondered if there were more iguanas ready to drop.

I looked back at the iguana. "How did you get here? Did you swim of your own accord or have some help? Why are you and your friends here all of a sudden?"

I stared into the creature's eyes, hoping to learn or see something that would help me find Rodent.

It took a step toward the windshield, cocked its head, and stared into me. *"Be careful what you ask for."*

"Wha—?" Rodent hadn't told me the near-wild iguanas could talk. "Excuse me?"

"Bulldozers. Golf courses. Communes for old people. You make us move too much. Selfish, lazy beings. You can't even catch your own food."

The iguana was talking to me, and it had a good vocabulary.

"It's too cold here. But I like the top of your BMW, Xena."

It surprised me the iguana knew my name and recognized my driving machine. "How long have you been on the island?" I asked.

The iguana took another step closer to the window. *"One set of hatchlings."*

I spoke without moving my head. "Where'd you come from?"

"*I don't know,*" it replied. "*It was light, I felt drunk, it was dark, then I was here in this frigid place. A few others, too. Not my friends. I almost lost my tail.*"

If this talking iguana was telling the truth, and I had no reason to doubt it, Rodent had been on to something. Could it be that the iguana felt drunk because someone had drugged him? Might make it easier to relocate and then dump a bunch of green iguanas on Galveston Island.

I gazed into the iguana's small, dark eyes. "Are you a girl or a boy?"

The iguana extended his snout and rotated its head in a small circle. *"I'm a male, of course. You know nothing about iguanas."*

"No," I admitted. "I'm trying to find a friend. He drives around in a van with a picture of a rat on the side."

"Hate rats. Ugly rat bit and ate one of my toes."

I looked, and sure enough, he was missing a toe on his front right foot.

"No, I won't grow a new one," the iguana continued. *"I'm not a frog. Rats gang up on the little ones. Rats are bad news. Rat Man is no friend to iguanas."*

"Perhaps."

The iguana poked his head toward the glass and touched it to my windshield. *"Why are you here? Are you an iguana killer, too? I love flowers. Got any flowers?"*

I shook my head and smiled. "No, I'm not a killer, I came here to think. I don't have a flower for you; I didn't know we'd be meeting like this."

He moved his head back and his snout up and down. *"I love the way your car feels. It's too cold on this crappy island."* The iguana turned away and said nothing more.

The sound of a slamming door in the next parking spot startled me. I sat up, shook my head and slapped my cheek. An iguana was running down Jenkins Trail. He waddled his tail and backside as he bolted out of my view. A couple dressed like birdwatchers got out of their car, fiddled with their cameras, and walked toward the observation deck at the end of one of the trails.

I looked around, woozy, and wondered if that was the iguana I'd talked to. I assumed so but decided not to tell my team about my conversation with Doug just yet. That's what I named the iguana on account of his Doug-y-ness.

My phone rang. It was Sparky. I sucked in a deep breath. "Yep."

"Where're you at?"

"Stop it," I said. I knew he would've tracked me before calling.

"You OK? The last time you went to that side of the park was after you and Ari broke up."

"I'm fine, just tired. I've been driving around all

afternoon looking for Rodent. No sign. What's up?"

"We got a possible sighting of the rat mobile."

"Excellent."

"Not exactly," Sparky said.

"Where is it?"

"If my drone buddy's right, it's in the middle of a stand of bushes off the end of Indian Beach Drive. It's covered so it might be a different commercial van."

I pushed the car's start button, looked in my rearview mirror, and selected the MEDIA button on my sound system so I could keep my conversation with Sparky going in hands-free mode. "That's just a few miles from me. I'm on my way. I'll confirm that it's Rodent's vehicle before deciding whether to call Ethan. E-mail me a copy of the video?"

"Already on it. Want me to bring the surveillance van out there?"

I backed out of the parking lot and left the park, careful not to run over Doug or any of his pals. "I'll let you know. Not much light left. If it's his, it'll soon be crawling with cops who'll rope off the area. Not much we can do then."

"Do you have your night vision gear?"

"The FLIR scope. Replenished my ditty bag yesterday. Glad I doubled up on the MoonPies, too. I might need to bribe the authorities."

"Xena?"

"Yea."

"I hope we've found it, but that Rodent isn't inside."

My heart sank. I made a right turn onto Termini-San Luis Pass Road and slammed my foot on the gas pedal. "Me, too."

Chapter 10

7:30 p.m.

The Indian Beach subdivision featured swanky houses on oversized lots, most with both bay and gulf views from their upper floors. Many of the homes were owned by rich folks who let property management companies offer them as vacation rentals when they weren't on the island. The community was quiet, populated by strangers, part-time residents, and empty houses. Not a bad place to stash a vehicle.

There was a turnaround circle at the end of Indian Beach Drive where the buildable land ended and the marshland began. Beyond this point were bushes, marsh, Ostermayer Bayou, and then the West Bay. I got out of my car and looked at the bushes. If there was a vehicle in there, it was well hidden. I put on my headlamp and grabbed my ditty bag.

The ground was spongy and moist, as usual. That was one reason it wasn't more populated. And mosquitoes, which were so numerous their swarms could change the weather. Thankfully it wasn't yet mosquito season.

Waterproof hiking boots were a standard part of my daily wear because there were a lot of deep puddles and squishy spots on the island. Even my tiny front yard pooled rainwater, and Twenty-Ninth Street flooded whenever we had heavy showers.

Sparky had given me approximate directions to reach the covered vehicle. One hundred feet northeast of the edge of the gravel circle. I saw multiple sets of tire tracks going along the west side of the bushes and guessed that was how they got the vehicle in there. Fishermen and birders might've come here, too.

I entered from the west so I could walk faster and quieter. I jogged about forty feet along the brush line and then another fifty down the northern edge of the treed area, following the tracks until they led to a small clearing to my right.

Although tan-colored tarps concealed the vehicle, I knew it was Rodent Roger's van because I could see a fuzzy cockroach leg peeking out from the bottom of the covering.

Damn. What happened here, Rodent?

I crouched about twenty-five feet away from the van and pulled the FLIR scope from my bag. With it, I could see pictures based on the heat that objects emitted. (In the summer, I would've had to wait a few more hours to see distinct images because everything would've been hot.) The van itself didn't light up as very warm, telling me it had been there a while. This made sense, given it was two days since anyone remembered seeing Rodent. And I felt relieved that

I didn't see a blob of heat coming from inside the van. Even a dead body emitted some heat.

One thing was evident: If Ultima Roger was involved in her husband's disappearance, she had some help. There's no way she could've gotten the large tarp over Rodent's van by herself. I wasn't sure even I could've pulled that off.

I scanned to the left and the right of the vehicle and didn't see any hot spots. The space beside the van looked empty as well until I looked about five feet from where I had been crouching.

Did you know, dear readers, that you can see snakes at night using thermal imaging technology? You can.

And I did. The coiled-up object looked dark gray compared to the lighter gray-to-white of the surroundings. It hadn't rattled (sometimes they don't) but I presumed it was a rattlesnake because it had been a bountiful mating season and the northwest part of the island was crawling with them.

I remembered rule number one when dealing with rattlers: Stay calm and still. Don't jerk or move fast. The snake doesn't want to attack you but will if it feels threatened.

I placed one hand on the ground while using my other hand to watch the snake through my scope. I pivoted on my heels so that the bottoms of my boots faced the snake and my butt rested on the ground. The cool and wet gooey marsh soaked through my pants.

The snake didn't move, but I heard a short, weak rattle.

That's not a proper rattle. You must be a young one.

The rattlesnake's rattle, which is made of interlocking

segments of keratin (like our fingernails), gets longer (more segments) with each shedding of the snake's skin. I looked through the scope and tried to estimate its length and therefore age. Maybe three to four feet; not full grown. On the upside, younger rattlesnakes have less venom and their bites aren't as dangerous. On the downside, these adolescents may not've learned the composure and judgment situations like these demanded.

I had no idea of the critical thinking skills of snakes or if that last point had merit, but it made sense to me.

Sick of sitting in the wet muck, I went on the offensive.

I slid my ditty bag from my back forward and next to me on the ground. Yes, as a barrier between me and the snake, but also because I needed something from inside it. I placed the scope on my lap and slid the zipper open. I put my hand inside and explored the contents until I found the small Ziploc bag I kept in a side pocket. Then I eased open the bag and grabbed one of the small plastic ampules inside. Once outside the bag, I pressed down on the smelling salts to break the inner capsule and release the ammonia mixture.

Rattlesnakes hate the smell of ammonia. I put the ampule between the soles of my boots and extended my legs toward the snake. It slithered away in the opposite direction.

I stood and looked around with my scope. No more snakes, but my butt was soaked with icky marsh. I started walking back to my car the way I came in. My first text went to Sparky to confirm that the vehicle was Rodent's van. Then I texted Ethan.

It's Xena. Can you meet me at the end of Indian Beach

Drive? We found Rodent Roger's van. His wife said he was missing, so we were looking for it. It's covered with tarps and branches; somebody didn't want us or anyone to find it.

Ethan responded within a minute. *Don't touch anything.*

I know. Did he think I was born yesterday or just printed out my certificate of completion for the online private investigator training program like some other hacks in town?

I don't want you getting close to it.

I know.

Any sign of Mr. Roger?

No. And no heat signature inside the van. He's not in there or has been dead for a long time.

How did you

His text was incomplete.

Never mind.

I stared at my phone and shook my head because my brain was buzzing from the smelling salts. *You on your way?*

ETA ten.

Ethan lived in the Palms at Cove View condos. No, readers, I've not been there, not inside anyway. Get your mind out of the gutter. I make it my business to know stuff about the people with whom I work. We're all Peeping Toms, aren't we? We look into windows as we pretend to walk the dog, watch the people behind us from our car rearview mirror, and stare at our security camera feeds for hours. That last example might just be me, but I bet you'd stay up late, too, if you had the gear I have hooked up. Our interest in being private voyeurs is why awful reality TV shows get better ratings than well-written crime dramas. The question we should each consider isn't whether we're Peeping Toms, because we know the answer to that question. The unsettling but more useful question is who might be watching you?

But I digress; we were discussing Ethan. The condos at the Palms were affordable, smallish, and owned mostly by full-time residents. The crime stats were higher than I'd expect, considering the head of the GPD Major Case squad lived there. Maybe he preferred to keep a low profile.

Ethan drove up in his personal vehicle, a white Chevy SUV. He hopped out and grabbed a long flashlight from his back seat. He extended his hand and gave mine a firm but friendly shake. "It's been a while since our paths crossed. Good to see you. What's the situation?"

I told Ethan that Rodent had asked for our help, and that two days later, his wife hired us to find him. I admitted I didn't know whether any crime had been committed, other than the illegal dumping of a vehicle.

"Might as well check it out, since I'm here. Where is it?" He looked around, pulled out his revolver, and held it at his side.

I still had on my headlamp and ditty bag. "Behind that batch of bushes, covered. We can walk around this way." I started walking and Ethan followed.

I panicked inside when I realized he would see my wet pants. I stopped and pointed to my butt. Ethan pointed his flashlight right at it.

"I didn't pee my pants," I said.

"Yeah, OK." I could see Ethan was smiling.

It was getting dark. Ethan moved his flashlight back and

forth in front of him. “It’s well hidden, how’d you find it?”

“Drone picked it up. I can show you the video when we get back to our cars.” I stopped when we got to the clearing and pointed. “There.”

Ethan took a few more steps forward and illuminated the vehicle. “How’re you sure it’s Mr. Roger’s van?”

I walked up to him and guided his flashlight to the bottom right side where the tarp didn’t cover a second clue it was Rodent’s ride: an enormous pink rat’s foot. “It has a ten-foot rat decal on each side.”

“Oh. I’ve seen that vehicle around town.”

“Most islanders know Rodent or have needed his services.”

Ethan looked around and shifted back and forth a bit. He looked impatient, but then put his revolver back into its holster. “And then you used thermal binocs?”

I grabbed the FLIR scope from my bag and handed it to him.

Ethan looked through it toward the vehicle and around the area. “Nice piece.” He gave back the scope. “How close did you get?”

“No closer than this.”

“Good. We shouldn’t be here. Let’s return to the road.” He turned and then stopped. “I see something.”

I walked over and blushed. It was my used smelling salts ampule. I bent down and picked it up.

“Wait—that’s evidence,” Ethan said.

“No, it’s mine, sorry. I should’ve picked it up.”

“But why —?”

"I used it to deter a rattlesnake."

Ethan cocked his head. "Huh. That works?"

"Thankfully, it does."

"I should start carrying some of those."

We walked back to our cars. Ethan made a few calls and then walked over to me. It would be fifteen minutes before most would arrive. My plan was to be gone by then.

I leaned on my front driver's side fender. Doug had pooped on the top of my grill. I'd need another car wash. "Calvary coming?"

"Something like that. You found this by drone?" He banged his flashlight, now turned off, against his leg.

I pulled my phone out of my pocket and showed him the three-minute clip Sparky had e-mailed me. "Amateur operator from the local club. Sparky is their unofficial leader and asked them to be on the lookout for the rat mobile. Nothing within five miles of the airport, of course."

He nodded while shifting back and forth. "You got a theory about whether we'll find Mr. Roger's body inside his van and what might've happened?"

I put away my phone and rested my hands on my hips. "Hope not, and nope." I looked at Ethan. "If I'm honest, I just started looking for him a few hours ago. All I know is that he was concerned about the iguana calls and new pest control competition, and that his wife is a knockout and successful romance novel writer who doesn't look his type but seems worried sick because he didn't come home." I stood up straight. "You're not going to let me get close to the van until forensics is done, right?"

He nodded. "You know the drill."

I sighed and kicked at the dirt. "Then I'll skedaddle."

"If you move your car over there" — he pointed down the block and away from the circle — "you can stay until they look inside the vehicle. At least you'll know whether he's in there."

I straightened and moved toward my car door. "Thanks."

"Stay in your car, OK? It could take a while. I'll come to you when we know something. If he's in there, you can provide an initial ID and save the wife from having to do it until morning." Ethan looked down the road, then motioned for me to move.

Red flashing lights turned onto Indian Beach Drive. I placed a beach towel on my leather driver seat and then got in. I then parked my car a block away and waited.

Chapter 11

11:30 p.m.

I was listening to my Dale Carnegie book while documenting case notes on my phone. Mostly questions. *Why did Rodent, or someone, dump the van? Who would know about this dump site? What did the neighbors see?* I looked down the street. The only light came from a house at least two blocks away. I put an answer next to my last question. NOTHING.

Was it irony or a paradox I was listening about smiling, while the police were searching Rodent's van? *Smile more* was principle #2 of six for how to get people to like you. Dale Carnegie suggested it was our facial expressions, not clothing, accessories, or wealth, that most affected what people thought of us. I believed there was more to first impressions than this but agreed that actions spoke louder than words.

I watched myself make funny faces—exaggerated smiles—in my rearview mirror as the narrator told me a about a man who'd started smiling more for a week. He smiled at his wife, coworkers, and the people he encountered in shops and his neighborhood. And after seven days, the man said his life had changed and that this one minor difference had brought more happiness into his life than anything else he'd done in the previous year.

I talked back at the narrator. "Really? Life transformed? Was this guy super grumpy before he became happy?"

I didn't buy that people wanted to be around happy, pleasant, or smiling people all the time. I'd made a concerted effort to show more interest in people and it freaked them out. Maybe I didn't do it right, or perhaps Carnegie's entire book was just bunk.

I was a serious gal who felt more comfortable using neutral-heading-toward-negative nonverbal expressions. Why force it if it's not natural, right? But Carnegie disagreed. He wrote that people who didn't want to smile should force themselves. And if they were alone, should sing or whistle or do something that might make them feel more jovial. He also suggested they act as if they're happy and that doing so will make them feel happier.

I made more faces in the mirror. "I feel happy. I feel happy. I'm happy!" I yelled in the closed cocoon of my car. The book cut off when my phone rang. It was Dora.

I pushed the button on my left earbud. "Hey, Dora."

"Sparky told me you were waiting in your car for Captain Slaughter, otherwise I wouldn't have called so late. Got a minute?"

"Sure. Especially if you have pleasant news. I could use some of that. It's been a bewildering day, and no amount of forced smiling has changed that."

There was a pause on the line. *"I found an iguana expert."*

I slapped my hand on the steering wheel. "Now that's great news, set something up."

"That's the thing, Xena. I already have because she works on one of the cruise ships that's coming into Galveston tomorrow morning. Dr. Quintana Flores is her name, and she's apparently a big deal when it comes to reptiles, especially iguanas. She's agreed to meet you at the port but is only available first thing in the morning."

I put my hands over my ear buds to make sure I was hearing Dora correctly. "The iguana person works on a cruise ship?"

"Yes, and your choices for when to meet with her in person were tomorrow or five days from tomorrow. I assumed you wouldn't want to wait."

I keyed her name into my phone's browser. Google returned 3,257 articles. Papers she'd coauthored, speeches she'd given, even one book she'd written called *The Sex Lives of Blue Iguanas, and other Evolutionary Disadvantages of this Near-Extinct Grand Cayman Treasure*. "Looks like the real deal. I don't want to wait."

"I checked her out before I called you. She's got a good pedigree."

"But a scientist who works on a cruise ship? That's odd."

"She does an iguana show onboard and takes passengers on an in-depth shore excursion on Grand Cayman to see endangered blue iguanas and promote their conservation. She's a board member for the nonprofit trying to save them."

"That's admirable and interesting. I'll be there." I looked

in my rearview mirror. No movement, which meant they were all still in the clearing with Rodent's van. "E-mail me the details."

"I already have, and I've included a set of questions I think you should ask her," she said.

"Thanks. And excellent work, Dora."

"I appreciate that, I hope you don't have to stay there too much longer. Your meeting is at seven thirty."

"No problem. I'll be there." I hung up and started reading the e-mail Dora had sent me. I felt lucky to have someone so thorough on my team. Lord knew I wasn't that person.

A knock on my window made me jump and drop my phone. It was Ethan. I opened my door and bent to pick up my phone.

"Sorry," he said. "Didn't mean to startle you."

"It's fine, I was engrossed in an e-mail." My heart pounded and stomach tensed. "Well?"

"He wasn't in the van and there was no sign of struggle."

I let out a long breath.

"Fqrensics is still processing it and will go back later this morning to take pictures before removing the van."

This morning… I looked at my watch and saw it was 1:10 a.m. No wonder Dora was worried about tomorrow's…or rather today's meeting time. "That's good news. He might be OK somewhere, but I'm worried about what might've happened."

Ethan had put his hands in his pockets and was looking toward the clearing. "They said nothing looked out of place.

The van is filled with equipment and chemicals."

I lowered my head. "So…no signs it was a robbery."

He shook his head.

"Points to something else."

"That'd be my guess." Ethan shrugged his shoulders and then looked at my face. "You've got something on your cheek. Dirt or chocolate, maybe."

My face felt warm as I brushed off gooey crumbs. "It's been a long night; I had a snack." I grabbed my bag from the back seat and pulled out a tissue to wipe my cheek. "Would you like a MoonPie to hold you over? I still have one banana and two vanillas in my ditty bag. I ate the chocolate one, goes without saying."

He walked closer, smiled, and looked into my bag. "Sure. I've not had dinner. Vanilla's my favorite."

I handed him the wrapped pie.

"FLIR scope, smelling salts, and MoonPies…that's quite the combo. I remember all the stuff you pulled out of there on that birder murder case."

He was referring to the first time we worked together.

Show an interest, use their name.

"That's right, Ethan. You started your new job in the middle of that whacky case."

He chuckled. "Never a dull moment."

I held up my bag. "I've several ditty bags that I curate for different seasons and situations. Stop by the spy shop sometime and I'll show them to you. I'd love to learn more about the tools or gadgets you've found most helpful for solving crimes." I pointed to his massive flashlight. "You might downsize your torch. I've got several compact tactical flashlights in stock."

"This thing of beauty? I'll never let it go. Doubles as a club." He held up his flashlight and swung it like a baseball bat. "Got a few minutes to go over the facts again? Might help me determine whether it's time to assign department resources to this case."

"Sure." I hoped he would get his team looking for Rodent. "Have you ever met Rodent Roger?" I pulled up a picture of him on my phone and showed it to Ethan. "This was him after he de-infested—his word, not mine—my spy shop when I first bought it."

"We've not met, but I've seen him around."

"He had his first name legally changed to Rodent."

"That's dedication."

"More than you can fathom. He came by the shop to tell us about the iguana cases, and I promised Rodent I'd look into it. I owed him."

Ethan smirked a half smile. "Your shop critters were that bad?"

"He called it a miscreant zoo. Found out when I stayed the night on the day I closed on the place."

Ethan smiled widely this time and chuckled. His belly, which was neither huge nor tight, twitched a bit. And in that moment, I realized Dale Carnegie was right. Smiles, and the physical changes that went with them, showed us who people were inside. Ethan seemed friendly and more attractive when he smiled.

Smiles *are* good. In moderation, of course. Like

chocolate, Scotch, and sex. He-he-he.

I nodded, pushed my lips together, and managed a closed mouth smile. "Maybe someday I'll tell you about the Ghost Rat." I put down my ditty bag. "Rodent's wife seemed worried when she came to see us this morning."

"Did she file a report at the station?"

"Said she tried and that a detective told her it was too soon to file anything."

"Other than the van, do you have any leads that indicate something bad happened?"

I felt weird talking to Ethan about this because I preferred to verify case information before briefing our law enforcement partners. This situation was still fluid. "Not yet, but two things are worrisome. First, no one I've talked to on the island has seen Rodent for the last couple of days. You know how people like to be all up in each other's business here."

"I'm learning that," Ethan said. "Maybe he's not on the island. Business trip to Houston? Or maybe a fling?"

"And he dumps his precious Rat Mobile? Perhaps, but he's not answering texts or calls and that's unusual. Also, there's something not right about this whole iguana situation; they seem to have appeared from nowhere and in a hurry."

"I had one on my car the other day for the first time."

I shrugged. "Metallic heat rock. We interviewed one of Rodent's clients. Iguanas crapped in his pool. He said it was a recent issue. And now the Lizard Liquidators are in town."

"That's Rodent's new competition?"

"Yes. We'll tail them, see where they go, what they do." I scrolled through the notes I'd been taking on my phone. "I'm also concerned about my client's motives. She's…interesting."

Ethan listened while monitoring the bushes that hid Rodent's van. "Tell me more."

"Nothing concrete yet. Seems charming, intelligent, gorgeous, and in love with Rodent. She's a successful romance novelist. Probably makes more money than he does."

"Too perfect?"

"Maybe. She wasn't truthful with us about the timing of things."

"Most people are liars." Ethan chuckled. "That sounds cynical, but you know what I mean."

I nodded because I did, and that some lies mattered more than others.

Ethan looked at his watch. "It'll be another hour or two before they pack it up. We'll leave two uniformed officers here to keep an eye on things. You might as well go home." He turned like he was getting ready to leave.

I put my hand up to stop him. "Ethan, please assign your team to look for Rodent."

"The major cases squad is on another assignment…" Ethan took a step closer. "Let's see what forensics comes up with on the van. Send me any information you have, and I'll have someone check it out."

"That's fair. I'll keep working it from my end. The iguana situation, Rodent's whereabouts, and my client's potential involvement."

"What is it about marriage that brings out the worst in some people?"

"Maybe they weren't smiling enough." I knew as soon as I said it that Ethan would wonder where that comment came from. I was wrong.

Ethan snickered and clapped his hands once. "You might be right. I've been divorced five years."

You shared a personal fact, Captain Slaughter…I believe you might like me. As a professional colleague, of course. This is a mystery novel, not a romance.

Chapter 12

Day 4, Saturday, March 3
7:25 a.m.

The Terminal Two building at the Galveston cruise port buzzed with frenetic energy whenever ships were docked. Throngs of tired, fattened, disembarking passengers competed for porters and cabs while eager new cruisers lined up early at security so they could get first dibs on the free hors d'oeuvres and sparkling wine.

My instructions from Dora were to meet Dr. Quintana Flores at 7:30 a.m. just outside the terminal, near a concrete bench at the west end of the long building. I found and sat on the bench at 7:25 while slurping the large drip coffee I'd picked up at the Starbucks on Harborside. It wasn't the same as the Mod, but super convenient and fast, which was important since I'd gotten home at 2:30 a.m., to sleep around three, and then back up at 6:00 a.m. The hot shower helped, but I still felt ditzy and out of it.

The bench was far enough away from the main entrance door that it was one of the few quiet spots in view. At 7:35, a short-roundish man bounded in my direction, I stood as he got close.

"Are you Xena?" he asked.

"I am," I said. "Dr. Flores can't make it?"

"She'll be here soon. Just running a few minutes late. She mentioned she was meeting you here and told me what you do."

"What I do?"

"For a living."

I nodded, but this change in plans worried me. I was leery of unfamiliar people who popped into my life. The man dressed in a ship's officer uniform looked pleasant enough and was so far.

He walked closer to me.

I stepped back and swayed a bit.

He leaned forward and nodded. "I've an issue…on the ship with my staff… I was hoping to talk to you about it."

I stepped back again. "Issue?"

The man looked around. "I think one of my employees is a gigolo."

It took a minute for me to realize what he was saying, but when I did, my interest level went from *try to escape* to *tell me the details.* "Turning tricks on the ship?"

He covered his eyes with one hand and gave me a silent *shh* signal with the other. "Yes."

"I assume you have security or police on board?"

The man stepped closer again. "We have a very capable team. Mostly ex-military." He leaned into me and whispered. "I'd rather not involve them in this situation."

This guy was invading my personal space with all his leaning. I stepped back half a step instead of a full one because I was at the edge of the sidewalk. "You don't know if he's a gigolo?"

He held up one finger and tilted his head. "Pretty sure, but he's my best lounge singer. Think Sinatra meets Steve Perry. People love him." He paused and rocked back on his heels. "Some maybe too much." He rubbed his thumb and index finger together. "New-jewelry-after-every-port too much."

I nodded. "I understand. What is it you'd like me to do?"

"Quintana said you're a private dick."

I snorted a laugh and bent over, almost spilling my coffee. "We don't call ourselves that any longer."

The man's cheeks turned red. "Sorry, I was trying to be cool."

I was starting to like this awkward little man but was prepared to hurt him if he got any closer to me. "Happens to us all. How about we start with an introduction? I'm Xena Cali, spy shop proprietor and private investigator." I extended my hand. "And you are?"

The man placed both hands on his cheeks. "Oh, my goodness, where are my manners? I was just so nervous." He grabbed my hand and shook it for a long time. "This entire thing has me in a tizzy. I've been cruise director for twenty years on five different ships and never had to deal with something like this. Rascal is —"

"His name is Rascal?"

"Yes, Rascal Romano, I know that sounds bad, but he

got that name from his mommy, not the ladies from Cougars International and —"

"Cougars International?"

"Yes, I know that sounds bad, but they generally bring their own men, I mean —"

I put up my index finger to stop him. "What's *your* name?"

He lifted his head and eyes. "Oh! Sorry, what am I thinking? I'm Anthony Strangelove. That's not my actual name, it's my stage name, my real name is Hal Roach Jr., but people call me Ant."

"Ant?"

He nodded.

I wondered what would happen when I introduced him to Rodent. I smiled inside. "It's a pleasure to meet you. Let's go back to my initial question. What is it you want me to do?"

Ant nodded several times, moved to the side, and leaned into my ear. "I'd like you to come on board and determine if Rascal is moonlighting with the Cougars. Get me evidence I can use to get him to stop for good. I can't lose my best singer or let this continue." He straightened his head and looked at me. "Do you take Discover Card? I'm hoping to keep this under the corporate radar."

I laughed. "You want me to go undercover on the ship?"

"All expenses paid besides your fee. Upgrades galore." Ant winked. "Sis."

"Sis?"

"As my visiting sister, I can give you uncommon access.

Even to some crew areas. This is an amazing ship. Like nothing you've ever seen."

"I'm sure it's lovely —"

"Like nothing you've ever seen," Ant repeated.

I nodded. "— but I doubt Rascal will hit on someone who he thinks is your sister, unless he's also stupid. Is he... stupid?"

Ant waved his hands. "Oh no. You're far too young and, may I say, beautiful to be one of his special customers. But maybe you can observe the business transaction as it goes down?"

This seemed like a terrible idea. "An undercover stakeout."

He nodded and grinned.

"I'll need to think about it and look at my availability. Can I get back with you in a day or two?"

Ant nodded and smiled.

"I'll e-mail you. You get e-mail on the ship, right?" I don't know why I didn't just tell him no. Perhaps it was the way he pleaded or because I'm drawn to weird cases.

Ant handed me his business card and asked me to e-mail as soon as possible. He lifted one arm toward the door of the building. "There's Quintana now. Perfect timing, as always. She's a delightful person and an absolute gem of an entertainer. Her show is among the most popular on the ship. We love her to bits! I'll leave the two of you to talk."

Ant walked away. He patted the woman he said was Quintana Flores on the shoulder when he passed her. As she walked toward me, her long, dark brown hair flowed and flapped in the wind. She was short, about five foot three, and well-rounded in all the preferred places. Voluptuous, but also strong because I could see muscle tone in her arms and legs.

When she was just a few feet away, Quintana beamed. She looked about thirty years old. "Xena?"

I stepped forward and offered my hand. "Yes, thank you for meeting me on such short notice, Dr. Flores."

"No problem. You can call me Q. Everybody does. Sorry I'm late. I see that Ant kept you busy in the meantime."

"We had a pleasant chat."

Quintana walked over to the bench. "Let's sit. I'm afraid I don't have a lot of time. There's so much to do on turnaround days."

I sat next to her and pulled out my notebook, pen, and phone. "Sure, I'll get right to it. I understand you're a reptile expert?"

"Herpetologist. I got my PhD in Evolutionary Biology from Manchester University in the UK."

"That includes iguanas, right?"

"For sure. Much of my research and conservation work has focused on saving the endangered Grand Cayman blue iguana."

"I was hoping you could help me understand more about green iguanas."

"OK, that's surprising. You're the first private investigator I've met with an interest in iguanas. Or is your inquiry personal? Perhaps your child is asking for one?" She patted my hand and smiled. "They're a handful and nothing like the cute lizards found in the movies." Her plump pink lips stood out next to her medium brown complexion.

"No, my interest is professional. I'm looking into an uptick of complaints on the island. People have been finding iguanas on their property."

"Xena—I love your name—you've heard about the issues that Florida and Mexico have had with invasive iguanas, yes? If the climate is tropical, the trees will be filled with green iguanas. They're insidious. Grand Cayman, where I was born, has been struggling to contain green iguanas for decades. They're part of the reason the blue iguana numbers have been in decline. The cats, rats, and dogs don't help, either."

I double underlined the word *insidious* as I wrote it. "What makes them insidious?

Q pulled her hair into a ponytail and then released it. She had a lot of shiny, bouncy hair. "Green iguanas, also called common iguanas, are excellent swimmers, so they get around. And they have a healthy fear of other animals, including humans, and so are quick to escape danger. They spend most of their lives up in trees or in bushes and lay lots of eggs. They're the rabbits of the reptile world."

I showed Quintana pictures of the iguanas Rodent had caught.

"May I?" She reached for my phone and then zoomed into and out of each of the images. "Yep, those are greens."

"Can you tell if they've come from pet shops or the wild? I've a contact who believes these animals were wild or near-wild."

Quintana raised an eyebrow and handed my phone back

to me. "Who said that and what does near-wild mean?"

"A local pest control expert," I said. She seemed put off by my question.

"Does he or she have a biology degree?"

"No, just professional experience. Are you saying he's wrong?"

"I've been around iguanas all my life and wouldn't be able to tell you where these iguanas did or didn't come from. And keep in mind that the gene pool is quite mixed. Where do you think the pet trade gets their iguanas? They take them from the wild, of course. I'm sorry, but this man couldn't know where these animals came from just from looking at them. DNA tests might narrow it down." She shifted and turned her body to me. "What does it matter where they came from?"

I raised my shoulders. "It might not matter at all. I'm just checking out the information I have, which isn't a lot. Is there anything that might cause a sudden increase in the iguana population here on Galveston?"

She paused for a moment to think. "Favorable breeding season, availability of food, fewer predators. The usual things. Also Galveston had a warm winter, so that's likely a factor. It'll be interesting to see how they do next winter."

"But you're not surprised they're here."

"If I were an iguana, I'd come to this island. Less competition for food!" Q laughed out loud. "In Florida, they have to dodge the pythons and wild pigs. Not to mention the snowbirds who keep bulldozing their habitat."

"Hmmm, good to know."

"Iguanas are sneaky and can stay hidden when they want

to." Q smiled and rocked back and forth. "Maybe a discarded female pet found a discarded male pet and they've been building their family tree on the west side for a while."

Quintana Flores was opinionated, but her assertions seemed to come from knowing stuff. She obviously knew something about Galveston Island, too. "May I ask what a herpetologist researcher is doing working on a cruise ship?"

She put her hand on my leg. "My mother asks me this question every time I call her! I continue to work on research projects, but my focus is on prevention and conservation. The shows I do onboard and the tours I lead on Grand Cayman educate people about the dangers blue iguanas face. I like to tell rich people how they can help." She rubbed her fingers together and raised her eyebrows. "Since working onboard, we've tripled donations to the Blue Iguana Foundation. When people see these amazing animals up close and learn how Westerners caused the problems we now face, they open their hearts and wallets and buy T-shirts for all their grandchildren. So, although pedestrian, the show is excellent use of my time to help the blues."

Quintana stood and looked at her watch.

I popped up beside her. "Good for you, I'm sure your shows are fascinating. I know you need to go." I shook her small but strong hand and gave her one of my cards. "You've been very helpful. Thank you for the offer to meet again, I might just take you up on it."

Q turned and walked away. Slow at first but then speedy as if she had somewhere to be. Halfway down the sidewalk, she turned and waved. "Bye, Xena!"

Quintana didn't need to read Dale Carnegie—she embodied it.

As I walked to where I'd parked along Harborside Drive, the quart of caffeine I'd consumed kicked in. I thought of all the questions I should've asked Quintana but didn't. I wondered what she did during her show on the ship and the obvious hygiene issues. But most of all, I wished I'd asked Q if an iguana had ever talked to her.

Chapter 13

10:30 a.m.

I was lost in thought about Ant's onboard gigolo situation when I blew past the spy shop's parking lot. This type of case, with all its tawdry elements, would generally be right up my alley. I loved catching sexually motivated slimeballs in the act and then ceremoniously ending their decrepit little careers. *You want exposure? I'll give you lots of exposure...just not the kind you're hoping for.*

He-he-he.

No, it's true. I've said those exact words, and it was awesome.

With a few left turns, I was back at the shop. I sat in the car for a minute while I collected my things and thoughts. I wanted to take this case, even though I knew it was a bad idea. We didn't have any big cases at the moment, so I had the time to go undercover. But I didn't want to be in the middle of the Gulf of Mexico while this thing with Rodent was going on. We weren't friends in the usual sense, Rodent and I, but we shared a connection akin to the relationship one develops with her gynecologist or urologist. They've seen you naked and touched your icky bits, so you might as well get real together. You know what I mean? Rodent had gone way under the hood of my spy shop and manhandled the numerous nasty infestations enabled by years of neglect. Perpetuated by the previous owner, readers, not me. They had boarded up the place two decades before I bought it.

Rodent hadn't shied away from the smells, decay, or angry pest interlopers. And this means something. After everything we'd been through to get this shop in shape to open, I would be there for Rodent Roger.

But the gigolo, if this guy was one, needed to go down. I could imagine his approach. A good-looking lounge singer hits on older women with his je ne sais quoi charm and enough alcohol to ensure the encounters fit his packed schedule. The ladies feel alive and desirable. They take his not-so-subtle hints and reward the rascal's efforts with expensive gifts and big cash gratuities. And no paper trail. It wasn't a unique con game, but one that required guts and creativity to pull off in the confined ship environment.

I tripped over the small step up and nearly dropped my second coffee as I opened the door to the shop. I then headed to the back where Dora and Sparky were waiting for me.

Get it together, Xena.

There were a lot of pros and cons to taking this gig. Once onboard the ship, I could spend time with Quintana. I had more questions for her and was eager to practice my Dale Carnegie. On the other hand, I knew from experience that iguanas crapped all over the place and could be mean. Iguanas...Rodent...Ultima...Rascal the gigolo.

I had to accept it wasn't the right time for me to leave the island. I'd resolved to e-mail Ant to decline the case when the perfect solution hit me like a lightning bolt.

"Dora, I'd like you to take a cruise." I sat down at the table in our meeting/stock room. "Can you be ready to board this Thursday?"

"Is this a trick question? A new bonding technique?" Dora paused and looked around. For what, I did not know.

"Nope, just business. You'll be undercover. I need you to check out a suspicious situation."

Dora's eyes got wide while her toothy smile told me she was up for it. "I love this job."

"Lucky dog!" Sparky said. He raised his eyebrows and glared at me, perhaps hoping I might dole out a dream gig to him, too.

I smirked and put my hand on the table. "Before you get too excited, let me tell you about your assignment." I gave Dora and Sparky the rundown of my surprise visit with Anthony Strangelove, aka Ant.

"Rodney is Rodent, and Anthony goes by Ant? What's wrong with people these days?" Dora asked. "Two guys with perfectly good names." She was looking all around the room like she does when she's making a mental list. "Whatever his name...I'm ready to solve crimes on the high seas!"

Sparky tapped at his keyboard. "The ship's name is *Twisted Ambition*?"

"That's right, Sparky." I knew using his name sounded

lame the second it came out. But Dale Carnegie said people love hearing their name.

"Did you...go onboard?" He was staring at his screen, his face crunched up as if he was looking at a picture of fungus.

"No, I met them outside the port pavilion. I assume they have the usual bad buffets, smoky casinos, and way off-Broadway shows. Plus, an iguana show, which is unique and apparently a fund-raising campaign."

Sparky projected the company's website on to our seventy-inch presentation monitor. "This is no ordinary cruise line."

The three of us stared in silence at the bright leotards, painted faces, a human cannonball, and what might've been the world's largest opium pipe. The vibe of the page was a mash-up of Cirque du Soleil, *Fear Factor*, and the Kama Sutra. A plump middle-aged woman in a velour jogging suit held a contraption that looked like a hamster habitat but was surely sexual since it was red and appeared to have a power button. A smiling man sporting a yellow spandex onesie hung in a hammock.

My stomach tightened. Had I checked out Ant or his ship? No, I had not. In my defense, I'd been up all damn night, and he wore a starched white shirt with three gold stripes on his epaulettes. He seemed, while not normal, legit for a ship's officer. I looked again at the screen. "This might not be such a good idea."

Dora's face was pale, and her smile had fallen. "How...weird can it be? I'm sure it's...fine."

Sparky clicked on the ABOUT page.

We created the Audacious Cruise Line to serve off-beat adventurers looking for a better vacation. Our travelers aren't interested in following hordes of people from bad buffets, to second-rate shows, and into pissed-in pools. They expect the unexpected, are prepared to be shocked, and eagerly participate in activities no other cruise line would dare offer. What happens in international waters...will blow your mind. Some call us twisted, outrageous, or eccentric. We reply, REBEL HELL YES. Your life will forever change the moment you become an Audacious Tribute.

I cocked my head. "What? Ant said the ship held twenty-five hundred passengers and sold out every season. He didn't use the words *twisted* or *audacious* or *rebel hell* anything. And if this is what's on their itinerary, I'm surprised he cares about a little gigolo side action going on."

Sparky snorted coffee out of his nose. "Maybe it's the *side* part that's a problem. They're not getting their cut."

I shook my head several times as I contemplated the emerging weirdness of this job offer. "Sorry, Dora, you don't need to do this. I'll contact Ant and give him a piece of my pissed-off mind." I stood and started pacing beside the table. "What I don't get is how an iguana expert fits into this craziness."

"I'll be all right," Dora said, muffled through the hand that was covering her mouth.

Sparky projected another page of the website. "Check out their onboard activities."

I walked up to the screen. "Pole dancing lessons. Do-it-yourself tattoo parlor. Live leech therapy. Audience participation Sumo wrestling."

"And macramé." Sparky caught my arm as I walked by his chair. "If Dora doesn't want to go, can I?"

"Do you have a cougar costume?" I winked at Sparky and sat down at the table and remembered the reason we were meeting on a Saturday. "We need to move on. I'll see if I can get Ant on the phone after this meeting. They've got Skype capabilities while at sea, right?" I looked at Sparky.

"I'm sure they do, but guests might have to play strip poker to earn minutes." He started laughing.

I gave Sparky the *zip it* gesture. "Dora, let's deal with this later. I won't ask you to go on that ship if it's too weird."

Dora sat still and stared forward. "I appreciate that."

I glanced down at my notes from the morning and saw Ant's words. *Like nothing you've ever seen.* I should've asked him to expand on this point.

My head hurt and I needed something to counterbalance the caffeine buzz. "Take five and then come back ready to discuss what we've learned about Ultima, Rodent's van, Lizard Liquidators, and Rodent's whereabouts. I'm ordering a Hangover Burrito from Bubba's. Shall I get them to deliver three?"

Sparky nodded with his entire body.

Dora raised her finger. "I'll pass. My stomach doesn't feel so good right now."

Chapter 14

8:30 p.m.

I don't always surveil my clients, but when I do, I take extra precautions to ensure I'm not seen. There's something about discovering you're being spied on, and then billed for being spied on, that tends to delay prompt payment. After dressing head to toe in black, I jogged the two-point-three miles to the Roger residence, so I could count it as a workout. It was a decision I regretted after strapping on my large surveillance/break-in ditty backpack.

I wanted to observe Ultima in her natural habitat to assess her involvement in, or concern for, Rodent's disappearance. After working their sources and organizing our intake data, Dora and Sparky uncovered information about Ultima that raised my suspicions. Key finding 1: We found out from Sparky's cousin, who worked at the county court, that Mrs. Roger, through her attorney, had filed a Petition for Divorce and paid the three-hundred-dollar filing fee not once, not twice, but three times in the last year. She withdrew the petitions before the court mailed the legal notices or heard her petition in court. It was unclear whether Rodent knew his wife had filed for divorce. Key finding 2: A phone number Sparky had recorded from Ultima's call log was from a Houston-based pest control firm and one of Rodent's biggest competitors. Ultima didn't seem interested in the business when we talked with her. Key finding 3: Ultima Roger had joined three Los Angeles–centric Facebook groups. We couldn't find a record of her ever living in Los Angeles or being connected to the region. Was her interest related to an upcoming vacation or something more substantial? While these leads didn't rise to the level of smoking gun—not by a longshot—they piqued my interest in observing Ultima without her knowing we were watching.

Locals knew which house was Rodent's on account of the tall snake tree out front. Their house was a lovely yellow two-story Victorian with a vibrant blue trim and matching storm shutters. The large home sat on a corner lot and had a wraparound porch on the main and second levels. Two concrete lion statues on pedestals framed the wide, red-painted staircase that connected the front lawn walkway to the elevated first floor. The snake tree towered above the second-story veranda and was to the right of the red stairs.

But before you google *snake tree* (I know you were thinking about it), I need to clarify that Rodent's snake tree was the dead trunk and main branches of a large live oak that had been carved into a snake. A diamondback rattlesnake, to be exact, with a pissed-off looking rat in its mouth.

There are dozens of beautiful tree sculptures on Galveston Island carved to look like mermaids, dogs, pelicans, dolphins, angels, and other things. Most were commissioned by wealthier homeowners and nonprofit organizations after Hurricane Ike flooded the island in 2008. The tidal surge uprooted many trees, and the saltwater killed hundreds more. When you visit the island, pick up the free Tree Sculpture Tour map offered by the local visitor's bureau.

You won't find Rodent's snake tree on the tour map however, as his live oak died several years after Ike and had been made by combining materials from multiple trees. That was presumably the only way to include the bulbous rat body high up the sculpture. The local paper did a story on the exceptional piece, calling it a "gruesome reminder of the island's two most hated residents." But most of the residents I'd talked to thought it was cool.

I walked past the front of the Roger residence from the sidewalk across the street and then crossed the intersection to get a look at the east side and back of the house. Interior and exterior lights were on at the bottom floor, but the second story was dark. I scooted down the alley that ran behind the home. The backyard was framed by a four-foot-tall chain-link fence and a small garage. There was a staircase on the back of the house that accessed both the first and second floor verandas.

Piece of cake.

After looking around to ensure folks in neighboring houses weren't watching, I climbed over the back fence, lurked around, and looked in the windows along the back and both sides of the home. Unfortunately, the best view inside was from the wide-open front of the house because

Ultima had most of the other window blinds drawn.

I inched up the back stairs to the second-floor veranda and moved slowly and carefully to the front of the house. I crouched behind the snake tree sculpture for cover from those who might walk or drive by. It was about ten feet from the house but seemed closer. The snake's wide-open mouth clamped onto the doomed rat as its slinking body turned and twisted down a large branch and the oak's broad trunk. It went diagonally, then down. Or up then over when standing on the ground, as if the snake had jumped in the air to catch the rat. I marveled at the rat's anguished expression and the snake's diamond-patterned skin. The artist had sanded and polished the sculpture to a furniture-like sheen. It was a masterpiece.

My ditty bag was also something to behold—a mini spy shop filled with the latest tools of my trade. I pulled out one of my newest gadgets. It was a flexible telescoping wand that could extend up to thirty feet. It had a tiny and powerful video camera at its tip and a sound cone that could be opened like a mini umbrella from the handle. With the paired Bluetooth video camera headset, I could hear and see my surveillance target.

I crawled to the outer edge of the veranda and laid down on my stomach. After powering up the wand and checking the image on my headset, I eased it through the railing spindles. I'd shaped the wand so it would hug the porch ceiling and then drop several inches to reach the front window where I'd seen through the curtains a person—presumably Ultima—sitting.

Although the sheers fuzzed up the image, I could tell that Ultima was sitting alone in the living room, looking at her phone or iPad, and listening to vintage Garth Brooks. I could control where the video camera focused and take still images with a click of a button. I made a mental note to thank Sparky for finding this sweet new rig.

Someone knocked on the door, and I nearly jumped out of my headset. I held the wand still hoping they wouldn't notice it above their head. Ultima greeted the person after he announced his name. It was Captain Ethan Slaughter. They went into the house and stood in the middle of the living room.

I couldn't make out what Ethan told her, but Ultima's scream blew out my eardrums. She then doubled over and flopped onto the chair. Fearing the worst—why else would she have screamed?—I pulled the wand back onto the veranda and took off my headset. I looked for the quickest way down.

The snake tree.

I left my ditty bag behind and then climbed onto the porch railing. I vaulted toward the snake, aiming for the flat and smooth part. Instead, I landed with a thud just below the rattler's mouth. One of the rat's outstretched feet smacked me in the nose, which instantly began bleeding. While I slid down the length of the snake, I wiped with my sleeve, smearing blood all over my face. As my body hit a large curve near the end of the sculpture, it launched me in the air and onto the red steps.

The front door opened, and Ethan and Ultima stared at me.

I popped up. "What a coincidence!" I looked around and tried to come up with something better to say. I pointed like an airline employee. "That's an amazing snake."

Ethan looked at me as if I was a stripper who'd showed up at a wedding. "Xena, now's not —"

Ultima pushed in front of Ethan and reached for me. "He's gone!"

We hugged, though I was careful not to allow my bloodied face to touch her clothing. I stepped back and looked into Ultima's eyes. "Gone where?" I knew what she meant but didn't want it to be true. My stomach cramped up and my eyes watered.

"He's dead." She plopped down on the steps, dropped her head to her knees, and cried.

Ethan stepped closer. "Why's your face —?"

I shook my head and lifted my finger to stop him. I motioned him to follow me away from the stairs.

"Mrs. Roger, take your time." Ethan patted her on her shoulder as he walked down the steps past her. "We can do the official identification whenever you're ready. I'll be right here."

My heart sunk and mind raced. Was it an accident, or did someone murder Rodent? Could I have prevented his death?

Ethan watched me as he walked up. "We found his body in the water against one of the bridge pilings at San Luis Pass. Fisherman called it in."

I stared into Ethan's eyes to control my crying. "Shit. Shit! This is terrible. What more can you tell me? Are you sure it's him?"

"The investigation has just begun, and yes, we're sure. No answers yet as to the manner of death. The body wasn't in good shape. Some damage looked to be post-mortem, but I'm not the expert." Ethan widened his stance, put his hands on his belly and looked down. "Sorry, I know he was your friend."

"Thanks," I said.

"I'll want to get with you tomorrow to go over what you might know."

"Of course," I said.

Ethan stepped closer. "Why are you here, and what happened to you?"

"Went for a run and got kicked in the nose by a rat." I shifted back and forth, and my legs felt wobbly; it was sinking in that Rodent was dead.

Ethan turned toward the house. "OK, so that's how you'll be." He seemed perturbed.

I touched his arm, so he'd turn back toward me. "I was surveilling Ultima when you arrived."

"Yeah? Then where's your magic bag of tricks?"

I pointed to the second-level veranda. The large black lump of my ditty bag was barely visible. "I was on the veranda when I heard Ultima scream. I rushed down so I could find out what was going on."

"You fell down the stairs?"

I pointed to the snake tree. "Landed wrong. My adrenaline must've been surging."

"And the rat kicked you in the nose." Ethan nodded and then groaned.

I took in a deep breath, walked over to Ultima, and sat next to her on the steps.

She wiped her eyes with her hands and transferred her tears and mascara onto her khaki pants. "They want me to go to the police station. Will you come with me, Xena? I don't think I can get through this on my own." She looked at my face but didn't mention the blood.

"Of course." I said, knowing I couldn't be with her during police interviews. "I'll meet you there."

We stood and then Ultima got her purse and locked the house. As she walked by me, Ultima put her hand in her purse and gave me a packet of wet wipes. "What the hell happened to you?"

Ethan then helped Ultima into his car. He closed the door and walked up to me. "Where's your car?" Ethan looked around. The street was empty.

"I told you I ran." I managed a partial smile. "I want to see the scene and have my team involved in assessing what happened to Rodent."

"We've got to do this right," he said.

"Ultima hired us to find her husband. She's my client; I need to ascertain how Rodent died." I stood straight and put my hands on my hips Wonder Woman style. "And I want to figure it out for myself. I didn't think he was in danger."

"I know, but we must let the forensics team do their thing. They should be done with the scene by tomorrow."

"Have any initial ideas?"

"No, except that I can't fathom an accidental reason he'd end up beaten and in the water under the bridge. I've asked for a scene recreation and tox screen."

I pointed to the back seat of his car. "How long will you have her occupied?"

"You've got at least two hours before she'll miss you."

"Thanks." I stepped closer and looked up at Ethan. "We're working this together, right?"

"With some important guard rails." He stepped back and turned to leave. "Guard rails, Xena. It's my investigation now. Stay away from the scene until I say so. Tomorrow earliest. Tell me about any persons of interest before you engage them. Share every lead before you act. Got it?"

"Guard rails." I nodded. "You sound like BJ, by the way."

"He warned me about you." He opened his car door.

"Glad you found Rodent before he floated into the Gulf." I waved and turned back toward the house. As Ethan's car left, I crossed my arms because they'd begun shaking. I walked to the back stairs and up to the veranda to where I'd left my ditty bag. I sat and cried. My nose ached and my arms stung where they were skinned up from sliding down the snake tree, but nothing hurt more than my heart.

I texted Sparky and Dora and filled them in with what I knew about Rodent's death, which wasn't much. I asked them to meet me at the spy shop in the morning so we could go to work tracing Rodent Roger's movements over the last few days.

I needed eyes and ears on the scene that wouldn't break my promise to Ethan, so I texted Steve Heart. *Turn on your police radio. There might be something happening at San Luis Pass. Take a videographer. Can't say more.*

. . . Who's working it?

Slaughter's team.

I'll check it out. Thx.

I knew Steve would share with us his raw footage and stills from the scene and any tidbits he could get from those he interviewed in exchange for an exclusive when we broke the case.

I sprinted the whole way home while I talked to myself in my crime fighter voice. It was time to compartmentalize. To focus. To put personal feelings aside, find Rodent's killer, and bring him, her, or them to justice. But first a drink.

Once I got home, I sat on my second-story screened porch with the lights off. An Edradour in hand, I toasted my friend Rodent before the silky spirit slid down my throat, calming my shaking body.

Chapter 15

Day 5, Sunday, March 4
7:00 a.m.

I'd scattered the contents of every ditty bag I owned throughout the spy shop—on top of the front counter, spread across the retail floor, under my desk, and in meeting room chairs. Cellophane MoonPie wrappers spilled out of the small trash can we kept near the coffeemaker. I'd filled the whiteboards with scribbles, lists, taped note pages, and pictures: Rodent in his hazmat extermination suit; Rodent waving with his body stuck out his van's driver-side window while driving by the shop; Rodent dancing with the Ghost Rat that first time. And questions, lots of questions. WHAT HAPPENED? WHY RODENT? COULD I HAVE PREVENTED IT? WAS I EVER CLOSE TO FINDING HIM? WHO IS SKEETER? Hours of pacing around the store in alternating fits of anger, guilt, and determination had made my head throb.

I bet you're wondering why all the drama. Why a cool and composed crime fighter like me seemed to be falling apart. Or perhaps you're thinking *Get it together, Xena.* Although Rodent and I hadn't been close, his death had triggered emotions inside me I'd worked hard to suppress—fears of inclusion and fears of attachment.

Mine is messy work. Slimeballs and crooks don't like it when I shine a light on their decrepit actions. Occasionally perps fight back, hold grudges, or seek revenge. The crazy situation with Agatha and the Houston execs is an excellent case in point. And why do you think I have a top-of-the-line security system around my house? Post-bust revenge.

I'm willing to take these risks.

For *me.*

Rodent wasn't an investigator, and he didn't know—in a palpable way—the potential consequences of kicking the hornet's nest of a criminal mind. And while I didn't encourage Rodent to investigate the lizard people or know if they had anything to do with his death, the possibility haunted me. Could I've stopped him, and would doing so have saved him?

And my meltdown wasn't just about Rodent. It worried me that I'd allowed Dora and Sparky—my employees, my responsibility—to become more involved in front-facing parts of our investigations work.

Inclusion. Letting others into my eat-or-be-eaten world, knowing they might get hurt.

Attachment. Owning what caring ought to look like in action.

I'd always sheltered others from the gnarly bits of investigations to avoid emotionally complicated relationships. I was learning perhaps there was no other kind.

The morning edition of the *Galveston Post Intelligencer* hit the glass front door of the spy shop. I placed it and a box of tissues on the meeting room table and plunked down. My hands shaking from caffeine, sugar, and emotions, I picked up the paper and read Steve's front-page story. I already knew most of the details about how the police found Rodent Roger's dead body, but seeing the words printed made it somehow more real. Or final. Something I couldn't undo or reimagine.

I was glad Steve's editor had given him above-the-fold placement for the story. Rodent had been a fixture on the island and deserved no less. Steve included a touching quote from Ultima, which I'd helped broker late last night after I met with her at police headquarters. His piece was funny in parts, too, such as sharing his first-hand experience with Rodent's uncanny ability to find and capture a family of mice who liked living inside Steve's exotic cowboy boots. The piece ended with a tasteful but gruesome description of Rodent's body and an appeal for anonymous tips about Rodent's death or how his van ended up in the marsh at the end of Indian Beach Drive.

Sparky and Dora arrived together, or perhaps one had waited for the other before coming into the shop. We exchanged hugs, kind words, and glassy-eyed looks of understanding. We'd all been Rodent Roger-ed a time or two. Like the time Dora found a colony of bats in the attic of an old Victorian she and her friends had purchased to flip. Or Sparky's showdown with a wily squirrel who liked the taste of the lead pipe that vented his roof. And me and my precious and formerly infested spy shop.

Sparky looked around. "What's all this?"

I picked up a bundle of zip-ties and dropped them again. "Needed to check and replenish my ditty bags, make sure I'm ready."

"You've already had breakfast, then?" Dora pointed to the MoonPie wrappers.

"Most of those are from earlier. Late dinner."

"How long have you been here?" Sparky asked.

Do I tell it like it is, or pretty up the story to make my actions seem more rational? *Be real, Xena; your team deserves that.* "Ultima identified Rodent's body, and then Ethan asked her some questions. I sat with her afterward at GPD and then drove her home. Came here to drop off my ditty bag and then one thing led to another."

"You've been here since last night?" Sparky asked.

"Yes…" I said. "I'm OK. I slept a wee bit in my office."

"You've worked late the last two nights," Dora said. "Let's get through our business so you can go home and get some sleep."

I gave her a thumbs-up. "You read my fading, foggy mind."

Sparky made a pot of coffee. Dora opened another case of MoonPies and placed an assortment in the middle of the table. Yes, we have a corporate account with the MoonPie Company; I know you were wondering. Dora and Sparky then push things out of their way, sat at the table, and waited.

I dumped a mountain of used tissues in the trash bin before washing my hands in the bathroom sink. I looked at the chaos I'd created and sighed. "Dora, will you clean off the whiteboards and put up new case charts? Leave the pictures where they are."

We organized our information and listed POTENTIAL SUSPECTS, POTENTIAL MOTIVES, WHAT WE KNOW, and WHAT WE NEED TO KNOW on large sticky notes that we could move out of public view. We updated the charts throughout the case and used them to divide and conquer.

My ditty bag contents were still covering all the flat surfaces in the shop. I looked at Sparky. "Help me pick up all this crap?" I grabbed a chocolate MoonPie and moseyed out of the meeting room. "Then we've got a murder case to solve."

Truth be told, we didn't yet know if Rodent's death was a murder or an accident, but it was better to assume the worst rather than risk allowing a killer to walk among us.

By 9:00 a.m., we'd compartmentalized our grief and rallied to brainstorm the case charts with what we knew or suspected so far, which wasn't a lot. We navigated between computers, charts, phones, whiteboards, and one another like drunk coyotes to compile and confirm our notes. I stood at the back of the room and raised my arms behind my back. The stretch felt good, although I was still wobbly from two sleepless nights. "Let's pause and go over what we have. See if we're ready to make assignments."

Dora pointed to the Potential Suspects chart. "Our suspects are Ultima Roger and Zorin Montaño/Lizard

Liquidators. Plus, we've listed as placeholders other competitors, unsatisfied clients, side action, and people who Rodent owed money. Also, I added a question you'd written on the whiteboard before I cleaned it off. *Who is Skeeter?*"

I hadn't remembered writing that question, but Sparky reminded me that Rodent mentioned a Skeeter the day he came to the shop.

"Oh, right," I said. "He said Skeeter was a guy he knew who agreed the iguana situation was bonkers."

Sparky pointed at the chart. "It might be a complete coincidence that the island is suddenly being overrun by iguanas at the same time our most established pest control professional ends up dead, but I think we need to assume they're connected until we can prove otherwise."

"Rodent seemed concerned, so I am, too," I said. "I'd also like to determine if there's anything to this 'near-wild' nonsense or if that's a distinction that even matters."

We all looked at the charts for a moment.

"And then there's our client, Ultima," I continued.

Dora raised her right index finger. "Filing for divorce three times? Even her fictional characters aren't so fickle. The attorney she's hired has a reputation for securing big divorce settlements and retainer fees. Something significant was going on between the Rogers."

Sparky nodded. "And she contacted Rodent's competitor in Houston, but we don't know anything about him or why. Harold something..."

"Harold Knowles," I said. "I wonder if Ultima and Harold know each other."

"Such a mysterious woman!" Dora said. "What did a successful, high-profile writer like her see in a goofy no-frills guy like Rodent? No offense to weird guys." Dora grinned at Sparky.

Sparky twirled his stringy hair between his fingers. "None taken."

I lifted my arms up and down several times—like jumping jacks from the waist up—to increase circulation. "They were an odd couple, but some of the best pairings are like that. Put *wife* on the list for a potential motive. What if one of her crazy fans—not you, Dora—didn't want Rodent in the picture?"

"Ooh, yes. Obsessed reader becomes killer." Sparky rubbed his hands together and raised his eyebrows.

"It's time I had a long talk with our client. Next chart: Potential Motives." While I'd seen my share of abhorrent behavior, I'd concluded that love, money, or fame motivated most killers and it helped if we analyzed case information through these three filters.

Dora shifted over to the second chart. "Life insurance or other inheritance? A love triangle…though we've no evidence of hanky-panky."

Sparky cut in. "—The iguana dispositioning business."

"That could be a money-related motive," I said, "but I'd like to understand how much we might be talking about. Enough to inspire murder?"

Dora updated the What We Need to Know chart and then returned to motives. "Maybe wrong place, wrong time? Shouldn't we entertain the idea that this wasn't pre-meditated?"

"Perhaps," I said.

Dora joined me at the back of the room. "Here's a potential motive I know we don't want to think about. Related to fame. What if Rodent did something stupid because he was obsessed with being the go-to guy for pests on the island?"

"We've seen Rodent's erratic and spontaneous side," Sparky said. "When he gets a burr up his butt..."

"He was driven." I smiled at Dora and nodded. "Fair point, Dora. We should assume that the most important clues aren't yet on any of these charts." I touched her arm. "Add it as a potential motive and let's keep an open mind."

She returned to the chart. She stood tall and seemed satisfied. Another win for Dale Carnegie's suggestions to smile, use people's names, and show an interest in them.

"Sparky, you and I should stake out the Lizard Liquidators," I said. "I want to see them in action. How they find iguanas, their sales techniques with clients, where they go after they've captured them, and what happens to the iguanas."

"Right on," he said. Sting and surveillance operations tapped into and challenged Sparky's strengths for putting spy gadget technology into action.

I ate another MoonPie—vanilla this time—even though I was feeling sick to my stomach. I shifted back and forth to stay alert. "What do we know?"

Dora moved to the next chart and read our list. The bell on our front door clanged. We all looked up at our security monitors. It was Steve Heart.

Chapter 16

9:30 a.m.

Steve had been to the spy shop many times and knew where to find us. He ambled into the meeting room and held up his hand before plunging it into the pile of MoonPies. "May I? All I've had since yesterday is a stick of sugar-free gum." He poured himself a cup of coffee and sat down at the table.

His *S*-shaped goatee looked like an exploded cattail and he had bags under his bloodshot eyes. I guessed he'd been up late getting the feature story to press in time for the morning edition.

"Nice job on the story." I sat down at the table next to him.

He lifted his chin. "Gut-wrenching stories about murdered locals seem to be my specialty. I tried to strike a balance between the raw, cold facts and warm memories. Appreciate you encouraging the Mrs. to share a few words on the record." He looked up at our charts and unpackaged the MoonPie. "I see you guys were in the middle of something. You want me to leave?"

I knew—because we were alike in this regard—he was pretending to be polite and had no intention of leaving. His astute investigative instincts had brought him here for a reason. Perhaps it was the MoonPies and friendly faces, but more likely he was working on his next story. Even so, I was glad to see him and didn't call him on his bluff.

"No need," I said. "We were just making assignments. Anything you can tell us we don't already know?"

Steve scanned the information we had on our charts and on the whiteboard. He chuckled when he saw the pictures of Rodent. "That guy was a character… I don't see mention of the City Council meeting tomorrow."

Sparky started typing. "What's going on tomorrow?"

"Rodent and the other people…Lizard…" Steve was pointing at the charts.

"Liquidators," Dora prompted.

"Yeah, them. They were both scheduled to present their services and credentials. The agenda said the city needs someone to get rid of the iguanas at the county jail and other municipal properties. Not sure what's going to happen now. Maybe they'll postpone it."

"Prisoners fighting iguanas," I said. "I'd pay to see that show."

Sparky projected the City Council's website. "It's still listed on the agenda."

"We can watch it here on CCTV, but I'd like you to attend in person," I said to Sparky. "Chat with Zorin if you can. But don't tell him your name or where you work. Let's keep the option open for you to go undercover." My stomach clenched as I said it.

"Cool." Sparky nodded and his eyes narrowed as though he was thinking.

Steve looked at me. "Is Zorin their lead guy?"

"We think so. Thanks for the tip about the meeting. Anything else to add?" I was expecting some inside scoop or juicy gossip.

Steve looked up and bobbed his head like he was scanning through his thoughts. "I heard Ethan tell the forensics lead he was putting his team on the case."

"That's great, I asked him to do that."

"And Melissa told me that at first glance most of the damage to Rodent's body looked post-mortem. But she warned me not to mention it, because that was just her first impression."

Melissa Romero was the medical examiner, and her initial interpretations about things were generally accurate.

Steve looked back at me. "That's all I can think of, but I've got some irons in the fire. You read my story… Did I miss anything you know?"

I drummed my lips and looked up at the charts. "Our investigation's just beginning. No clear motive yet. Lots of questions. Everyone's a suspect."

"Even the wife, I see," Steve said. "Isn't she funding your team's work?"

"That's why we bill in advance." I tapped on my temple. "We always include our clients on the potential suspect list, but we're particularly interested in the mixed vibes we've gotten from Ultima."

Steve snickered. "Ah, well let me know if I should talk to

her again. I see you've written several facts about iguanas on your charts. Where'd you find your information?"

"Mostly online, but Xena met with an expert yesterday," Dora said. "A herpetologist."

Steve took out his phone. "Can I get a number? I'd like to interview him."

"She's a her," I said. "And the next time she'll be in town is Thursday. She works on the *Twisted Ambition*. I'm hoping to meet with her again. Wanna tag along?"

"Heck yeah. I've heard that ship is ridiculously bizarre with a capital *B*."

"I was going undercover on the ship until all this happened," Dora said and then radiated pride. I wondered if she was showing off to Steve or still interested in going onboard.

"Who said anything's changed?" I looked at Dora to gauge her reaction.

She opened her eyes wide and nodded. "Oh."

"It might be nice to have ready access to our herpetologist," I said. "While making a few bucks taking care of the Ant issue."

"Ant issue?" Steve asked.

"Just a little gigolo named Rascal," I said. "Nothing related to Rodent's case. I'll fill you in over drinks. I think it's your turn to buy."

Steve grabbed his ragged beard segments and tried twisting them back together. "If the stories are true, that ship offers unconventional entertainment. I wouldn't mind taking an assignment aboard the *Twisted Ambition*." He tipped his head and smiled at Dora. "You're a lucky lady."

"I'm jealous of Dora, too." Sparky winked.

"First, neither of you are Rascal's type. And second, we'll have no trouble finding occupational mischief here on land." I held up my coffee cup to Sparky.

Sparky nodded.

"I'll make a fresh pot," I said. "Then let's discuss how we should trick out the surveillance van for our incognito exploration into the world of the Lizard Liquidators. I'd love your ideas about any new equipment we should install."

The van was Sparky's pride and joy. He'd outfitted it with state-of-the-art equipment for capturing video and audio in challenging conditions. Like low-light situations, while hanging from a tree, or in the middle of a raucous crowd. And now, men chasing fast-moving reptiles. I knew discussing the van would refocus Sparky's mind away from the outlandish cruise ship.

And, dear readers, did you pick up on how I asked Sparky for his ideas and used his name? I even smiled at him, but I know you didn't see that.

"You guys are way too cool. Got any job openings?" Steve then stood and pointed at one of the video monitors. "Looks like you have two large iguanas sleeping under the light in your parking lot. I almost ran over one when I left the office. Bizarre times. I think I'll be focusing on this lizard paroxysm for my next big story. Let me know what you discover about them, OK? I'd like to interview the lizard people, too."

"Paroxysm? That coffee must've kicked in real good." I stood and patted Steve on the shoulder.

"It means a sudden attack or uncontrolled outbreak." Dora gloated.

"Oh, I know what paroxysm means…" I opened my arms and grinned. "I once used it during a board meeting to describe employee-generated sabotage clusters that popped up after leaders held lame events like cupcake giveaways, free car wash coupons, and cheery town hall meetings just before the employee satisfaction survey launched. Employees told me they felt bribed and had had enough. Fun times, those corporate paroxysms were."

"Show off," Steve said.

Although running on fumes fueled with caffeine and MoonPies, I felt a fresh burst of energy. I gazed up at our video monitors and noticed the iguanas in my parking lot hadn't moved. "Anyone want to spot me as I take a stab at handling an iguana? They look like they're sleeping."

"I'd like to see that," Steve said.

Sparky stood. "I'll videotape you."

Dora handed me a bottle of hand sanitizer. "Do you want me to google some iguana handling tips?"

"I'm good." I shook my head and sprinted in place for a few seconds. My instincts for dealing with wild animals were Grade A rock-solid. "I'm going to come up behind them like you would a gator then jump one."

Chapter 17

Day 6, Monday, March 5
10:00 a.m.

Never approach an iguana from behind. It freaks it out and makes it try to sprint away while whipping its long, spined tail back and forth. Green iguanas have a lot of sharp edges. Nails on their four feet and spikes all over. Even sleepy lizards can slash a person all to hell. Steve tried to help but stepped back and gave up when blood started dripping from one of my hands. Ever the steady hand, though, Sparky got it all on video, including the part where the iguana I refused to let go of crapped all over me. In its defense, I might've squeezed it a bit too hard. Dora got the Lysol wipes and first aid kit to help me clean up and treat my wounds. When was the last time you embarrassed yourself in front of your friends and employees?

I then went home to take a much-needed shower and nap and slept for hours. After reviving myself with a smoothie and stretching out my stiff muscles, I went for a run. March was a glorious time of year to be on the island. The highs and lows were in the sixties, and tourists had not yet flooded the town. Not that I disliked visitors, it's important to be clear about that. I relied on tourism for 55 percent of my sales at the spy shop. It's the resident in me that prefers the quieter times.

I knew I had a case to solve, and that I'd not find Rodent's killer while on a run. But I did my best thinking when in movement and needed new ideas. Plus, I'd gotten way behind on my training for the triathlon. I started mid-island and went west to the end and back—just shy of twenty miles—and then threw in a bit of parkour razzle-dazzle near the end to stimulate my deductive and inductive reasoning skills.

Parkour is the most-watched extreme sport on YouTube. It's true, you can google that. The term *parkour* was derived from *parcours du combattant*, which means obstacle course like those used for training the French military. Parkour practitioners such as me used our training to get through a complex environment quickly and efficiently. No help from machines or vehicles. We ran, swung, jumped, crawled, climbed, rolled, flipped, grabbed, or did whatever was needed to keep moving forward.

It suits my compact and boxy body style. Small hips, boobs, and subtle contours. I'll never win a bathing suit competition or bodybuilding award, but I can out-maneuver everyone I meet. And although I've been doing parkour since I was a teen, practicing is crucial to my private investigation work. It comes in handy when up against larger criminally motivated slimeballs who overestimate their physical advantage over me.

I sometimes wish I was a voluptuous woman. Because, let's be honest, bouncy boobs and swingy hips are appealing. But can they do tricks with all that jiggly baggage getting in the way? I had perfected many uncommon bedtime moves.

But back to my non-sex-related razzle-dazzle. After I got back to where I'd parked my car, I downed a blue Gatorade and then practiced jumping over my car with one or no touches. Turned off the alarm, goes without saying. Vaulting from the rear hatch to the front. One touch. Rolling over my vehicle from side to side. Constant contact with my back. Getting aerial by cartwheeling over the front of the car without touching it. I was a gymnast before I discovered parkour. And although my bandaged hand throbbed and my legs felt like noodles from the run, I did well. As for my mental productivity, let's just say I'd renewed my interest in the primary crime scene and whether there were others we'd not yet uncovered. It was again time I put boots on the ground and look for more evidence related to how and where Rodent was killed.

A phone call caused the Artic Monkeys tune playing in my AirPods to cut off. I looked at my watch and saw it was Ethan. I pushed the button on my left earpiece. "Hey, Ethan."

"You sound out of breath. I can call back later."

I walked in a slow circle in the parking lot to bring down my heart rate. "It's fine. I just finished my twenty."

"Minutes?"

"Miles. I'm training for a tri." I smiled because it was fun sharing that with Ethan. "What can I do for you?"

"I was hoping we could meet up today. I'd like us to get clear about what you and your team are doing on the Roger case. So we don't mess up the evidence chain."

I groaned inside because our case plan was still forming, but also applauded Ethan's command and clarity. "Sure. How about the Mod in two hours? I'll be looking for another shot of caffeine by then."

"Fine. See you there."

I called Dora and Sparky and asked them to e-mail me with any new updates so I could decide what to share with Ethan.

As I drove home, I saw several iguanas lying flat on side streets. They were using the asphalt as a gigantic heat rock. Rodent sensed the sudden increase in iguana calls was a warning signal for a bigger problem on the horizon. How did he put it?

Whole other can of worms.

Chapter 18

12:30 p.m.

I ordered my usual cortado—a double shot of espresso and half as much soymilk—and found a table in the side room. The Mod was three blocks from my spy shop and in the middle of downtown and the historic Strand area. It was a large coffee shop with a hip-meets-rustic front room and a large side room with lots of tables. They baked fresh scones and muffins that were to die for. When you visit Galveston, go there and tell them I sent you.

I had some time to read before Ethan arrived, and I wanted to work on my Dale Carnegie during our meeting. I thumbed through my book and re-read the section on smiling. The last two days had been tough, and I was ready to test the transformative powers of a smile.

I looked up from my book and across the room. There were about a dozen wooden tables, each with mismatched wooden chairs. Small original paintings for sale from local artists filled the painted beadboard walls. The painted concrete floors gave the place an industrial vibe. Another customer had taken a table toward the back of the room. He sipped the tallest glass of coffee they sold and was reading the *Galveston Post Intelligencer*. The man had gray curly hair and looked about sixty. His red sweatshirt accentuated his enormous belly.

"Hey," I said.

The man looked over at me.

"Do you think smiling is important? If I sat across the room from you smiling like this"—I grinned so my teeth were showing—"would you want to be my friend more than if I didn't smile?"

The man lowered his paper, stared at me without expression, tilted his head, and shrugged. He seemed amused, and familiar to me, perhaps from previous visits at the Mod.

"Exactly! It depends, doesn't it? How about now?" I stood up, walked to his table and sat in the chair across from him. I put my elbows up on the table and rested my chin on my hands and smiled. "What do you think of me now?" I mumbled without moving my teeth. "I'd like to know your honest opinion because I'm trying to make more friends."

The man's mouth cracked open. "Uh…" He swallowed and sat up straight. "I'm not sure what you want me to say." The man sipped his coffee and then stared at his cup.

"I'm sorry… This is freaking you out and I don't mean to interrupt your reading. I'm just trying to get a feel for whether this psychological mumbo-jumbo about smiling has merit. Does it make a difference?" I leaned toward the man and grinned. He maintained constant eye contact with his coffee.

"Sir, would you like to file a disturbing the peace complaint against this woman?" Captain Ethan Slaughter was standing under the door frame with a coffee cup in his hand. He'd pulled back his jacket, revealing his gun in its holster all badass style.

The man's eyes got big, and he shook his head.

I stood and returned to my table all cool-like. "How much of that did you hear?"

Ethan sat down at my table and smiled so wide I saw all his teeth.

I groaned and felt like a dork, then tapped on the cover of my Dale Carnegie book. "I'm reading a classic. Trying to get better at peopling."

The man with the curly gray hair got up and left in a hurry.

"Good for you for working on your skills. I think smiling is an important tool for investigators like us." Ethan blew on his drink and gave me a quick nod.

I liked that he said *investigators like us.* Police detectives often view PIs as little more than a nuisance. "You think so?"

"We need people—witnesses, POIs, victims, partners—to trust us. Likability plays a big part in how we're perceived."

POIs. Persons of Interest. "You make a good point, Captain Slaughter."

"Thank you." A softer smile this time. Warm.

This wasn't the first time I'd noticed that the captain was gentle on the eyes in a way that said *brother's best friend* versus heartthrob. My theory: He was tanned from fishing, not tanning. His hair was well kept because he got regular trims, not because he styled it every morning. He was strong because he worked hard, not because he worked out. He had brown eyes, salt-and-pepper hair, and was clean-shaven. He dressed professionally, but his clothes were neither fashionable nor outdated. Just smart.

If Ethan were a car, he would've been a Volvo, or maybe a Saab if they were still making them. Steve Heart is a temperamental Fiat, although he'd likely self-identify as a Jaguar. Dora is a VW—steady and fun. And Sparky? That's a tough call, but I'll say he's a Subaru: principled, adventurous, but nothing fancy.

What kind of car am I? I know you were wondering. I'd love to hear how others describe me, but since this is my story, I'll take a stand for being a Jeep Wrangler. Stick shift, of course. Sahara trim in forest green with a tan soft top. I drive a BWM X3 for practical reasons.

Or maybe I'm a Tesla, because they're quiet, speedy, and expensive.

Ethan looked around and seemed satisfied with the level of privacy in the side room. Most everyone was sitting outside on this lovely spring day. "Thanks for meeting me here. What happened to your hand?"

"Tried and failed to make friends with an iguana," I said.

"No...what really happened?" Ethan's eyes narrowed.

I found it interesting that after everything he'd seen me do, he still didn't think I'd do something so ridiculous. "I was on the losing end of a boxing match at my gym."

"That's more like it," he said. "Here's to better luck next

time." Ethan raised his glass to me.

It was clear he never boxed in his life. "I never rely on luck." I smiled.

"Touché." Ethan looked around again. "Can we step outside for a minute?"

I followed Ethan out of the coffee shop and half a block down Post Office Street. He stopped near where I'd parked my car.

"I assume you're still working this case for Mrs. Roger?" Ethan said.

"She hasn't fired us yet, although I might have to smooth things over if she realizes I've been watching her."

"She seemed quite intelligent when I talked with her."

"The night you found Rodent?" I asked.

"And yesterday." Ethan looked up and down the street. "Let's chat about how we're going to handle our shared goal of solving this case."

I walked to my car and put my book in the back seat and coffee on the roof. Ethan followed. "Sure," I said. "We've only begun our investigation, but I can tell you that right now our focus is on Ultima and the Lizard Liquidators. I don't know if either is involved. Who are your POIs?"

Ethan chuckled and shook his head. "You know I can't get into that. We're just getting started, too."

"No suspects, then."

"Not yet," he said.

"Do you know where he was killed?"

Ethan tilted his head and shook it.

It didn't surprise me that Ethan didn't share more. Cops

act like cops. And precocious PIs were…well, somewhat forthcoming and always mysterious.

"Do you have a copy of the autopsy yet?" I straightened and put my hands on my hips to show I meant business. "I want to get a copy from the ME as soon as it's available. Because I wonder if it's possible he died or was killed near where his van was hidden and floated to the bridge."

"Another day or so before the report is out, I suspect. That's a good question, though."

"Sparky is researching the tides, water levels, and any drone footage along the bay."

Ethan nodded. "Share that info with me?"

"Of course," I replied.

Ethan looked at my car. "There's a handprint on the roof. Someone giving you a problem?"

I laughed. "No, I was vaulting over my car earlier."

Ethan sighed and frowned. "Come on, no bullshit. Someone harassing you?"

I looked up and down the street. No cars were coming. I grabbed my coffee and handed it to Ethan. "Hold this a minute?"

I walked across the street so I could get a running start and then jumped and twisted to somersault in the air over my car without touching it. Then I bounced up, leaped toward the car, and placed my hand on the same place on my roof as the print and levered over the car a second time.

"Damn," Ethan said. "And you practice this?"

I smiled and walked closer. "Yes, I know it's crazy, but I love it." I held up my forearms. "And as I said the first time,

I cut the hell out of my hand and arms trying to catch an iguana." I accepted my coffee back.

"Huh." He looked at me and raised his eyebrows. "I'd love to hear that story, but I'm late for a meeting."

Do not let yourself become interested in a cop.

Do not let yourself become interested in a cop.

Do not let yourself become interested in a cop.

I took a sip of my coffee and gave Ethan a thumbs-up. I overslurped and had coffee foam on my lips. "Let's do this again sometime soon."

Chapter 19

3:00 p.m.

When I called Ultima and asked if we could meet, she said she was just about to call me with the same request. Was she about to fire me, or to say she didn't need us working the case because the police had it under control? Perhaps she'd found Rodent's secret journal with all the answers to our most pressing questions. Dora had prepared an invoice for the work we'd done in case Mrs. Roger was letting us go. We accepted checks, cash, all major credit cards, and Venmo.

It surprised me to see movers at the Roger residence as I walked up to the open front door. I walked in and found Ultima in the empty living room, directing the movers as they took out boxes.

"Xena, there you are," Ultima said. "I'll grab us a drink and join you out on the patio. It's my only place to sit. Beer or wine?"

"Wine. Whatever's open is fine." I dodged several guys in blue overalls and made my way to the backyard. I sat in one of the four chairs around the teak table in the shade of an old oak tree. A swift breeze put a chill in the air.

Ultima walked out with two beers. "Sorry, they've packed everything except what was in the fridge. I hope you like IPA." She sat across from me and sighed. Ultima wore a gray sweatshirt, jeans, and a lot of jewelry. I wondered if she was afraid the movers would steal her baubles.

I accepted the beer and took a sip. "You're moving?"

She rolled her eyes. "Yes, I am, and I know what you might think about that."

"You do?"

"Yes. Before we talk about the case, I need to clear the air with you."

I was getting fired. "Sure, be direct." I always tell clients I'd rather just get it over with, but most meandered their way through giving bad news.

Not Ultima.

She took a slow sip of her beer and leaned back. She seemed calm and confident. "In the publishing world, you're what we call an unreliable narrator. Do you know what I mean?"

There are two strategies I use when faced with conflict—mirror or shock. I mimicked her nonverbal cues and rested my elbows on the chair's arm. "I've not heard that term, but I can guess."

"An unreliable narrator is a character who"—she put one finger up and wagged it—"one, lacks credibility, or two"—a second finger went up—"is evasive or deceptive, or three"—a third finger—"is naive to the point of blurring reality and fantasy. You are not naive, Xena."

I swallowed hard. "I try to stay informed."

Ultima didn't move. She looked at me and smiled. "But deception is your forte."

"Well—"

"No, no. I'm not angry that you were spying on me the night I found out my husband was dead. But I'm disappointed you felt the need to hang from my balcony and peek into my windows when you could've been looking for Rodney."

I placed a hand on the table. "Ultima, it's standard—"

Ultima put up her hand. "I'm sure it is, Xena, and I'm not interested in hearing your explanation. The thing with unreliable narrators is they add conflict and tension to the story. I'm seeking less of both."

She's firing me…

"Before I hired you, I checked out the press coverage from your previous cases. You get exceptional results, but your methods are sometimes unconventional. That's fine—preferred even. But before we move forward as a team —"

She's not firing me…

"— I want to make sure we're on the same page. I'm not the antagonist in this story." Ultima raised her arm and pointed to the house. "And my rather sudden move isn't a cause for your concern. I can't be in this house. His house. Our house. I've moved into the Tremont and am putting everything in storage. That's right up the street. You'll have ready access to me, although only through the door to my room."

Did I tell my client I've spied on plenty of people who

were staying at the Tremont House hotel? No, I did not.

Ultima remained calm. "I can't spend another night here, and I don't want to step foot in this place again."

It was my time to mirror her again. I grabbed a pen and notebook from my bag. "Let's get on the same page; I think that's a terrific idea. I have a couple of questions."

"Of course." Ultima held up her beer, toasting this new chapter in our relationship.

"When you came to the spy shop, you said you hadn't called Rodent until the morning when you woke up and saw he'd not been home. Your phone records indicate you'd been calling through the night. Which is true?"

A soft smile came across her face. "The phone records you have are correct."

"Why did you lie?" I asked.

"It was a test."

"Bullshit."

She gazed at me but said nothing.

I looked down at my list of questions. "How did you and Rodent meet? Was it love at first sight?"

Ultima laughed and leaned on the table. "Are you kidding me? Do you want the short or long version of the story?"

I picked up my beer. "Still full, so I've got time if you do."

"It's a great story; one of my best. My house had mice. I called Rodney, and he took care of the problem with great flair. He was entertaining and an interesting character. I have a nose for characters. A month later I called him again and said I had another mouse in my bedroom. I didn't."

Ultima paused and looked up at the sky. "Rodney left some traps and came back a week later. They were empty. By this time, he'd started flirting with me. He asked me out. I said yes. Not because I wanted to go out with him, but because I needed a model."

"Model?" I asked. "Like a nude model to paint?" I was trying not to imagine Rodent with no clothes on.

Ultima tilted her head. "That might be closer than you'd think, but for writing, not painting. I take writing romance novels seriously. With detailed love scenes that I can only create right after I've acted them out. I publish three books every year, so I need a lot of models."

Once more I was trying not to imagine Rodent naked, but what a brilliant way to live. Screw. Write. Get paid. Screw. Write. Get paid. I started thinking about changing professions.

Ultima spun her wedding rings. "Rodent became my most eager and productive model. He would do anything I asked and loved it when I coached him during our love-making sessions. We even got to where I e-mailed him the scenarios I wanted to act out so he could practice and prepare."

"Impressive," I said. I was still trying not to imagine Rodent in the buff.

"Yes. This went on for over a year. Much longer than any previous models held my attention. I broke up with him after I'd gotten all the love scenes written for a trilogy of books that featured his character."

"Oh no," I said. I was getting caught up in Ultima's story and had to remind myself I was interviewing her. But then I realized I'd get more information if I let her riff.

"It was sad," she said. "Rodney was crushed but continued to call me every month. When the Hope and Chance books came out—they're the principal characters, Hope and Chance—the feedback from my most loyal readers was better than I'd ever received. They wrote that they loved these two characters and hoped I might bring them back. They had chemistry and seemed very much in love."

Ultima's eyes were tearing up. "I realized they were right. As odd as we were as a couple, we worked. It was the best and most explosive love I'd experienced."

"Wow." I didn't know what to say, but her story had me hooked.

Ultima wiped her eyes. "I called Rodney and asked him out again. I took him to Houston for the weekend and proposed after our second night back together. Ro had started out as my roleplay lover but became my soulmate." She sighed. "And that's how we met."

I looked down at my next question but paused.

"No more questions, Xena?" Ultima asked.

I looked back up at her. "Then why did you file for divorce?"

She gazed at me for at least a minute.

I resisted the temptation to fill the silence.

"Fear," she said. "It worried me that I'd not be able to write new romance stories without being unfaithful to my husband. My books are better than most because I did my research. Myself. I've whipped people, been penetrated, and hung upside down for foreplay. You've heard of method actors, well I'm a method writer. I knew my readers would recognize it if I cheated on my process. I've sold twelve million books. It came down to my marriage or my career. So, I filed for divorce because I was unwilling to give up my career."

"You never went through with it," I said.

"I ultimately chose my marriage," Ultima said. "I thought I might try my hand at writing a mystery series before Rodney went missing. Not sure what I'll do now."

My mind went to the dark side. What if killing Rodent was part of her research? Or research that went wrong?

"That's fascinating," I said. "Perhaps we could work together on a mystery story."

Or, Mrs. Roger, perhaps we already are.

Chapter 20

6:00 p.m.

"In my defense, I was channeling you when I deviated from our plan," Sparky said and then smirked as he cued up the video from the Galveston City Council meeting. "And you said to leave open the option for going undercover. I'd say it's now wide open." He fidgeted with his water bottle and pen, looked at me, and then around the room. Sparky seemed nervous, perhaps because he didn't know if I'd be pleased with what he'd done.

Dinner from Mama Teresa's Flying Pizza arrived, and we splayed open the boxes on the front counter. We each got a couple of slices and returned to the meeting room table.

"I don't think it's that bad," Dora said. She smiled at Sparky. Dora had watched the live stream of the city council meeting while I'd been interviewing Ultima at the Roger residence. Although I'm sure you'll agree that *interviewing* isn't the best word to describe what happened at Ultima's soon-to-be former house. *Performance* might be a more apt description.

"Without further ado!" I pointed to the screen. "I can't wait to see what all this buildup is about." I tucked hair behind my ears and navigated a slice of pepperoni and jalapeno pizza into my mouth.

Sparky played the video. The secretary to the council introduced the topic and then acknowledged that Rodent Roger, of Rodent Roger's Pest Control Service, was no longer available to appear because he was, in fact, now dead. And he acknowledged that Zorin Montaño, very much alive, was present.

Yes, the secretary used those exact, awkward words; I know you were wondering.

The council opened the topic for discussion. One member suggested they select the only remaining alive provider and not wait to seek additional bids because the detention center employees had threatened to call out sick if the iguana problem didn't get solved this week. Apparently green iguanas loved the steamy conditions in the facility's laundry room and had mistaken the bins of linens and towels for nests. Another council member asked Zorin to step forward and then asked him to share information about his firm.

"So that's Zorin," I said. He looked to be around fifty-five years old, just under six feet, meaty but not fat. A hat he'd removed had flattened his mostly gray hair. He wore yellow-tinted aviator glasses and had a friendly smile.

He removed his glasses. "Hello, I'm Zorin Montaño, owner of Lizard Liquidators of Texas. We are a part of a larger company headquartered in Florida. We have all the required licenses and permits needed to operate in Galveston County. We responded to new demand from customers looking for help with nuisance iguanas. My employees are experienced, professional animal trappers, and we'd be happy to help catch and disposition the unwanted iguanas. Pythons and feral pigs too, if they become a problem."

Sparky paused the video. "So, you can see, the council members were all nodding their heads, and I feared they were going to give the contract to Zorin."

"And that'd be bad why?" I asked. "Rodent is gone. And I doubt the iguanas will go away on their own."

"It seemed disrespectful so soon after Rodent died." Sparky strummed his fingers on the table, which was his tell. He was anxious. "And I saw an opportunity to shake Zorin's tree."

"Show me the rest. It's clear you're not going to tell me what you did." I grinned at Sparky and then pointed at Dora. "And let's see what we can find out about their parent company in Florida."

Sparky clicked the PLAY button.

The secretary asked the council members if there were any additional comments or if they wanted to move to a motion. A voice from the back of the room interrupted the council and requested to speak. Sparky walked up to the lectern on the opposite side of the room from where Zorin stood.

The secretary asked Sparky to state his name and purpose addressing the council.

"I'm William Wiley—"

That's Sparky's proper name.

"And I'm here representing Rodent Roger's widow, Ultima Roger. She would like the council to postpone a decision on this contract until she can present her firm's credentials."

"Rodent's widow intends to continue the business?" a council member asked.

"Yes, with qualified iguana catchers," Sparky told the council. "Mrs. Roger is committed to helping her late husband's clients—which includes most of the island's residents and businesses—through this recent crisis. My team is assisting her."

Sparky paused the video. "So that happened."

"I see," I said. "None of it is true, of course." I leaned back to think about what I'd just watched. Although most of the people in that room knew Sparky and where he worked, Zorin didn't. And if I put myself in Zorin's position, I might've thought Ultima had hired William Wiley to take over Rodent's clients.

"Sparky…" I paused for effect. "That was brilliant."

Sparky let out an enormous sigh.

"We've got some thinking and fixing to do, though."

Sparky nodded.

"And we must get Ultima—the grieving widow who wants NOTHING to do with Rodent's business—onboard," I said.

Sparky nodded again.

"And we're going to need to create some online presence for William Wiley," I continued. "The sooner, the better. If

Zorin googles you, we want him to find something that confirms any suspicion he might have that you've stepped into Rodent's role."

Sparky nodded once more. He typed on his keyboard and then pointed to the screen. He'd already created a website for Wiley Animal Services. "And I'm listed on the Texas Secretary of State website."

"Nice," I said. "Great, in fact. But you know what this means, right? You're going deep undercover. Are you sure you want to do that?"

Sparky shook his head. "No. Not at all. But from the moment I stood in that city council meeting and at this moment, this feels like the right thing to do. For Rodent."

"Your website looks convincing," Dora said.

And it did. It featured Sparky and three other guys standing in knee-high water. Wiley Animal Services had a contact form and a detailed list of services, including iguana trapping and removal.

"That's your team?" I asked. I recognized the three other men as his brothers and cousin.

"The Wiley boys," Sparky said. "That's a picture from the last time we went fishing together. Let's not tell Zorin these guys no longer live in Galveston."

I went to get another plateful of pizza and sat back down. "Sparky, have you ever tried to catch a lizard?"

"Nope," he said.

"Didn't think so," I said. "And as I recall, snakes freak you out."

"Yep," he admitted. "I'm quite jittery around reptiles.

And big bugs. I called Rodent for all that stuff."

I'd gone from being the only investigator who performed the mucky, front-facing tasks to having both my employees work undercover. I wasn't at all comfortable with this, but I knew it wouldn't be fair or right to stop them.

"All right," I said. "Let's see if we can limit your role to a discussion or two. Spare you the hassle of wrestling iguanas."

"I'd appreciate that," Sparky said. "Didn't work out so well for you. No offense."

Dora tried and failed to keep from laughing.

Chapter 21

Day 7, Tuesday, March 6
7:00 a.m.

Galveston Island was long and skinny—twenty-seven miles along the Gulf of Mexico and three miles wide on the more populated east end, which included downtown, most of the city, Galveston County municipal buildings, the Strand Historic District, and my spy shop. The western two-thirds of the island shrunk to less than a mile wide. Although some iguanas had made their way east, the more open West End was where most had been found.

We'd already planned on surveilling Lizard Liquidators, and William Wiley's emergence as a potential competitor made learning about their operations more important. We parked a couple of blocks from Zorin's small home to test our feeds and prepare the surveillance equipment, so we'd have several options for how we'd observe Zorin and his team.

Tailing someone on the West End was a challenge because it was open and there wasn't a lot of traffic to use for cover. We knew Zorin would notice the van if we followed him around all day, even from some distance. We'd staged our personal cars at the Jamaica Beach Circle K and put my city bike in the van. I brought a couple of outfits I could change into if I wanted to walk, run, or bike by the Lizard Liquidators while they were in action.

According to Dora's research, the iguanas would start moving around after the sun warmed things up. At 7:30 a.m., lights went on at Zorin's house. Zorin walked out of the front door and down the steps just before 9:00 a.m. A black cowboy hat covered his gray hair, and he was wearing a lime-green, short-sleeve shirt, jeans, and cowboy boots.

"He'll be easy to find in that bright shirt," Sparky said.

"I wonder how colors affect the iguanas, if they do." I watched Zorin on the video feed from the camera we had mounted on the back of the van. "He's limping. Maybe a bad hip?"

"I noticed that yesterday, too," Sparky said.

Zorin opened the side van door and was arranging several cages we assumed were for iguanas. We had questions: How did he track and trap the iguanas? How many people worked for Zorin? Did he kill the iguanas or otherwise disposition them?

"Looks like he's getting ready to leave." Sparky started the van.

I took off my jacket, climbed to the front, and sat in the passenger seat. I put on a blue cap that matched my T-shirt. Outfit number one.

We followed a couple of vehicles back after Zorin turned

east on San Luis Pass Road. He took a left on 12 Mile Road and then pulled into the parking lot of a small beige industrial building. Two other cars were parked in that lot. We drove past and into the visitor spaces at the fire department, which was next door.

Zorin got out of his van and went into the building through an unlocked door.

"Maybe this is where they keep the iguanas," Sparky said.

We'd figured the Lizard Liquidators had another location; Zorin's house was too small to hold a sizable iguana capture business and the equipment and space that might require.

I texted the address to Dora. "That'd be my guess. There's no signage out front, but I've got Dora searching for information."

A couple of minutes later, Zorin and two other guys walked out of the building and got into Zorin's van.

"Must be his team of highly qualified iguana hunters. Do you want me to follow?" Sparky put his hand on the keys, ready.

I held out my hand. "Wait. They locked the front door. No one is inside."

Sparky scanned the area around the building and then pointed. "You wanna get a look-see?"

I smiled. "You read my mind. I wish there were some windows I could peek into. It's too light now, anyway. Let's wait a minute and then catch back up to Zorin."

We tailed them from a few cars back. They turned left on Trinidad Way in Jamaica Beach.

Jamaica Beach was a city that occupied a large slice of land just west of the state park. Galveston, the city, was both to the east and west of this planned community, which had a cluster of stores and restaurants, a few dozen streets and canals, and about a thousand residents.

"Gordy lives on this street," Sparky said. "We can park in his driveway."

I tucked my hair into my cap and put on my sunglasses. "Cool. I've got my GRD5 cap cam ready to go."

The GRD5 was like a GoPro, but smaller. I sometimes used them to document my training sessions. It recorded a sharp and stabilized video picture, whether I was still or in motion.

We edged up to Trinidad Way and saw that Zorin's van was parked in a driveway about halfway down the block. The house was on the north side of the street and backed up to a canal.

"I'll get a better view from the next street if they're working in the back," Sparky said.

I strapped on my mini ditty bag. "OK, let's try that. I'll get out here. We can coordinate on cell."

I jogged most of the way to Zorin's van and then slowed to a walk. I called Sparky on my cell phone and spoke to him using my earbuds. We had a routine. When I was undercover, I could say anything into the audio piece or phone, and he'd ignore me and provide coaching or visuals as needed.

"Hey, Mom," I said. "I don't think I can come up there this weekend."

I stopped and looked around, like I was focusing on the call. They must've been in the back or far yard.

"I've parked in the driveway of a house that looks vacant and am walking to the dock to get a look at what's going on."

I took a few more steps toward where the van was parked. "Haven't I met him before? I'm not looking for a boyfriend."

"Don't worry. Zorin won't recognize me. I intend to stay out of view and I'm wearing a floppy fishing hat."

I stopped and wiped the back of my neck. "Where does he work?"

"I see them. They're at the canal. One guy has a long pole with a wire loop at the end. Another is down the seawall a bit. He's got a pole, too. Zorin is standing talking to a woman. The homeowner."

I edged closer and kneeled down to fake tying my shoe. I still couldn't see anyone. "Jerry wants to go fishing and angry —"

Sparky cut in and whispered. *"There's an iguana swimming in the canal."*

I put my hands on my earbuds because it was hard to hear.

"The taller guy just snagged it. It's on the lawn now and they're heading tomas yon torfado..."

"What the hell!" I yelled.

A guy carrying a writhing iguana on the end of a stick nearly smacked me with it.

The man stepped back and lowered the captured iguana to the lawn. He looked like a body builder with a good tan. Early thirties. A few tattoos, but he was not my type.

"Oh, sorry, ma'am."

I'm sure I looked startled because I was. I stared at the iguana. "Is that thing dangerous? What're you doing?"

"He can't get loose. We catch unwanted lizards. That's my job."

I stepped toward the animal and bent to look at it. "What're you going to do with it?"

The man was looking at my butt, but then he raised his head when I stood up straight. "That's up to the boss. This one's not very big."

Sparky could hear my conversation with the guy because we were still on the cell phone with each other. *"Smile at him, Xena."*

I smiled. "That's fascinating. Do you have a card? In case I need you to capture an iguana?"

The guy nodded. "Yeah, sure. Hang on a minute." He picked up the rod and swung the iguana toward the van. He then opened the side doors and pulled out one cage.

I followed him and looked in the van. "Wow, how many do you catch in a day?"

"There's another iguana in the canal that the other guy is trying to snag," Sparky said. *"Zorin is still with the woman in the backyard. You've got some time."*

The guy cackled. "We fill up this van two or three times a day." He slid his large hands down the rod and grabbed the iguana around the base of its neck and supported its body with his other hand. He removed the loop of wire and then maneuvered it into the cage.

So that's how to grab a big lizard. "Impressive handling

skills." I winked. "We didn't use to have these animals here. Do you know why they've become a problem?"

"No, ma'am." He put the caged iguana into the van and slid the door closed.

"Amanda."

He looked me up and down. "I'm Seth. My boss called me two, three months ago and asked me if I wanted the job here. Free rent. Decent pay. I worked with them in Florida."

I swung my arms and rocked back and forth. That was the only way to make my tiny breasts bounce a bit. "You were going to get me your card?"

He rubbed his wet hands together then dried them on his pants. "Right." He opened the passenger side door and grabbed a Lizard Liquidators flyer. He pulled a pen from middle console and wrote something on it. Seth handed me the flyer. "This is who we are, and that's my private cell number, if you want to call. I work from about nine to four. Iguanas are slow to wake in the morning."

"Second guy caught a little iguana. Oh, he lost it again. You're good."

"That's kind of you." I stepped closer and let my eyes wander up and down his body. He noticed. "You mentioned your boss decides what to do with them. What're the options?"

"Most people don't want to know, but I see you're a strong woman." He looked to see if the others were coming. "Big ones are good eating. Meat markets and taco trucks like iguana. And their skin makes nice boots after it's tanned and processed. Smaller ones are relocated or sold to another guy.

Don't know what he does with them. Maybe pet stores."

"That's fascinating. Head's up, Xena, the second guy caught the smaller one again. They'll be heading your way soon."

I took the flyer and folded it up. "That's quite the operation, Seth. Impressive… I should get back to my walk." I put the flyer in my fanny-pack ditty bag.

Seth nodded. "Hey, uh, is there a good place to get a big burger on this island?"

I started to leave, but then stopped and turned around. "I like Yaga's on the Strand. They've got two-for-one beers on Sunday, starting around seven. Maybe I'll see you there?"

"Yaga's doesn't have two-for-one anything on Sundays. You vixen."

Seth waved. "I'll be there. And you can call me anytime."

I turned and ran the opposite direction so I could loop back to the van and Sparky. He was climbing into the driver's seat as I hopped in the passenger side.

"I enjoy eavesdropping on your manipulative conversations," Sparky said.

I shook my head. "Men are predictable. No offense." I noticed the van going back down the street. "They're on the move. Let's hang back for a minute."

"None taken," Sparky replied. "We're rats. And promise me you won't ask me to lasso a lizard. It looks harder than reeling in a big grouper."

"Maybe that's how Seth got to be so strong." I batted my eyes.

Over the next three hours, we observed Zorin and his team catch and cage over twenty iguanas. Seth and his coworker did the hard work. They captured most using the pole routine but shot a few with an air gun, which I found unsettling.

They went back to their warehouse building on 12 Mile Road and unloaded the iguana cages and dead lizards that they'd stacked on top. After about an hour, they loaded up empty cages that were dripping wet. The three men then locked up the warehouse and climbed back into the van and left to trap more iguanas.

"What a learning experience!" I captured some notes from my conversation with Seth. "More iguanas than I expected."

"Global warming?" Sparky asked.

"Probably. I'll ask Dr. Flores. Or better yet, I'll get Steve to inquire. He's working on the invasive species angle."

Sparky started the van. "What's next? Pythons?"

The locked-up warehouse looked peaceful, but I couldn't help thinking of it as a hellhole of death. A condoned but barbaric place where animals were broken into parts to address a serious ecological imbalance. But two wrongs never make things right. Or do they?

Chapter 22

2:00 p.m.

Ant reassured me that, while the *Twisted Ambition* was an unconventional ship, Dora would enjoy great food, exceptional hospitality, and first-class accommodations in one of the larger rooms. To raise her onboard profile with the staff. He said that couples (or trios) looking for a romantic rendezvous preferred the Volcano Suite. It featured a faux-lava-filled bed with sensors that triggered a ten-foot-tall volcano on the shopping promenade to erupt when one or more people experienced a real (or fake, if done well) climax. Ant said word would get out if a single older lady booked the room. He promised no shenanigans that Dora didn't instigate.

Wink, wink…like getting hit on by the rascal named Rascal.

Shall we call Dora a cougar? In name only! Dora seemed relieved she wouldn't have to put out to complete her assignment. And based on what Ant had told me, his onboard gigolo targeted the women who ordered top shelf but dressed on the conservative side. Perhaps these snappy dressers treated the lucrative partnership in a more businesslike manner than the piña colada ladies.

Dora sat in the chair opposite my desk and took out her notebook. "I'm ready for my instructions. Thank you again for your confidence in me."

Since I'd called her early this morning to tell her she'd be going on the ship, Dora had given me a fern for my porch and a bag of my favorite chocolate-covered coffee beans. And while I appreciated her gratitude, the only reason I green-lit the case was that I'd figured out a way to do the toughest part myself—confronting Rascal such that he'd never again turn tricks while on the ship.

"Complete confidence," I said. "And I'm going to break down your assignment into very clear and achievable steps."

Dora beamed and bounced in the chair. "Excellent. I'm ready to take copious notes. May I also record your instructions? I'd like to listen to your voice throughout the mission."

She seemed exuberant, and I smiled because I knew her naivete would help her stand out. "Why not? Let me review each desired outcome, and then we can go over the details. First, Ant is going to give you privileges at the Audacious Club. That's where Rascal works most nights. Sit close to Rascal's stage and order a top shelf drink, take your pick. But nothing with an umbrella. Bring a dark-colored water bottle. Drink a bit of your cocktail, then dump some in the bottle, so you can order several drinks without getting drunk. Stay until the end of Rascal's shift, which Ant says is one a.m."

"Got it," she said. "Fake drink a lot of the good stuff and don't leave as long as Rascal is there."

I nodded. "And tip well. Ant will give you a thousand dollars in cash to tip Rascal in twenties."

"Should I request my favorite songs?" Dora asked.

"Terrific idea," I said. "Tip extra when he sings them for you. Chat him up between sets and make sure he knows you're rich and sailing alone."

Dora clapped with glee.

I held up two fingers and grinned. "Desired outcome number two. Tell Rascal you'd like to find a spirited sexual partner and ask him to let you know of any single, adventurous men. Offer him a finder's fee for the right encounter and say you'd be happy to compensate your date. Maybe a wink."

Dora gulped. I think it was hitting her that this assignment was all about sex.

"Are you comfortable talking about sex?" I asked.

She looked up from her notebook. "Would it be OK if I pretended I wanted to hire a bird-watching guide?"

I laughed. "If that's what'll light your eyes on fire."

"That'll do the trick," Dora said.

"Your aim is to get Rascal to be your personal birding guide." I went with Dora's preferred metaphor because she was more animated when talking about birding than boffing. "And when he offers himself to you, find out where he meets"—air quotes—"birders before the tour begins and any financial arrangements."

Dora was writing down every word I said. "Got it. Get

him to clarify the specifics of his booking process."

"Book an exclusive tour on one of the final two sailing days and request that he come to your suite," I said. "Then it's time for desired outcome number three."

I let Dora get caught up on her note taking before continuing. "When Rascal gets to your room, confirm the financial arrangements and then sit him in front of the computer. I'll take it from there."

Dora sighed and her shoulders relaxed. "That's all I have to do?"

"Yes, Dora, and we'll test the Zoom connection before he gets there. I'd also like Ant to be waiting right outside your suite so you can let him in once I've started my part. I want everyone to hear the same information."

Although I'd thought through the mission in my head, talking it out helped me feel confident it could work. The most unpredictable part of this operation was Dora. How she'd act and whether she could pull off the role of a rich, old nymph.

Dora stopped the audio recording. "I've never been a wealthy socialite type, but I have seen actresses play them on TV. I think this will be fun."

"And important, because we'll get one more gigolo off the streets...or the water." I laughed. "I know you'll be staying up late working this case, but I hope you can attend Dr. Flores's iguana shows. I'll e-mail a few questions I'd like you to ask her."

Dora leaned back and looked up at the ceiling. "I assume I should stay in character when talking with Quintana?"

I clapped my hands. “Glad you asked. Yes. Stay in character at all times, even with Ant, unless you’re in a private place.”

“I’ll get with Sparky later to put together a ditty bag that’ll make it through security. Is there anything else?”

“Enjoy the cruise!” I said. “I hope it’s not too deranged.”

“It’ll be fine.” Dora stood to leave. “I’ll send a case report at the end of each day.”

“Perfect.”

I sat at my desk for a few minutes because it felt weird handing the undercover role to someone else. I was the one who took action, spied on others, and played the role of a rich nymph. I specialized in throwing myself—not others—into the thick of things.

Shake it out, Xena.

I smacked myself on the side of the head because I had a murder case that needed my full attention and an early morning appointment with the mysterious Ms. Agatha Reacher.

Chapter 23

Day 8, Wednesday, March 7
11:00 a.m.

I parked outside the Flounder Run Bar and Grill, which was across the street from the Fisherman's Cove Motel on the Bolivar Peninsula. The small, periwinkle-blue building had seen better days. This was true of many buildings on the Bolivar because of the repeated storms that had come across and battered it and the lack of money to put things back together. I hoped the peeling paint, dirty windows, and muddy, uneven parking lot were not signs of how my lunch meeting with Agatha was going to go. I noticed her black Tiguan was the only other vehicle parked close to the front door as I walked in.

My eyes adjusted to the dim lighting, and it took me a couple of minutes to see where Agatha was sitting. She was the only other customer in the place. I waved as I walked toward her.

Agatha stood. She wore black boot-cut yoga pants made to look like dress pants. I had the same pair and recognized the logo. Her red hi-top tennis shoes, tank top, and half-zipped hoodie gave her a put-together-but-still-a-badass look. And several places to conceal weapons.

She extended her hand while her lips edged upward into a short smile. "Xena. It's good to meet you. Properly." She nodded and looked down.

"Likewise," I said. We sat across from each other in the dark wood booth with cracked black vinyl upholstery.

I felt my side to ensure my ditty bag was close enough to access. The seat bench was sticky. "It surprised me that you selected a place on Bolivar. Don't you live in Houston?"

She nodded and picked up a menu. "I'm here working a case. Something I'd like to talk to you about later." She waved the menu to get the bartender's attention. "I'm starving, so I hope you don't mind we order before we talk."

"Sure. What's good here?" I looked at the menu.

She huffed. "Not much, but the frying process kills any bacteria."

"Safety first. That's smart. I'll have the fish and chips, with extra vinegar if you have it."

"Sounds good. Me too," she said to the bartender, who looked like he'd just gotten up and forgot to change out of his pajamas. As he walked away, I noticed he had a gun strapped to his calf. That's the thing about PJs; it's tough to hide metal objects inside of them. Perhaps hiding the gun wasn't his goal.

Agatha noticed I was watching him. "His second job is drug dealer."

"That was my first guess," I said.

She put both of her hands on the table. "I need to go first. I'm sorry I hit you. My client wanted you to feel pain. It was nothing personal."

Be a good listener, I reminded myself. Many investigators enjoy boasting about their research and methods. "I'm not often surprised by people, but you got me good that night, Agatha. May I ask how you chose when to make your move and which move to make?"

She shifted her weight back and forth on the booth seat and then folded her arms on the table and close to her chest. She breathed in and out a few times. "I learned what I could about you, of course. The spy shop, the parkour, the unusual lengths you're willing to go to catch your target. It impressed me how you apprehended multiple people on that octopus case. I knew that given enough warning, you'd be hard to beat. Had to be a surprise."

"And you'd watched me, so you knew I'd be going for a run that night and you assumed I'd notice you parked on the side street."

"I did," Agatha replied.

"Tell me a bit about yourself," I said. "Where'd you learn how to fight?"

What? I might as well try some Dale Carnegie to break the ice.

Agatha tilted her head and looked up. "I started lifting and running early. Daughter of a high school basketball coach. He wanted me to go WNBA, but as you can see, I'm not tall enough. Anyway, I preferred inline skating."

I leaned in. "My mom was the gymnastics coach and a

star athlete in Scotland. I crushed her dream for me when I switched to parkour."

"Small world." She smiled and gazed into my eyes. "I'm curious about why you wanted to meet with me. You mentioned a win-win in your text."

The way she slid right into what she wanted to know was impressive. "Yes." I switched my brain from relationship building to negotiation. "I understand that some of my former work colleagues—"

"You mean the executives you set up to take a humiliating fall that ruined their careers and finances in an extraordinary display of trickery?"

"Yes." She was right, and I had no reason to deny it. "I understand that at least one or more of these pieces-of-shit have it out for me."

She puckered her lips and narrowed her eyes. "If I forced myself into their tiny brains…"

"Nice…"

Agatha nodded. "It's hard for them to read about your successes on Galveston. They're still licking their wounds."

Tell me something I don't know or should care about. "Right. You and I both know they had it coming."

"Based on what I've learned about them, I'll stipulate to that."

I looked around. We were still the only ones in the building except for the drug-dealing bartender. Good. "I want their interest in me to stop."

Agatha raised her eyebrows. "And I want a Ferrari. You got an angle? Something to offer my clients?"

Moment of truth. My stomach tensed. "A reduction in opportunity costs."

"I'm not following you."

"The Houston operation exposed some of their fraudulent activity and criminal decisions. But not all."

Agatha pushed back in her seat and smiled. "Clever girl."

"Jurassic Park," I said, recognizing the reference.

She rubbed her hands together and grinned. "Let me see if I have this right. There's more dirt and you've got it. Locked up in some safe deposit box somewhere."

"Something like that." I nodded and shrugged as if to say *of course.* "I'll give them—all of them—what I have in exchange for their guarantee they'll call off their thugs. No offense."

"Ouch. Why would they believe you'll be giving them everything? You could copy it all as an insurance policy."

"And I will. I'll share it so they know I'm serious and they're seriously screwed. If they keep pissing me off, I'll start turning over evidence to authorities. Life's good here on the island, and I've no interest in rehashing this old sting."

Agatha thought for a moment. "And how is this a win-win?"

"They get to prevent their lives from becoming a shitstorm. WIN. I don't have to worry about being clocked by buff and beautiful women who have nothing to do with my active cases."

"Win." Agatha bowed her head to acknowledge my compliment. "And you want me to sell your little plan to my client."

"And for him to get the word out to the others."

"What about a win for me? I'm not itching to battle you, but you're the subject of a well-paying gig."

I should've expected Agatha would look out for number one. "Oh, ah —"

"Relax. I've something in mind. Remember I told you I was here on a case?"

I worried about what was coming next because I had no time to do her dirty work. "I remember."

"My subjects are from Houston and this case is personal."

"And you want me to help you."

She nodded. "My brother Ward and sister-in-law Ginger live in Pearland. Ward and I are close. Both our parents have passed." She adjusted her seating position and seemed uncomfortable for the first time. "You know how we investigators have or develop a sixth sense about things?"

"I do." It was true, but not always welcomed.

"I think my sister-in-law is cheating on my brother. The idea is haunting me because she was my best friend and I introduced them."

"That's quite a tangled family web. Our intuition can be wrong."

The bartender delivered our plates and a bottle of malt vinegar. We both smothered our fries in it.

Agatha ate several fries and a bite of fish. "That's why I'm looking for confirmation—one way or the other—before talking to Ward."

"And you want me to get that for you."

"Yes. Ginger has been spending every weekend on

Bolivar at her friend's house. Says she's writing a book."

That'd make two writers I have to figure out. "Sounds plausible. Don't writers go on retreats a lot and write the costs off their taxes?"

"Ginger blew her high-school English teacher to get a passing C. She almost didn't graduate. I know this because I did the same thing." Agatha held up a fry like it was a sword. "Neither one of us could write worth a damn, but Mr. Bender graded non-verbal communication on a curve."

I tried to hold back a smile. "His name was Mr. Bender?"

She nodded.

"Who's the Bolivar friend?" I asked.

"This is where it gets interesting. He's allegedly a poet. Can't find anything he's published, but he teaches classes above a yoga studio in Uptown. I've followed him a few times, and he likes to surround himself with women."

"And he makes enough money as a poet and yoga teacher to have a second home?"

"The house isn't his. Some old biddy. Maybe a sugar mamma who likes hanging around poets. I was watching earlier when Spec's delivered a boatload of liquor."

"Has your brother mentioned anything about Ginger's writing group?"

"Ward's too trusting. He'll believe anything a woman tells him."

"But you don't trust your friend?"

"I don't trust most people. Best way to prevent disappointment."

"I agree with that. OK, Ms."—air quotes—"Agatha

Reacher, I'll find out what Ginger's doing at her Bolivar Peninsula weekend getaways."

Agatha raised her glass. "Then we have a deal. I'll pitch your trade offer to my client. I don't think it'll be a problem—he's a spineless twat." She laughed.

Spineless twat! Agatha spoke my language. "The whole c-suite was like that. But the board loved how the stock performed."

She pressed her chest into the table to get closer. "I worried that I was going to like you. We've a lot in common."

Was I making a friend? Might the person who beat the shit out of me be someone I could hang out with?

Best to play it cool for now, Xena.

"Shall we shake on it?" I asked.

We finished our fish and fries and exchanged information. I left the Flounder Run feeling optimistic that I'd be able to put the blowback from the *glorious incident that changed everything* in the past and maybe, just maybe, turn an adversary into a comrade.

As Agatha and I headed out of the restaurant, she stopped and turned to face me. "You wore a bear suit. I've not met anyone that committed to their plan. When this is all over, let's hang out. Maybe go for a run or get drunk." Agatha slid her hand down my forearm. "It'd be fun."

I felt light-headed for much of the ferry ride back to Galveston. Agatha Reacher was a mystery wrapped in a muscled enigma, and she intrigued me.

Chapter 24

2:00 p.m.

By the time I walked into the meeting room at the spy shop, Sparky and Dora had created a diagram of comings and goings at the Lizard Liquidators' warehouse on 12 Mile Road. They researched several leads, documented what we knew, and listed several open questions. The big picture was that Zorin and his team were bringing in fifty to seventy iguanas a day, for which they charged clients $125 a piece or $6,000–$9,000 in revenue per day. That was sixty grand each week before expenses. These numbers didn't include sales of iguana meat or hides. We figured their gross revenue was likely $180,000–$250,000 per month with a net of $150,000–$200,000.

Dora had confirmed that Lonestar Tannery and Burt's Meats—two of the companies that the Lizard Liquidators listed on their website under PARTNERS—were legitimate vendors who'd both been in business for several years. The Lonestar Tannery website showed pictures of boots and wallets made from iguana and other reptile skins and listed

Steve's custom boot maker in Houston as a customer. The Burt's Meats blog offered recipes for all its products, including iguana. Iguana Stew, Iguana Tacos, Caribbean Stew, Grilled Iguana, and Iguana En Pinol. And Dora had found detailed instructions for killing and processing iguanas for the do-it-yourself audience and several articles that touted iguana meat as an excellent source of lean protein.

I looked at our charts on the wall. "As unusual as this might be, it appears to be a legitimate business. Are we missing something?"

"We don't know what happens to the smaller ones," Sparky said. "Seth told you they might release some and that there's a guy who picks them up, but we we've not seen another guy."

"Let's go over the timing again," I suggested.

Sparky looked at the diagram they'd drawn on our large whiteboard. "Everyone is usually gone by five-thirty."

Dora sat and rocked back and forth with her chin in her hand. "Here's a theory. It's against the law to catch and then free invasive iguanas, or any invasive animal. Once caught, iguanas must be kept secure or killed."

"Makes sense," Sparky said. "If they were let go, it wouldn't help solve the problem."

"But here in Texas, green iguanas aren't on anyone's radar," Dora said.

"Yet," I said. "And is it therefore not something Zorin would get caught doing?"

Dora fanned her hands back and forth. "It's not a priority for law enforcement. Especially here on the island."

Since pirate Jean Lafitte discovered it in 1817, Galveston Island has had a reputation for being flexible with how people lived and recreated. The GDP held crooks and murderers accountable; I don't want you to think it's a lawless city. Just stop by the spy shop and pick up some pepper spray to be on the safe side.

"Little iguanas grow," I said. "They can sell them once they're larger."

"Zorin charges the same fee for catching younger iguanas," Dora said. "Maybe they keep catching and releasing them until they're big enough to process."

"Like blue crabs and trout," Sparky added.

Dora nodded. "And more new iguanas hatch. This could explain why we're seeing so many on the island."

"Who's releasing them and where?" Sparky asked.

I tapped on the table several times. "Perhaps *when* is the more important question?" I stood and walked up to the diagram. "When Sparky and I watched Zorin yesterday at his house, we noticed he had a few empty cages in his van. What if he releases the iguanas late at night and then drives home?"

"And what if Rodent figured that out?" Dora asked.

While this was an interesting and important discovery, it didn't add up to murder. Even if Zorin was releasing some iguanas to increase his revenue or solve the problem of what to do with animals he couldn't sell, doing so might not've interested the law. So, where's the motive?

"I don't know… Zorin is a cheater, but do we think he's a killer?" I looked at Sparky. "Think about how William

Wiley could use this knowledge as leverage while we keep working our other leads. I'll call Ultima and get her onboard."

I then turned to Dora. "See what you can find out about the parent company from Florida this afternoon. I'd like to know more about them."

I went into my office and called Ultima to explain what Sparky had said at the city council meeting and our plan. After a few dramatic sighs, she warmed up to the idea and agreed to play along. She said she was glad we were working the case. Our next challenge was to figure out how to fake being a lizard eliminator without doing the work.

Then it hit me. We need to subcontract the work. Maybe to a benevolent competitor. It seemed like the right time to ask Ultima a question I hadn't asked when I was at her house. "Our records show you called Harold Knowles. Can you tell me the nature of the call?"

I was hoping we might get Harold to fulfill requests under the guise of helping Rodent's widow keep the business going until she set up her own team.

"Never heard of Harold Knowles and sure as hell didn't call him." She let out an exasperated breath.

Another lie. "Are you sure? We found his number listed on your call log and traced it to a Harold Knowles, owner of Southwest Exterminators."

"From Houston?" she asked.

"Yes."

She started laughing. *"Oh, you must mean Skeeter. His real name is Harold?"*

Chapter 25

7:00 p.m.

According to Dale Carnegie, the fifth principle for how to make people like you is to *talk in terms of the other person's interests*. The trick is to do this from a mindset of genuine interest versus being a manipulative prick. Those are my words, not DC's. He suggested we try to provoke and evoke people with interesting questions inspired by research we completed before meeting them. And then, he said, let the other person talk about themselves for hours.

That seemed like a lot of effort and way too much listening to make a new friend. Wouldn't it be quicker to offer better booze? On the other hand, Agatha Reacher impressed me with how much research she'd done. And although we were talking business, I liked that our conversation touched on parkour and my previous case credits. We're all self-absorbed, don't you think?

And perhaps that was Dale Carnegie's point. The best way to befriend people is to honor and stoke their inner narcissist. But I wondered if he would've caveated his suggestion to research people if he'd lived in today's time of rampant social media and reality television shows. Where does effective research end and online stalking begin?

Amanda Reacher, with her fake name and unlisted burner cellphone, had made a mistake when she told me her sister-in-law's real name. Or maybe she knew exactly what she was doing. This piece of information allowed me to find her brother, and then her. The real her.

Hiba Olson. Forty-seven years old. Twitter handle @hibajeebees.

Yes, readers, I have a Twitter account. You can follow me at @… ha! Faked you out. I use Twitter to monitor suspects and follow my favorite journalists for just-in-time information when the worldwide shit was hitting the fan. Like during last year's coffee bean shortage or the Twinkie resurrection. Yep, I'm food-motivated.

Back to Hiba. I found pictures from when she completed the Houston Half Marathon, links to her favorite restaurants, her neighborhood (Rice Village) crime page, and a photo album from her vacation in Paris three years ago with her boyfriend. No local marriage licenses, criminal history, or active warrants.

I was about to look for Hiba Olsen on Facebook when Steve called.

"Hey," I said. "Is your *S*-beard behaving today?"

"Mostly," he said. *"Have you seen the Pelican Man's latest column?*

Ned Quinn, aka the Pelican Man, wrote a popular column for the *Galveston Post Intelligencer* called "Bird

Guts." Ned and I worked together on a case several months ago, one we now call the birder murder. Maybe you remember it?

"Nope. I've been focused on figuring out who killed Rodent Roger," I replied.

Steve grunted. *"Well, take a look. He's weighing in on the island's iguana explosion."*

I sat up in my chair. "Of course, he did. Damn, why haven't I thought to call him?"

"He's a bird guy."

"And a brilliant medical physicist and environmentalist with an informed and vigorous opinion about everything that happens on Galveston. Thanks, Steve. I'll pull it up right now."

"Are we still meeting with your lizard doctor tomorrow?" he asked.

"Seven-fifteen. Park in the Starbucks and we can walk over to the ship together."

I pulled up Ned's column and read his rant about how iguanas are an invasive species whose growing presence in Galveston is one more sign of our mass mismanagement of the environment. I sent him a text.

It's Xena. Saw your column. Can I come and see you tonight?

My phone rang. It was Ned.

"Xena, Xena, Xena! What a delightful surprise."

"Hello, Ned. Did I catch you at a bad time?"

"Never a bad time, unless you're the dead bird on my examination table." Ned snorted.

"Seriously. You heard about Rodent Roger's death, right?"

"Damn shame."

"I'm trying to find his killer and think the iguana situation might be related," I said. "Can I come over and chat?"

"Hell yes. I'll be in my lab another hour or two."

***

I sped to Ned's lab, called the Last Resort Flight School, after printing out Ned's column and underlining the parts I wanted to discuss. His bird sanctuary, laboratory, and home were at the end of Sportsman Road on the bay side of the island. I parked and pulled open the door to his large laboratory. "Times Like These" by the Foo Fighters was blaring through large speakers in each corner of the room.

Ned looked up and smiled. "Hey, Siri, stop playback."

The music stopped. I walked up to Ned and hugged him from the back, careful not to get any bird guts on me.

That's why his column was called "Bird Guts." Ned performed bird necropsies and then wrote a column about each bird's life. Except his most recent column, which was about iguanas.

Ned turned around. "Xena, Xena, Xena!" he said again.

"Ned, you're looking tip-top." And he did. At fifty-five, he looked forty-something. Ned was tall, strong, and his dark shaved head and cheeks glistened with vitality.

Damn, I'll be forty-something soon.

He covered the bird he was working on so it wouldn't dry out—not to hide it. Ned and I had done a necropsy together; he knew I wasn't squeamish. "I realize this isn't a social call, but would you like a drink?"

I followed Ned into his office and sat in the chair opposite his desk.

He put a bottle of Johnny Walker and a Costco-sized container of Cheez-Its on his desk. "Know it's not your brand of whiskey, but let's toast to Rodent."

I nodded, accepted the Solo cup of Scotch, and raised it high. "To Rodent."

We sat silent for a moment.

"I want to get to the iguanas," I said, "but first, tell me how you're doing. It has been too long since we talked."

Ned propped up his elbows and rested his head in his hands. "I'm doing well. You probably read that I stepped away from working directly with GIBA. . ."

That's the Galveston Island Birding Association. Ned was a board member and helped lead the staff."

"And that feels good and right," he continued. "I'm focusing on my column and this sanctuary. I'm thinking about writing a book."

"Wow!" I now had three writers in my life. "I'd buy your story. . .at full price."

Ned laughed. "Nonexistent love life, but I've always got my eyes on the lookout. How about you? Anyone since you and Ari broke up?"

Ari Pani had been my hot biologist boyfriend. He took a job in Washington state several months ago, and I missed him. "Nope, I'm not seeing anyone." I didn't want this conversation to go down any weird rabbit holes. "I should've called sooner once we took this case, but it wasn't until I saw your column that it occurred to me."

He took the bait. "Why're you working this case? Aren't the police all over it?"

I told Ned how my team got involved and what we'd learned about the Lizard Liquidators. We walked, drinks in hand, around his compound and he showed me where he'd installed electric fences to keep iguanas out of the large enclosures where injured or struggling birds lived while he was rehabilitating them. I'd jumped into one of those pens a few months ago and over a dozen pelicans, who'd assumed I was carrying food, had rushed me. We sat down on a bench on his dock that looked over West Bay and South Deer Island.

We didn't see any iguanas on our walk. "Where are they now?" I asked.

Ned pointed at a stand of trees on the west side of his ten-acre property. "In the trees, likely, or in burrows they've dug. Under vehicles, and I bet there's one hiding behind my AC unit. They slow way down at night and will go into a state of torpor if it gets into the forties or thirties."

"Like hummingbirds?"

"Yes. That's why iguanas fall out of trees and make the morning news in Florida. They'll be fine as long as it warms up the next morning. Otherwise, they'll die."

"Why is this happening here?" I asked.

"It's what invasive species do, Xena—they invade. Especially iguanas, because they're fast and can eat damn near everything."

"Why now?"

He turned to me and slugged the rest of his Scotch. "The

two most likely causes are warming temperatures, or someone dumped them. Maybe both. Think about it this way. You know saguaro cacti in Arizona?"

I wasn't sure where he was going with this, but Ned was a world-class storyteller. "Yep."

"They didn't use to be in Arizona, and you don't see them in New Mexico except in the far southeast corner. Why? Because it was too cold. But over time, the climate has become more hospitable for saguaro, and they've likely adapted a bit. Similar with iguanas. I don't think Galveston is the ideal climate for lizards, but they're making do." He lifted his arms toward the sky. "The quick answer is humans are to blame. We're accelerating global warming and stupid enough to buy Timmy a cute little pet lizard before doing five minutes of research where we'd learn that iguanas become big, biting, crapping, piss-poor pets that live fifteen to twenty years in captivity."

I chuckled. "If all it takes is human ignorance, I'm surprised this island isn't swarming with lizards, wild pigs, and pythons."

"It'll happen," Ned said.

Ned knew the waters in these areas better than most. He fished by boat and kayak and taught young pelicans how to fish. His property was six miles east of where we'd found Rodent's van and another ten miles east of where his body was discovered by a fisherman.

I looked out at the water. "I've been wondering whether Rodent's body might've floated from where we found his van at the end of Indian Beach Drive to where it was found.

The water is shallow, but do you think that could've happened?"

Ned shook his head and swung his legs to kick at the gravel. "Unlikely. Depends on the timing. If he went into the water during high tide, the currents might've pulled him toward the bridge. During low tide, the water in the bay goes out through San Luis Pass. Not sure a six-foot body would make it all the way in one cycle. Could've taken two low tides. But if he got stuck anywhere… I could look at the tide and lunar charts and let you know what the conditions were."

"I'd appreciate that. If we need to find a second crime scene where he was killed or dumped, I'd like to know. The police don't think Rodent went into the water at the pass."

"You're a fascinating woman, Xena Cali. You know why?"

I shook my head.

"You have the brains to keep trouble far away but the spirit that drives you into the middle of these perilous quagmires." Ned grinned and lowered his head to look over his glasses. "I bet you caused your mother many sleepless nights when you were a teenager."

Chapter 26

Day 9, Thursday, March 8
7:15 a.m.

Steve was leaning against the railing at Starbucks with a coffee in hand. He'd coifed his hair and *S*-beard and was wearing a trim black suit with a lime-green button-down shirt. Shoes, not boots this time. I felt underdressed in my jeans, black tank top, and Patagonia windbreaker. A cool but humid wind blew my short bob around like a garden spinner.

"Hey," I said. "I can't decide if you look cool or bad."

Steve stood up and walked toward me. "Both. Like Pitbull."

He meant Pitbull the Latin singer and dancer.

"I can see that." I lied.

We walked across Harborside Drive and then down two blocks to get to the concrete bench outside the cruise port. I sat on the bench.

Steve stayed standing and looked at the *Twisted Ambition*. "Too bad we couldn't meet her on the ship."

I looked down the walkway. Quintana was striding toward us fast; she looked in a hurry. I stood to greet her. "Dr. Flores, this is Steve Heart. Steve is an investigative reporter for the *Galveston Post Intelligencer.* He's doing a piece and asked to tag along. I hope you don't mind."

She hugged me and then hugged Steve. "Pleasure to meet you, Steve. I'm sorry, but I have just a few minutes today because I'm picking up some supplies and then preparing a new presentation for tomorrow's show. Please understand."

Steve flashed his whitened teeth in a big smile. "Dr. Flores, I'll take the time you've got."

"Call me Q, please," she said.

I'd told Steve he could go first because I figured I'd learn a lot from listening to his questions and thought Quintana might offer more complete answers for a reporter who might give her some good publicity.

Steve and Q sat next to each other on the bench and I stood with my notepad in hand. He summarized what he knew about the increase in iguana sightings on the island. He asked her whether the island was dealing with an invasive species and what residents and the government should do about it.

"Well, Mr. Heart—"

"Steve," he said.

"Steve." Q smiled. "We have a saying in my field. If you have to ask whether you're dealing with an invasive species, it's already too late. In my home of Grand Cayman, it took us many years and billions of dollars to get the green iguana population to a manageable state." She noticed me taking notes. "It was difficult, Xena, I can tell you." Q turned back to Steve. "There's prevention, eradication, containment, and management. Based on what you've told me, I'd say the door is closed for prevention but also eradication. Think of invasive species like a cancer. Once it spreads to many parts of the body, it cannot be cured. Eradication requires early detection and action. I don't think this happened, correct?"

Steve shook his head. "I've not gotten the sense that anyone in government is discussing the problem other than the city council who wanted someone to get the iguanas out of the detention center."

Q giggled. "That's funny, but I know it's also not funny. So answering your question about what to do, people need to focus on containing the iguana population and then manage it. Florida is trying to do this."

"How are they doing?" I asked.

"Not too well because there's more energy going into the python issue, which I think they view as a bigger problem because it's a predator and eats other animals, even pets and children."

Steve winced.

"I'll send you some excellent papers on this, Steve. Galveston doesn't need to reinvent the wheel. You're lucky that here you don't have pythons."

"We have coyotes," Steve said.

"Coyotes are everywhere, but they're not a problem like green iguanas."

I could tell Quintana was getting antsy, so I pulled a flyer out from the back of my notebook and handed it to her. "A company called Lizard Liquidators has been distributing flyers in a few residential areas. Have you heard of them?"

"These people, no," she said.

"What would you recommend residents do if they find iguanas in and around their home?" Steve asked.

"Iguana catchers, iguana hunters, lizard chasers—there are so many. They pop up wherever iguanas are a problem. Some companies do all the invasives. Snakes, hogs, lizards, even fish. I'd encourage homeowners to call them. They're likely better trained on the humane removal techniques. Faster and cheaper, too, than pest control companies who don't know. Iguanas are wildlife, not cockroaches. A problem, for sure, but better handled by people like your—" Quintana looked at the flyer again "—Lizard Liquidators."

She stood. Our time was running out.

Q turned toward Steve. "I spent a summer working with an iguana catcher in Mexico when I was in undergrad school. It was a tough job! And very helpful because they knew how to catch and repurpose the iguanas. Most are good, hard-working people." Q extended her hand. "I'm sorry, but I have to go. E-mail me if you have questions. I'm back in port every five days during the sailing season."

She looked at me. "Xena knows how to reach me, eh?" She winked and then gave me another hug. "You can give Steve my information."

We watched as Quintana blazed a path down the sidewalk and hopped into a cab. We walked back to our cars.

"Maybe I don't want to share her information with Steve," I said to Steve and then chuckled.

He looked at me and creased his Botoxed forehead. "What do you mean?" He looked at the ship again and took a picture of it with his phone. "Do you think she can take a guest on board?"

We compared notes and recapped the discussion in my car with fresh lattes. She'd told us a lot during the fifteen minutes we talked with her.

"I found Q quite impressive, overall," Steve said and raised one eyebrow. "And how cool is it to quote a PhD who goes by Q?"

I wondered what she meant by "repurposing" iguanas but didn't get into that with Steve. While we had common interests on this topic, I was careful about what I shared about the murder investigation. "I hope your story prompts the county and state to do something. Sounds like we've experienced a tipping point. What did she compare invasive species to? Cancer?"

Steve nodded. "And ours has metastasized."

Chapter 27

10:00 a.m.

Ant was a nervous wreck. He'd called, Zoomed, and e-mailed to confirm the details of our little sting operation on the *Twisted Ambition*. I guaranteed him we knew how to handle self-assured gigolos and that Dora was prepared and could reach me anytime. And I promised, again, I'd not inform the ship's captain. Ant cycled from gleeful and ready to solve this problem to depressed and questioning whether one existed.

And between you and me, readers, this was a small potatoes investigation. More complex than catching a cheating spouse, but simpler than most everything else. I guess Ant had never ambushed one of his employees while keeping his bosses in the dark. He also needed to cloak how he paid our expenses (Dora's onboard spending) and fees, but said he managed a sizeable petty cash slush fund set up to ensure he could make every passenger's experience "bizarre, surprising, and rebel hell extraordinary."

I was alone in the spy shop because Dora was boarding the

Twisted Ambition and Sparky was working leads in the Rodent Roger case. Thursdays in March were often slow in the store, which suited me fine. Lights on, door unlocked, Imagine Dragons on the stereo, and pancakes from Miller's gave me the feeling that this was going to be a terrific day. I sat at the front counter and googled Hiba Olsen and her sister-in-law Ginger Olson (Ginger Carrama, maiden name).

The front door clanged, and Captain Ethan Slaughter walked into the store. He'd been to the spy shop before for an intense meeting related to the birder murder, but never to shop. I walked around the counter and greeted Ethan in the nanny cam aisle with a vigorous handshake. "What a pleasant surprise. Or is it? I hope you're not here to share more bad news."

Ethan propped one hand up on his hip. His gun side. "No, I don't think so. I promised your reporter friend I'd update you on some information he'll be releasing in a couple of hours. I gather the two of you have an established relationship for exchanging information."

I felt my cheeks flush. "Someone once told me we investigators need people."

He smiled.

"I think you'll find that Steve Heart is the best investigative reporter in Galveston County and a tremendous source," I explained. "But I don't tip my hand until and unless it's safe and appropriate. He's researching a story on invasive species that could be helpful to our investigation."

Ethan walked around and up to the glass display case

where we kept the expensive stuff. "Is all this legal?"

"You know it is," I said. "I'd be happy to show you around, but how about we start with you telling me what Steve is publishing."

Ethan pulled a small leather note holder from his breast pocket. "Sure. In partnership with the medical examiner—also a friend of yours, I understand—our belief is that Rodent's death was a homicide. Tox screen results still pending, but the physical exam indicated the manner of death was suffocation. We don't know whether it was premeditated or a crime of opportunity. We're looking for leads from the public and Rodent's widow has funded a reward pool of $15,000, but I'm guessing you already know about that part."

Did I tell the captain I had no idea my client Ultima Rogers had established a reward? No, I did not. In three sentences, he'd shared information I didn't know from three of my contacts. Ouch. "I appreciate you telling me this, Ethan. Off the record, is Melissa looking for any particular toxin?"

He looked around. "No. The ME's preliminary report should be ready in a day or so."

I'm sure that wasn't *all* he knew but was grateful he'd shared something. "I understand." I placed a hand on the display case.

Ethan looked down into the display case and at my arm. "What's the story behind these tattoos?

"My first tattoo was a black mamba snake I have coming down my upper thigh." I picked up my leg and ran my finger along where the snake was. "I wanted something that came down to just above the knee so that when I wore a shorter—but still appropriate and professional—skirt the snake's head would be visible if I crossed my legs. Freaks people out, which was my intent."

Ethan tilted his head and seemed interested. "Why a black mamba and not a rattler or cobra?

"Black mambas are the fastest snakes in the world, and just two drops of their venom can kill you," I said. "They're twitchy and aggressive. My second tattoo runs down my spine. It's a quote from *Henry V*: *He who hesitates is lost*. It's my personal mantra."

"That's telling," he said.

I lifted my right forearm. "This one was my first highly visible tattoo. I chose the Celtic spiral to remind me of life's meandering, circuitous journey." I turned and lifted my left arm. "Bought this dragon while on a business trip in Singapore. I was born under the Chinese Zodiac sign of the dragon and admire their, albeit mythical, energy and determination."

Ethan shook his head. "You got a tattoo in a foreign country while on a trip? That was brave."

"I researched the artist." I smiled. "Here's my grandest tattoo. It's the only one I've gotten related to a case. It's Fred the Octopus, who had been charged with the death of a marine biologist. Fred was intelligent and precocious, and I will remember him always."

"I read about that case when it happened. And if I remember, you met your boyfriend while working that case.

He helped you on the birding case if I'm thinking about the right guy."

I sighed. "Former boyfriend, but yes, we met on the octopus investigation. Ari got a great job offer in another state."

"Sorry," Ethan said.

I turned over my left wrist. "And this is my latest tattoo. The leaping, creepy rabbit is a nod to parkour and my fascination with rabbits."

He looked closer. "Have you had pet rabbits?"

"My fascination is with the idea of rabbits."

"Huh. Aren't you worried your tattoos will sag when you get old?"

Ethan didn't know I was kicking and screaming into a milestone birthday year and that any mention of old age could trigger me to gorge on MoonPies. "Here's the glorious thing about tattoos; they can be refreshed and reimagined. A drooping clown becomes a Japanese landscape. It's important to find a tattoo artist who specializes in revitalization projects."

"This has been an education." Ethan turned and started walking toward the door. "I've got a meeting, but let me know if you come across anything helpful to my case." He turned back to me. "And tell me before you investigate anyone new."

"Count on it like a tattoo." I realized this made no sense the moment I said it.

After Ethan left, I texted Steve. *Captain Slaughter just left my shop.*

I saw the three pulsating dots telling me Steve was writing a response. *He made me promise I wouldn't tell you. Said he'd arrest me if I did.*

I laughed and turned up the stereo. *When has a fear of consequences ever kept you from doing the right thing?*

Chapter 28

Day 10, Friday, March 9
2:00 a.m.

Investigator Report—Thursday, March 8
Investigator: Dora Baker

The weather was glorious—58 degrees and clear—when I boarded the *Twisted Ambition*. No problems making it through security. I took your advice and told the agent inspecting my ditty bag I needed all those things for my uterine cancer. You were right! Men don't enjoy discussing female body parts.

As you know, Ant booked me into the luxurious Volcano Suite. It's a stunner! And larger than I expected, at 508 sq. ft. inside the stateroom with a 161 sq. ft. balcony space on the bow and port corner of the eighth deck of the ship. That's front, left. It's a two-story suite with the lava bedroom taking up the entire second floor. I did calisthenics on the bed to see if I could trip the model volcano on the shopping deck. It's connected by

Bluetooth. I was unsuccessful but will keep trying. I have a cashmere-covered conversation pit (how do they clean it?) and hot rock sauna I'm going to try. And if that's not enough, they have a Suite Genie named Filo—like the dough, but she's skinny—assigned to my room. She exists to improve my cruise, full stop. I can request anything! It's like an odd version of paradise, so thank you again for this assignment.

Captain Chablis Conner (a female at the helm!) stopped by my room to say hello. Not because Ant told her about the operation; she thought I was a rich customer. I assume she pops in to meet anyone in large suites. CC, as she asked me to call her, said the *Twisted Ambition* was a member of their Ambitions Class of vessels. It's 965 ft. long and carries 2,500 passengers and 840 crew. With an average cruising speed of 25 knots (about 29 mph), this ship is fast, slim, and maneuverable. The captain described the ship as elegantly zippy, like a floating Maserati. Even when going backwards up to 18 knots, which is a remarkable feat and handy when pathfinding new itineraries or escaping pirates. CC was delightful and invited me to dine at her table one night during the cruise. I accepted, of course. But I didn't tip the captain. Was that correct?

This must be what it feels like to be rich. People fawning all over you and saying that you're brilliant and special even if they know nothing about you other than you're rich. I'm not sure how I feel about all the attention.

After the captain left, I completed my onboard questionnaire, which the staff use to make dinner and entertainment assignments. I then walked around the ship to orient myself, including finding the dining room (aft, decks four and five) and Audacious Club Lounge (aft, deck ten). And I found the Wild Time Theatre (fore, deck five), where Dr. Flores will perform with her iguanas tomorrow.

I then walked along the shopping promenade (deck six), took a picture of myself in front of the ten-foot volcano (attached), and browsed a bit in the Hula-Hoop shop. So many colors and sizes to choose from. I bought a fuzzy green one to practice with in my suite. There was a Bearded Lady Barbershop Quartet singing. These ladies had impressive facial hair and sang quite well.

I noticed several people dressed in head-to-toe yellow leotards. I thought maybe they belonged to a circus act, and so I introduced myself to a yellow man who was sitting having coffee. His name is Beauregard, and he said he wasn't in any act, but that he was a twelve-time Stowaway. Audacious Stowaways—they happily answered to ASS or Hey ASS—are budget conscious cruisers who book one of the 55 sq. ft. cabinettes. Beauregard told me this unique cabin category was perfect for risk-takers like him who planned on being out of their cabin most of the time. And he said that those who're cash-strapped qualify for Audacity's sweat equity program for cabinette-level accommodations. Stowaways who work two hours per day or one entire day per cruise pay only port fees and taxes (about $179 for the five-night itinerary). Work assignments vary based on the needs of the ship but are consistent with the motto of the cruise line, which is *Embrace the Unconventional.*

Staff notify Stowaways of their daily chore every morning by 5:00 a.m. Assignments are non-negotiable. Those in the Stowaway program wear a yellow unitard while fulfilling their work duties so the staff knows who they can boss around. Stowaways wear their own clothes other times. I asked Beauregard if it embarrassed him to wear the leotard and he scoffed at me and said wearing it was a golden badge of honor and proof that he's living a courageous and exciting life. He also said the leotards were comfortable, stretchy, and flattered most body types. Beauregard got up to leave so he could continue his afternoon job of signing up passengers for Friday's contest. He asked me if I'd participate, and I agreed without asking what type of contest it was. I'll ensure my involvement doesn't compromise my cover as a filthy rich woman looking for a gigolo.

Because the staff needed time to process our onboard questionnaire answers, dinner on the first night was the same every cruise. Starting from the highest decks to the lowest, passengers reported to deck ten and selected one of the 2,500 yellow duckies floating in the pool. The number on the ducky determined the dinner entrée they gave us. They let us put the first duck back and select another if we didn't like the result. But we could only do this once. I was lucky enough to go early in the draw because my suite is on deck eight, I can only imagine what was left for the poor folks sleeping on the third deck. My second ducky, lucky number 367, awarded me a colorful pre-sushi platter. Pre-sushi meant everything was still alive. It was delightful and scary. I loved the mini pineapple, salad ingredients, and oysters, but liberated the snapping crab back into the ocean. I hope it has a happy life. Beauregard texted me to say he was enjoying his tire jerky with chocolate cheddar fondue. He'd had it before and knew to pick the rusty screws out of the tread before eating.

I went to the Audacious Club after dinner. Ant had already told me it was Rascal's night off, but I thought I'd establish my character so my reputation might precede me. My outfit for the evening was a white pantsuit with a camel-colored shirt. I'm saving my best pantsuits for Rascal to see. I ordered a Pappy Van Winkle fifteen-year-old, neat (I thought you'd approve!). It was the perfect drink because its low overall volume made it easier to dump into my black matte water bottle. I chatted with the server and established my favorite seat, right next to where Rascal will perform tomorrow. I gave the server, Trish, a generous gratuity and she confirmed that she'd reserve my table for the rest of the cruise. I've pre-purchased the rest of their Pappy inventory (one bottle) so they'll not run out of my drink. Word of this will get around. To test the strength of the crew communication pipeline, I told Trish my favorite song was a slow version of “Fly Me to the Moon” by Tony Bennett.

I should’ve asked, was there a budget you wanted me to stay within?

End of report.

Chapter 29

9:45 a.m.

Ultima had pissed me off. When she and I talked on the phone, I'd emphasized it was critical we talk with Skeeter before she reached out to him. She'd agreed. Why was this order of events important? First, Harold Knowles, aka Skeeter, was a person of interest in our investigation. He and Rodent had talked shortly before Rodent went missing and was killed. They'd apparently discussed the iguana issue. Skeeter was at least tangentially involved in this case, and I needed to interview him to ascertain his role. And if we cleared Skeeter as a suspect, we needed to get him onboard with our little Wiley Animal Services ruse to make sure he'd say the right things if he ran into the Lizard Liquidator guys. We had a rock-solid plan for how we were going to handle Skeeter.

It had become crystal clear that my relationship with Ultima was one of convenience. Not partners and not trusted allies. Steve was right. To build trust, we must share information. Ultima moved and said nothing. She'd failed to mention she set up a $15,000 reward fund. And now this.

When Sparky called, Skeeter shared that he and Ultima had already struck a deal and that his team would be servicing Rodent's clients three days a week.

"I know you're not happy." Sparky looked at himself in my passenger visor mirror. "But Skeeter seemed amiable and open. Said Rodent was a buddy."

I grumbled as I drove to where Skeeter had a 10:00 a.m. appointment to catch a couple of iguanas. "I don't know what to think. Ultima is an unreliable client-slash-suspect one moment and a fascinating client the next. She's a self-proclaimed method writer, and I can't help but wonder if we're unwitting models in her forthcoming crime novel."

We pulled up behind the Southwest Exterminators van and pickup truck and got out. Skeeter was working on an iPad while sitting in his truck. He got out when he saw us. He was a roly-poly guy with a black mullet haircut and thick mustache. We shook hands and introduced ourselves.

"Rodent was salt-of-the-earth good people and what happened to him's not right," Skeeter said. "Ultima said she'd hired y'all, and I told Ultima I'd help however I can."

"Appreciate that," I said. "How long had you known Rodent?"

"Five years, give or take." Skeeter gave instructions to one of his workers, as they got pole snares and cages ready. "He gave me my start, then encouraged me to start my own outfit in Houston. I loved that man. He gave me my nickname, too. Skeeter, 'cause I was a mosquito magnet. Followed me everywhere."

"And did Ultima ask you to take care of his customers?" I asked.

"Much more than that," Skeeter said. "She's selling the entire business to me for the cost of the equipment. Our lawyers are talking. Just wants to be done and out of the business, I understand. I'll be forever grateful to Rodent and the Mrs."

Ultima was nothing if not fast.

"So, you don't normally work Galveston?" Sparky asked.

"Nah, only overflow for Rodent during the busy season."

"When had you last seen Rodent?" I asked.

"Couple of months," Skeeter said. "We talked on the phone last week. That's when he told me about the iguanas. I've not seen them up in Houston yet."

"Did he ask for your help?" Sparky said.

"No, and besides, I was in Cancun when he called. Tenth anniversary with my wife and kids." Skeeter pulled his phone out of his pocket and showed us pictures from his trip. "That's my oldest son right there." He pointed to a young man carrying a cage to the back yard. "Was an outstanding trip, but I'd given it up if I thought I could've helped Rodent."

"When did you come back?" Sparky asked.

He waved his crew on to go ahead with the work. "Sunday."

"When did you first hear from Ultima?"

"She left me a voicemail at work. Friday, I think. She was looking for Rodent." Skeeter sighed and shook his head.

Skeeter excused himself for a moment so he could check

on his workers. Sparky and I took a look in Skeeter's van. They'd left the side door open, presumably to air out the stench because it smelled. Four live iguanas were in cages stacked on the floor of the van. I wondered what Skeeter did with them.

I walked up to the cages and looked in. "Oh no."

Sparky stepped closer. "Something wrong?"

It was Doug. I recognized his face and missing toe on his right foot. I kneeled and looked into Doug's eyes. "I know this one."

"From the shop?" Sparky asked. "Is that the lizard that crapped on you?"

"No," I said.

I stood and looked around. Skeeter and his men were still in the back yard.

"I need you to keep them in the backyard. Ask them to show you how their equipment works or something. Anything." I pointed to the backyard. "Go!"

"OK, OK." Sparky shuffled across the front lawn and along the side of the house.

I lifted the caged with Doug inside out of the van. I looked around. We were on Cade Lane in the Lake Como neighborhood, which was just east of where I'd met Doug in the state park. I thought about opening the cage and letting my friend go, but what if he ran in the wrong direction? He'd soon get caught again. Doug's chances would be better if he went back into the park.

I approached the cage from the front and started talking to Doug. "Hello Doug, I'm going to get you out of this predicament, but you need to stay calm and be nice to me." I opened the top of the cage just enough to slip my hand into the cage from the side. "Hold him behind his head and support his body," I whispered to Doug. I remembered seeing Seth using this method.

The large iguana flinched. But I held my hand open, moved it closer, and wrapped my fingers around Doug's thick neck. He jerked but then calmed down after a few seconds, so I opened the cage top and scooped him up like a linebacker carrying a football with my right arm looped around his body and my left hand gripping his neck. Doug's tail whipped behind me. I took off sprinting while carrying Doug across the street toward a stand of trees at the edge of the park.

"Doug, you're going to need to trust me. Stay in the trees and marshes. If you don't, you'll become a pair of boots. I know you're just trying to have a happy iguana life, but this isn't a good place for you."

Doug said nothing, and for a moment, I wondered if I was saving the wrong iguana. When I got to the trees, I stopped and looked down at his lumpy, spiky face.

I placed Doug on the trunk of a large tree and let him go. The iguana scurried up the tree and climbed onto a low branch. He stopped, nodded his head, and then continued up the tree.

It was Doug. I turned and ran back to the van with just enough time to put Doug's empty cage back into the van before I heard voices coming from the side of the house.

"Xena!" Sparky yelled. He was leading the pack of people

and was carrying a pole with a little iguana dangling from the pole's end. "I got one!"

Skeeter and his two workers followed Sparky back to the van.

"Took him a few tries, but he got 'im," Skeeter said and patted Sparky on the shoulder.

Skeeter's son grabbed a cage and took the pole from Sparky. "Hey, Pa, I thought we had another iguana in here. Did you let one go?"

"No, sure didn't." Skeeter looked at us and shrugged. "Boy doesn't count too good."

Skeeter didn't notice I was sweating and had dried weeds on my pants from running through the field.

I asked Skeeter to play dumb if he encountered the Lizard Liquidators, and they asked questions about Rodent's business or a guy named William Wiley.

"No problem. I don't know nothing." He smiled and shook my hand.

"One last question." Sparky pointed to the van. "What do you do with them?"

Skeeter snorted a laugh. "Sweet deal with a buddy of mine in South Houston. Takes them off my hands for five bucks a piece. Said lizards make a fine stew."

As we got in the car, Sparky scowled at me. "I missed catching that damn iguana on purpose at least ten times. I assume you did what you needed to?"

"Yes," I said. "His name is Doug. We met at the state park."

Chapter 30

4:00 p.m.

A downpour put a damper on my plan for a long training ride. The rain didn't bother me but it made drivers more unpredictable. I slid open my garage door and warmed up for a ninety-minute ride on my stationary bike. Not the same as being on the road, but better than no ride at all. To help pass the time, I listened to my Dale Carnegie book. The reader told me to *make others feel important,* which was principle #6 for how to get people to like you. He suggested we admire their work, be polite, and communicate their importance in your life.

Although I initially pooh-poohed Carnegie's recommendation to smile a lot, I had no problem buying into this principle. It made sense. We want to make a difference and love hearing someone tell us we matter to them and are special. The reader pierced a metaphorical arrow through my heart when he challenged listeners to consider that most people suck at making others feel important. And that most of us fit into the category of most.

Message received. I'll try harder.

After listening to more examples than I needed—I'm cold and aloof, not stupid—I switched over to music from Awolnation. Halfway through my favorite song for training, "The Best," an incoming call cut in on my AirPods.

I looked at my watch and recognized the number. "This is Xena."

"Hey," Amanda/Hiba said. *"I've called during a workout."*

I held my arms up toward the ceiling to stretch. "Stationary bike. I'll slow down a bit so you can understand me. I'm training for a tri."

"My butt is too big for bikes, or I'd be right there with you."

"Nonsense," I said. "What's up?"

"I've two bits of news. First, Ginger left for her writing retreat this afternoon. She'll be on Bolivar all weekend."

"Great, I was going to head out there tomorrow." I lied. But maybe I could combine the trip with a training ride if the weather was good.

"Super!" Amanda paused. *"The second thing is that my client seems receptive to your offer but would like to see a sample of the information you have. Something small will do as long as it leaves him suitably terrified."* She laughed.

I took a drink of water, then rested my hands on my handlebars and slowed my speed again. "Yeah, OK. I think I can do that. Give me a couple of days, ah… Would you prefer I call you Agatha or Hiba?"

There was a pause on the line.

"Surely you knew I'd figure out who you were…"

"Surely," she said. *"It took me a minute to decide. Let's stick*

with Agatha. I selected it because it's my favorite name."

"Agatha, it is." I stop peddling and got off the bike and sat on my weight bench. I focused on my breath for a few seconds. "And I want to thank you. The work you're doing is making a significant difference in my life, and I'm more optimistic about things."

I realize that maybe I'd poured on the Dale Carnegie a bit too strong. At least I'm practicing on real human beings and not just talking to my punching bag.

"How kind of you to say."

"Well deserved, Agatha." Yikes, that sounded stiff.

"Xena, can I ask you a personal question?"

"Sure," I said.

"How old are you?"

My stomach clenched. "In my thirties."

"Oh, sorry. You don't enjoy talking about your age?"

"Maybe," I said. "And this year especially. I'm thirty-nine with a birthday next month."

Agatha sighed. *"I had a hard time with forty, too. But you know what helped?"*

"Tell me."

"An epic trip that challenged me physically, mentally, and spiritually."

"Cool, what did you do?"

"Dog sledding in Alaska under the Northern Lights. And not just the fun parts. I fed the dogs, cleaned up after them, and hooked them up to the sled. Even had to pull a couple out of icy water. And driving a dog sled is HARD work. The end of every day was glorious. Warm fire and a brandy. And here's why this

trip was just what I needed. It took me way out of my comfort zone and helped me put my entire life into perspective."

I stood up and ran in place for a few seconds to ensure my muscles didn't stiffen. My workout was far from over. "Epic journey. That's what I need. You've got my mind working on overdrive, Ms. Reacher, but I need to get back to my workout. I'll be back in touch soon with a tease…for your client."

"I look forward to that."

Chapter 31

Day 11, Saturday, March 10
3:00 a.m.

Investigator Report—Friday, March 9
Investigator: Dora Baker

This was our first full sailing day in open waters, and it did not disappoint. The weather was partly cloudy and 63 degrees, with a swift wind created by the moving ship. Captain CC was right: the *Twisted Ambition* is a peppy steel steed.

It was a jam-packed and productive day. I'll spare you all the details and focus on the parts I know you're most interested in. Filo recommended I arrive early for the *Live Like You're a Kid Again* breakfast where I enjoyed cold pizza, mac and cheese pancakes, and banana pudding. Why have I not thought of this? I then burned 765 calories (according to my Fitbit) practicing with my green fuzzy Hula-Hoop for an hour. I even tried doing the Hula-Hoop on my lava bed to see if I could make the model crater erupt. Strike two, but I'm determined to make it happen because I want word to get to Rascal about my vitality.

Before lunch, I attended Dr. Quintana Flores's *Wild World of Iguanas* lecture and show. Her presentation was out of this world, and I took over twenty pages of notes. You were right, Q is brilliant and passionate. Did she tell you she got her PhD in Evolutionary Biology from Manchester University in England by the time she was 29 years old? She's 31 now. And she studied under several renowned herpetologists and was a research intern before joining the research staff at the Blue Iguana Conservation Society on Grand Cayman. I'm glad she's our iguana expert.

I feel I know much more about iguanas, including why your initial attempt to handle them by approaching from the back backfired. Has your hand healed? It could've been so much worse if they hadn't been sleeping. Dr. Flores showed us several types of young and old iguanas, including a baby hatchling green iguana that was only three inches long.

And I'm in love, absolute love, with the endangered Grand Cayman blue iguana. They're deep teal/aqua blue and can grow to be quite large. Blue iguanas seem chill, like the Snoop Dog of lizards, and the complete opposite of the spastic greens we're dealing with in Galveston. Q says this is because Grand Cayman didn't have predators like cats, dogs, and rats until humans brought them to the island. Blue iguanas are innately unafraid, even if their environment is now more dangerous. She lifted two mature blue iguanas during her presentation, one in each arm, with her forearm supporting their body. They looked six feet STL—snout to tail—and weighed close to 30 pounds. Such a powerful woman.

Although nothing like you, Xena.

Saving the endangered blue iguana is Q's passion and driving force. Their plight is heart-wrenching. I did as you suggested and stayed in character, but I worry my enthusiasm might make Q think I'll be writing her foundation a huge check. In the meantime, she's invited me to her very exclusive on-the-ground tour to see wild blue iguanas when we're in Grand Cayman. We'll also learn more about the foundation there. I'll be attending, of course, but will have to be careful when answering financial questions. How do I act rich without spending money? Perhaps I'll assign writing checks to my fictitious personal assistant. Let me know if you have other suggestions. And don't forget to e-mail me the questions you want me to ask Dr. Flores.

For lunch I took Filo's suggestion and tried one of their engineered entrees. It was like a newfangled smoothie and very Jetsons-with-a-Vitamix. I had a delightful medium rare prime rib with Yorkshire pudding smoothie with horseradish whipped cream. No need to use a toothpick to get meat out of my teeth. It tasted superb and like the real thing.

After lunch I reported to the promenade deck to take part in the *Whose Underwear Is It?* contest. Thankfully, Beauregard had put me down as a player not a donor, because my underwear isn't interesting. Here's how it worked. One hundred passengers donated a pair of clean underwear for free casino credits. There were five heats of twenty. During each round, players would look at the twenty undies while the corresponding donors stood and introduced themselves on stage in random order. Players used a hand-held console to match the people to their underwear. Every correct match earned a point, and the top thirty players moved on to the second round. The top twenty competed in round three, while the top ten and five played against one another in rounds four and five. Matching undies to people was harder each round. The winner of round five became the Grand Champion for the cruise.

And guess what, Xena? I won! Here's a clip of my in-character acceptance speech.

> Videotape: Dora wins *Whose Underwear Is It?* tournament.
>
> I'm thrilled and humbled. Winning the Grand Champion prize for the Best of Five Rounds in the *Whose Underwear Is It?* tournament is one of the more interesting moments of my life. You asked me to share my strategies, and I'm happy to oblige.

Toby, you almost had me stumped with those pink polka-dot briefs without the fly flap until I remembered seeing you drink a vodka martini. That was a dead giveaway. Vodka martinis shouldn't exist, much like men's underwear without fly flaps.

And I'll be the first to admit that I got lucky when I matched the stainless-steel chastity belt with Bobby. Who knew such a fine male specimen could fit in one of those contraptions? Wink, wink. There was just something about the way you smiled that said *metal panties*.

But my pièce de résistance was Mrs. Bogart. As you stood on the stage braless and sagging in your see-through shirt, you oozed inner-confidence and verve. Guessing the lime-green, crocheted G-string belonged to you filled me with a rush of adrenaline and secured my final win and designation as Grand Champion. I applaud you!

And I can't forget Rita and Dagnet, my dear departed parents, who taught me how to judge people with pinpoint accuracy based on their looks and actions. While you can't always judge a book by its cover, people are completely predictable. I'll remember this award forever.

I had a latte with Beauregard after the competition. He told me that my performance was inspiring, and I was the first seasoned woman to win. I think he intended this to be a positive remark. He looked handsome in his khakis and red turtleneck (no yellow leotard because he'd completed his task of singing wake-up calls earlier in the morning). He has short-cropped gray hair and bright blue eyes that look enormous behind his thick but stylish round glasses. And he still has his real teeth. Beauregard is a retired history schoolteacher.

But don't worry, Xena, I've stayed in character and focused on the case. In fact, Beauregard has turned out to be a terrific source of information. I mentioned I was looking forward to hearing Rascal Romano sing, and he told me to watch out because he walked in on him and a lady passenger last year. The staff assigned Beauregard to her cabin to play a human ottoman for two hours. He didn't expect to see an aroused lounge singer in one of the Audacious robes (which are transparent when wet, he advised).

Rascal's reputation precedes him.

An item on our onboard questionnaire asked us to list countries we wanted to visit, and then the culinary team created tonight's dinner based on our selections. I enjoyed an exhilarating oxtail stew, pap-pap (maize porridge), and spiked ginger beer gelatin. Can you guess which country I listed first?

The Kingdom of Lesotho, of course.

And now for today's big news. I met Rascal tonight. I walked into the Audacious Club wearing a black pantsuit with a charcoal gray silk top and some costume jewelry that Ant loaned me. As I walked in, the bartender nodded, and a man who I now know is Rascal watched me as I made my way to my reserved table. My Pappy was on the table before I leaned back in my chair and Trish greeted me with a big smile.

I've never experienced this level of service. Is this what life is like for rich people?

Rascal is a beautiful man in a Fabio-meets-Paul-Newman kind of way. He's muscular, tall, has long dark hair, and the face of an angel. Dark evil eyes, however. He looks about thirty-five years old. I understand why women throw money and jewels at him.

Fascinating fact: His mother named him Rascal because he kicked her a lot when she was pregnant with him. Or so he said. One look at his sly smile and any mother could see he was going to be trouble.

He's slick, which we knew and expected. Rascal must've kissed my hand a dozen times tonight. And guess what song he played at the end of his first set without my prodding? The slow version of "Fly Me to the Moon." Extra slow, and he looked right through me as he sang it. That confirmed the ship's informal communication pipeline was in tip-top shape.

Just like Rascal. We'd chatted during the night—polite chitchat, but with flirty questions and answers. After his last set he kneeled down beside me, touched my leg, and told me to let him know what he could do to make my cruise exceptional. And that he specialized in exceptional.

I imagined he was the most famous birding guide in the world and then told Rascal that I was a woman of action, believed in possibility, and that I'd love it if he'd consider taking me on an exceptional—pause—birding tour. And then I winked and told him I'd like to learn about his services when I come back for drinks tomorrow. I encouraged him to be daring and that I'd be willing to compensate extraordinarily for extraordinary efforts.

Rascal accepted my invitation to think big. I predict our conversation tomorrow, or rather later today, will get into specifics.

Is that the way you wanted me to do it, Xena?

It's going to be a big day for me, and I need to prepare. Time for me to sleep.

End of report.

Chapter 32

10:00 a.m.

Sparky and I got the spy shop opened and tidied up the meeting room so we could update our case charts and reassess where the investigation needed to go next. I shared Dora's second update with him. "Have you heard of Lesotho?"

"After reading all that, Lesotho is your first question?" Sparky laughed while he poured another cup of coffee. He pulled the tin foil covering off the glass container of brownies he'd brought. "They're still warm."

"Fair point. The underwear contest and lizard show were pretty spectacular." I cut an inch square brownie and popped it in my mouth. "Fudgy and intense. This batch is your best ever."

Sparky bounced his head up and down a few times, spread his arms wide and smiled. "Practice makes perfect. And who's this Beauregard guy? She's mentioned him twice. You think we should worry?"

I pulled the tray of brownies closer and cut another inch square. "I don't care as long as we bust the gigolo and collect our fee. Dora will keep her head in the game when it counts." I slid the brownie in my mouth and raised my eyebrows in delight. "She always does."

We watched again the drone footage of Rodent's covered van because I wondered if it would tell us anything about the tarp and inform our investigation. It was larger than most tarps, and not the usual blue type people put on their roofs after storms. It looked more like what an exterminator might use to fumigate a house.

"What if the tarp came from inside Rodent's van?" I asked.

"Could mean that the killer hadn't intended to dump the van." Sparky said.

"What if Rodent drove his van there?" I tapped a marker on our chart of questions and added anything we blurted out as long as it was relevant. You might imagine with our brownie consumption that some questions didn't deserve a spot on the wall. Why aren't cookies considered a school-lunch vegetable? And how do planes fly? When the page was full of legit questions, I sat back down, took some notes, and cut another inch-square brownie and ate it.

Did I tell Sparky I was going on a thirty-mile bike ride over to the Bolivar Peninsula in a few hours? No, I did not.

Sparky leaned back and grabbed the pages I'd just sent to the printer. He gave me one copy and kept one. It was the ME's preliminary autopsy report on Rodent. We both started reading.

I slapped my forehead. "Whoa, confirms manner of death is suffocation, but no compression damage to the throat, which I find really puzzling. Did they wrap him in plastic? And Rodent had ligature marks on his wrists. They tied him up. That's totally murder."

"Consistent with zip-ties." Sparky circled something on the report. "All wounds except bruising to cranium occurred after death. Someone whacked him on the head, then bound him up. Man, that just sucks. He didn't deserve that."

"Melissa gave us her A game on this report," I said. "I'd worried she'd not be able to gauge time of death, but she's saying they killed him last Friday, but that the bruising to the head appears a day or two older." I stood up and posted a fresh page from the flip cart on the wall. "So… Where were we? Let's create a timeline."

Sparky and I spent the next hour charting out the movements for all our key players: Rodent, Ultima, Zorin, and us. Less impaired people could've done it in fifteen minutes. We then created a list of potential scenarios and open questions.

"We need to find and then focus on the crime scene," I said. I pointed to our list of questions and underlined: WHERE WAS RODENT KILLED? "I know forensics went through and cleared the marsh area where Rodent's van was left, but I don't think we can rule out he was killed there."

My theory was that they used zip-ties to secure him, but then cut them off when they dumped his body in the water. I made a circle with my hands and extended my arms toward Sparky. "Put your mind in the head of a killer. Assume killing Rodent wasn't your goal. Do you take the zip-ties with you after you cut them off? No, they could be found and connected to you. Do you leave them on the ground or in Rodent's truck? No, that puts law enforcement on your trail right away."

Sparky handed me another inch-square brownie, just like I like it. "You dump them."

"Right." I positioned the brownie on my tongue and pointed to the monitor. "Bring up the satellite picture of the end of Indian Beach Drive. In the middle of a marsh on the edge of the bay, your only choice is to get rid of the ties in the water. Throw with all your strength."

"Do zip-ties float?" Sparky asked.

I shook my head. "They don't. How likely is it that the killer, or killers, would know that?"

Sparky shrugged. "Depends on how much they use zip-ties. Don't dominatrices use them?" He giggled.

"Wouldn't know, but I if I were in that line of work, I'd carry several sizes." I smiled, picked up a marker, and cleaned off a spot on the white board. "I've four questions for Ethan. One: Did forensics search the water for evidence? Two: Did they find unused zip-ties in Rodent's van? Three: Was the tarp over his van consistent with the type exterminators use? Four: Did they find evidence that Rodent was unconscious or incapacitated when he suffocated?" I started walking around the meeting room. "I'm betting his answers will be no, yes, yes, and yes. I want to go back to that marsh. See if we can find any clues forensics might've missed.

I plunked down and let out an enormous sigh.

"You should wait a little while before calling the captain." Sparky cut a sizeable brownie and started eating it. "Wrong place, wrong time? Or maybe he caught someone doing something wrong and one thing led to another?"

I cut and ate my ~~fourth~~ fifth square of brownie. "Like dumping little iguanas."

Chapter 33

2:00 p.m.

According to Google, the best ways to stop feeling high include hydrating, chewing on a peppercorn, taking a walk, and distracting yourself. I wondered how they determined eating a peppercorn worked. Perhaps some high-as-a-kite magazine writer accidentally chewed a peppercorn and then was so distracted by his numb tongue that he forgot he was high.

Luckily for me, my brownie bonus wore off within a couple of hours and two sport bottles of cold water. Plan B was to ride to the ferry dock and hope the thirty-minute bumpy 2.7-mile journey across the pass did the trick.

Although the Bolivar Peninsula is nearly thirty miles long—making it an excellent choice for a longer bike ride—my surveillance assignment was at a house on Twenty-Third Street just a couple of miles from the ferry landing and close to where I had lunch with Agatha. It was a bright aqua-blue stilt house and looked newer, which wasn't uncommon. In 2008, Hurricane Ike wiped out over 60 percent of the buildings on the Bolivar Peninsula. There were few mature trees here for the same reason.

The house was on a small canal and near where a fleet of shrimp boats were docked. The empty lot next to the house had a pen with goats in it. I took my time riding to the house because I'd not yet formulated my strategy for getting inside. Faking a flat tire, or a mechanical malfunction perhaps. It must've been my lucky day because Mother Nature offered me the perfect story.

Like many stilt houses, this one had a large tiki bar and sitting area built under the house. I could see several people congregating around the bar when a fast-moving storm started to rain down hard. I jumped off my bike when I got to the house and ran with it up to the house.

"Hi, would it be OK if I stood here until the storm passed?" I smiled and tried to look harmless.

A tall woman with long gray hair came from behind the bar and waved me under the house. "Sure, honey, step right in. Would you like a beer while you wait?"

Brownies and beer. I decided I'd better pass on the alcohol.

There were eight people sitting in a loose circle of Adirondack chairs. One man, seven women. All had beers, or wine glasses, or what looked like mixed cocktails. The general mood seemed lively. Even the goats were making a good bit of noise, but then don't they always?

The man got up and walked over to me. "You live on the peninsula?"

"No, Galveston," I replied. "I'm training for a triathlon

and was hoping to get in fifty miles today."

"I'm Dylan."

"Geena," I said. I often used this as my fake name because I could claim they heard it wrong if they later found out my actual identity.

"We were just taking turns reading poetry." He pointed to an empty chair. "Please, have a seat and enjoy it."

I leaned my bike against a stilt and sat. Most of the women looked to be in their fifties and sixties. Two seemed a bit younger. One matched the description Agatha had given me of Ginger. Tall, long curly hair, medium brown complexion, lots of freckles. She said Ginger was biracial.

The woman who'd been standing behind the bar—maybe the owner of the house—pulled a stool next to me, sat, and whispered. "I hope you don't mind dirty poems."

I looked at her, puzzled.

"The poems are erotic. Just wanted to warn you." She smiled. "I'm Ida."

"I love erotica," I said in the same manner one might ask for a paper clip. "I'm Geena."

I'll not be sharing or summarizing any of the poems here, dear readers, because if I did, bookstore owners would move my story to a different section. I know you were wondering.

Soon it was Ginger's turn to read. She stood. Her hands were shaking a bit. She lifted her notebook. Her poem was called "In Ward," and it was dirty with a capital *D*. After Ginger finished, the other women offered feedback, like that her poem was luminous, vivid, lovely, sweet, and motivational. I didn't know if it was motivational, but I heard a few new ideas I thought I'd try if I ever got another boyfriend. I started feeling sorry for myself when I realized that wouldn't happen until I was in my forties.

Dylan stood next to Ginger and told her that this poem was her best yet.

I stood and acted as though I was stretching. I walked back to the bar where Ida was standing. "Thanks for letting me listen. I'm enjoying it. Is this your writing group?"

Ida shook her head. "We—my son, Dylan, and I—run a three-month intensive course in writing love poems for real men. We help participants with the entire process: writing, formatting, cover, and printing. They leave the class with something they can give to their real men."

Real men? What did she mean by that? Guys who were more likely to read Playboy than Robert Frost? That'd be a large target audience, I imagined. I opened my eyes wide and smiled. I took a step closer to Ida. "What a fascinating idea!"

She nodded while watching the next reader get ready. "Dylan is uniquely qualified to help coach them find the right words to provoke their men because he's gay. He's quite a famous poet of gay erotica under his pen name, Rod Erogenous." She smiled and put one of her hands on her heart. I thought it was cool that Ida seemed proud of her son. Maybe one sign the world is becoming a more tolerant place?

The rained had slowed to a trickle. "Is this something publicized that I could share with a friend who I think might be interested in attending?"

Ida nodded and bent down behind the bar. She handed me a trifold brochure.

I grabbed the water bottle off my bike, stood at the edge of the concrete pad, and listened to a couple of more readers. The poems were growing on me like the *Rocky Horror Picture Show* had. The nice thing about erotic poetry, I concluded, was that because there was so much symbolism and metaphor, the writer's description of how body parts performed sex acts didn't seem shocking or uncomfortable to hear. Like the distinction between sensual massage and giving someone a hand job.

After all the students had read and received feedback, they took a break. I got ready to go, but first walked up to Ginger. "I liked your poem. Is the Ward you mention in it your boyfriend?"

Ginger put her hands together and smiled. "Thank you. I'm out of my element, here. Ward is my husband. I'm going to give him the book on a trip to Cancun we've planned next month. To spice things up."

I touched her forearm. "If all your poems are like that one, I think they'll do the trick!" I winked at her and then turned to leave. After thanking Ida, Dylan, and the others and I got back on my bike.

Ideas for how to best describe to Agatha what Ginger was doing on Bolivar entertained me as I put in another thirty miles on my bike.

Chapter 34

Day 12, Sunday, March 11
2:40 a.m.

Investigator Report—Saturday, March 10
Investigator: Dora Baker

Filo brought me a brie cheese and grilled peach omelet that I ate on my veranda as the ship arrived at Grand Cayman. The water went from midnight blue to lapis to aqua as we got closer to shore. It thrilled me to watch Captain CC stand on the outside overhang from the bridge as her mates navigated the *Twisted Ambition* alongside the dock to get tied up.

Those going with Dr. Flores on her shore excursion, five including me, got off the ship first. We then took a forty-five-minute shuttle bus ride across the island to the Queen Elizabeth II Botanical Park. Grand Cayman is a British colony that is an equal distance between Cuba and Jamaica. Quintana was born on Grand Cayman, making her a Caymanian. She boasted she learned street smarts from her mother and uncles. Her father was a fisherman who was gone a lot. The shuttle driver took us through Q's childhood neighborhood, called Savannah Gables, and she pointed out the house she grew up in. It was a charming single-story vivid fuchsia blockhouse with white corner blocks (called *quoins*), a white roof, and solar panels. The yard had palm trees, agave, hibiscus bushes, and bright bougainvillea the same color as the house.

Many of the houses were colorful and chickens ran around everywhere like we've seen in Key West. Nobody bothers the chickens, but our driver, who was named Vincent, said some people eat the roosters.

The park was understated compared to other royal botanical gardens I've seen. But inside the small visitor center, there was a poster of Prince Charles petting a large blue iguana. Quintana hugged and said hello to the staff at the park and then took us down a wide path. Champagne-colored sand, low bushes, palms, and a thin forest of tall pines dominated the landscape. After we'd walked about ten minutes, I saw something up ahead lying in the middle of the walkway. Q said it was an endangered Grand Cayman blue iguana. We walked toward it, and she led us single file up to and by the blue iguana, who remained still. We walked in front of it, not behind (never go behind an iguana, Q said). The fronts of our shoes were less than two feet from its snout. After we'd cleared the iguana, we stopped to watch it and take pictures. It was dark turquoise all over its body and had a light blue-green snout and short spikes down its back. Including its tail, it looked five feet long. The middle of the iguana's body seemed about the size of a paper towel roll. Thick! The healthy-looking iguana yawned but never moved from the middle of the path. I've got video footage I'll show you back at the spy shop.

During our walk, we saw four other blue iguanas. All seemed relaxed, except two that were chasing each other. They waddled when they ran. Dr. Flores then showed us the nursery inside the Blue Iguana Headstart Facility, which is a breeding laboratory working to increase the number of blue iguanas that are born and make it through their first six months, when they're most likely to get picked off by predators. Q made a point of telling us that this is the important work that our donations would fund.

It was a remarkable day on Grand Cayman. I feel lucky because it seems only the wealthy passengers are invited to attend. The tour was $500 per person and the others in my group talked like rich people talk. *When we went up the Nile on a private yacht…* and such pompousness.

It was dinnertime soon after I got back to the ship. The chefs based tonight's dinner on the fantasy job we listed on our questionnaire. I didn't dare write *investigator,* even though I feel like I'm living in a fantasy world, because I didn't want to compromise my cover. My entrée was based on what I thought the rich and saucy Dora Baker would want to do—international food curator for the Prince of Monaco. They assigned me to Captain Chablis's table, and she congratulated me for what she called a spirited choice of jobs. My electric eel sushi, braised baby impala shank with morel mushroom soufflé, and violet lavender gelato was intoxicating! I tried not to think about how the baby impalas never got to grow up because I assumed my character ate baby animals whenever they were an option on the menu.

I went to the Audacious Club later than usual tonight because I didn't want to seem too eager. My outfit: an emerald green pantsuit with a deep purple button-down shirt and lots of fake bling. You might wonder where I got all these pantsuits. I had lunch with an always-elegant friend who wears the same clothing size as I do. I asked her if I could borrow some of her outfits and hit the jackpot with ten different color pantsuits from her days as a fundraiser for the Hillary campaign.

Rascal and I chatted in-between his sets. He said I looked powerful in my green pantsuit and I nodded (while gushing inside). I told him about my day on Grand Cayman and how seeing endangered blue iguanas in the wild had gotten me in the mood to experience something exotic. At the end of the evening, Rascal walked me out and onto a private veranda just outside the lounge. I asked him if he'd thought more about my interest in a private birding tour. He told me he'd love to take me on a birding tour if he and I are the only birds.

Obviously, I told him yes (I was feeling weird, but held it together).

Then I told Rascal that it was important he be clear and specific with me because the cruise was short, and I'd get someone else if he wasn't up to it. And I said it needed to happen in my suite.

I think he's done this—shift from flirtation to a business transaction—many times before. He neither hesitated nor sugarcoated anything. Maybe that's normal for those who buy and sell specialized bird-watching tours. Here's exactly what he said so you can make sure we got the information you need for your part: *For a $6,000 donation, you will receive my famous sensual massage and two hours of made-to-order seduction. I guarantee you will climax, and I'll earn a $500 bonus for each climax you achieve beyond three. My optional exotic dance is $500.*

I was freaking out inside, so I kept the conversation short. I told Rascal that I'd take all of that, including the optionals and bonuses. And I asked him to double-down on exotic moves because I'm not getting any younger. Tomorrow afternoon, 2:00 p.m., so I'm not late to dinner at 6:30.

Rascal gulped. I made him gulp! But then he told me we had a deal, and we shook hands.

I made sure my handshake was firm, just like you taught me.

I told him I was in the Volcano Suite.

He nodded and said he was familiar with that stateroom.

When I got back to my room, I drank the Pappy I'd been pouring into my water bottle all night. This assignment has pushed me out of my comfort zone, Xena, so I channeled my younger sister Sally. She's been a tart her whole life.

I think I did what you asked. Today we'll close this case, right?

E-mail me when you're ready to chat later this morning to go over the plan. I'll be available after 10:00 a.m. my time (because it's 3:00 a.m. now).

End of report.

Chapter 35

11:00 a.m.

Ultima handed me a cup of coffee and sat down on the couch. Her one-bedroom extended-stay suite in the Tremont House included a full kitchen and lots of open space. From the living room, she could see the Port of Galveston and north toward the mainland. Two Royal Caribbean ships were docked at the cruise terminal.

"Can we clear the air again?" I asked.

She twirled one hand and rolled her eyes. "If you feel the need."

"I thought we had a deal you'd let me talk to Skeeter first," I said. "What happened?"

Ultima thought for a moment and bounced her crossed leg. "Changed my mind. Thought Skeeter would rather hear from me. And I wanted to make sure you did nothing to mess up my deal with him to buy Rodent's business." She tilted her head. "What is your problem?"

"My problem," I said and pointed to her, "is that I'm trying to find your husband's killer and don't like being surprised by my client."

"Client. Am I your client or one of your suspects? Because you make me feel as though I'm the one you're investigating." Ultima stood and looked out the window. "I told you I'm not the antagonist of this story."

Time to mirror. I stood and stood at the window. "But everything you do affects whether and when we'll find who's responsible."

"What I do with my house or Rodent's business is of no consequences to this matter, don't you get it? I make more money writing romance novels than I'll ever be able to spend. I had no motive or desire to get rid of Rodney. His death is quite inconvenient and has ripped my heart in two."

So maybe you didn't want to share your fortune with Rodent if you divorced, I thought, but said nothing.

Ultima turned and looked at me. "This relationship isn't working for me, Xena, and I feel comfortable leaving this case in Captain Slaughter's hands. Send me a bill for services through today."

"I agree that's best." I lied. Not getting paid is never best.

As I walked the two blocks from the Tremont House to my spy shop, I reflected on what had just happened. Movement caught my eye, and I looked up to see a large iguana peering at me from the roof of the bank.

More iguanas.

I called and left a voicemail for Ethan. *"Please call me as soon as you can. I've a few questions and some new information about the Roger case."*

You didn't think I was going to stop investigating Rodent's murder just because my client fired me, now did you?

Chapter 36

1:30 p.m.

I hadn't told Ant or Dora about the research that Sparky and I had been doing to prepare for what we were calling Rascal Romano's "Come to Mama." It'd be better if they both reacted naturally to what would be going down. We were looking for an impact that'd ensure Rascal demonstrated lasting behavior change.

Dora joined me on Zoom, and we adjusted the camera view and where we'd place Rascal for my part. Close enough so I could see his nonverbal reactions, but far enough away so he couldn't touch the keyboard. I told Dora to relax, respond naturally, and deliver the following line once he was inside her suite: *"Show me you're not going to be wasting my time."* And then we practiced what she'd say to Rascal before turning the conversation over to me.

Did I know he was going to be wearing pants and a shirt held together by Velcro or that he'd yank them off with flair like he did? And that he'd be wearing nothing but leopard print underwear, white socks, and black shoes? No, I did not, but I'd hoped he'd undress to some degree.

"Good," Dora responded. *"I'd like to make a few things clear before we get down to business."* She guided Rascal to sit in a swivel chair that she'd placed four feet from her laptop on the desk.

Rascal complied.

"I'm going to give you a shitload of money for great sex, and I want to be sure you're experienced enough to earn your large fee." Dora's voice was shaking but controlled. *"Have you been with a woman like me before?"*

Rascal grinned. *"Satisfying sage women like yourself is my specialty."*

"As a gigolo," Dora said.

Rascal swallowed and nodded.

"Fine," Dora said. *"Let's begin."* She spun Rascal around.

I turned on my camera. I'd slicked back my hair with gel and put on rectangular black glasses.

Rascal's eyes opened wide, and he glanced back at Dora.

"Hello, Rascal," I said. "Dora, please ask Mr. Strangelove to join us."

Rascal started to get up as Ant came into the room.

"Sit your ass down, Rascal," I ordered, "or things will get worse than they already are."

Rascal complied.

I looked past Rascal to Ant, whose face had drained of color. "Mr. Strangelove, my name is Xena Cali, I'm a private detective, and I've been hired by your home office to investigate and resolve a situation on your ship that represents a risk to the corporation. I'd like you to serve as witness to this conversation and support its outcome."

Ant nodded. *"What have you done, Rascal?"*

Rascal's shoulders drooped.

I began the takedown. "Let's make this quick, shall we? I need to neutralize a murderer in an hour. You've already met Dora Baker, she's one of my finest investigators. Everything you've said to Ms. Baker has become a part of your case file."

Dora beamed.

Rascal slumped.

Ant stood at attention.

"Ercole Romano, that's your real name, right? The name your mother Angelica Romano gave you?"

Rascal put his hand on his mouth and nodded.

"Ercole, meaning gift from God. Your mother is quite a religious woman, as I understand."

Rascal's eyes looked glassy.

"She doesn't call you Rascal, does she?"

Rascal shook his head.

"You came up with that yourself, in fact, didn't you?"

Rascal nodded.

"Didn't you?"

"Yes," Rascal eked out.

"Your seventy-one-year-old mother, Angelica, living in the Red River neighborhood in New Jersey, cell number ending in 4123, would be surprised to hear people call her son '*Rascal,*' and she'd double over in pain if she knew her gift from God was a male prostitute who charged women thousands of dollars to have sex with him. Women her age, some older."

Rascal held out his hands and started crying. "*No, please. Please don't tell my mother. I'll do anything. Please.*"

Ant swayed like he might faint.

Dora beamed again.

I leaned closer to the camera. "I'm glad to hear you say that, Ercole, because the corporation is willing to give you one opportunity to save yourself from your mother's shame and disappointment."

Rascal whimpered, *"I'll do anything."*

"Here's precisely what you will do. You shall never take money for sex again."

Rascal nodded.

"Tell me."

"I won't take money for sex," he replied.

"Ever."

"Ever."

"Good. And you'll never have sex with a woman your mother's age until you're older, too."

Rascal nodded.

I waited.

"I won't have sex with a woman my mother's age." He began wailing.

"Excellent, you're doing well, but there's more. And you won't have sex, and that includes oral sex, Ercole, with anyone while working on this or any Audacious Cruise Line ship."

"I won't have sex with anyone."

"While working on board."

"While working on board."

"Now turn and apologize to your supervisor, for putting him, the ship, and the company at risk."

Rascal stared at me.

"Do it now!"

He turned to Ant and repeated the line.

"Mr. Strangelove," I continued after Rascal had issued his apology, "it is your duty to report any improper behavior or hints of improper behavior to headquarters. If you fail to do so, they'll fire you. Do you understand?"

Ant saluted. *"Yes, I understand."*

"Ercole, look at me."

Rascal turned back to me and looked into the camera.

"If my client hears that you've sold your body to their customers, vendors, or employees, you will be fired and prosecuted to the fullest extent of the law. Your mother and the entire world will learn who Rascal Romano is. A greedy and decrepit man. Have I made myself clear?"

Rascal nodded.

"Say it," Ant said.

"I'm clear." Rascal stared at me as tears continued to stream down his face.

"Now get your disgusting body out of my sight," I said.

Rascal looked around.

I got close to the camera. "NOW!"

Rascal jumped up, grabbed his pants and shirt, and ran out of the suite. Dora and Ant didn't move and looked stunned.

I sat back and smiled. "Hope you have a lovely day! I've got to catch a killer. Great work, Dora, see you soon." I waved and signed off the Zoom connection.

I closed my laptop and looked up.

Sparky gave me a standing ovation. "That gel really helped. You look badass."

Chapter 37

3:00 p.m.

We'd been tracking Zorin's movements for several days and had learned a few things. He was a creature of habit. He left the house at nine in the morning to go to the warehouse. He worked with his team until four in the afternoon and stayed at the Lizard Liquidator's warehouse until around 5:00 p.m. Zorin then got dinner from one of the quick shops near Jamaica Beach and drove home. He remained at his house until about 11:00 p.m., when he'd go to the warehouse, load up the younger iguanas, and release them. He'd then get home by midnight. Every day was the same, and this was important because we wanted Sparky to catch him at home.

Sparky and I agreed we needed to talk to Zorin directly, and after his performance at the City Council meeting, it seemed like an assignment for William Wiley. It needed to be tonight, because we were still working on Ultima's dime until midnight. Or that was how I'd interpreted her request.

I was nervous about Sparky going undercover alone, but we'd be keeping this first meeting simple and benign. He'd wear a camera and mic and carry a few items for self-defense. I'd be sitting in the fully stocked van a couple of blocks away in case he needed backup.

At 6:00 p.m., Sparky walked up the steps to Zorin's small home on Miramar Drive. Zorin answered, and Sparky reminded Zorin who he was. He asked if he could come in for a minute to discuss business.

From the camera on Sparky's glasses, I could see that Zorin seemed friendly but not eager to chat.

"Maybe we can agree to something that's a win-win for both our businesses," Sparky said.

Zorin stepped aside and invited Sparky in. *"No harm in talking."*

Sparky stayed standing and scanned the room so we'd have footage we could zoom into later if something looked interesting. *"I've noticed you and your crew working on the west side. You're fast and know what you're doing."*

Zorin motioned toward a small dining room chair. *"Sit. Want a beer?"*

"No thanks, man. I don't want to take up too much of your time." Sparky sat at the table.

"I'm going to drink one. Been a long day." Zorin got a beer from the kitchen and then sat across the table from Sparky.

Both men were quiet for a moment.

"Say something," I said into his earpiece.

"So, Zorin, I wanted to chat with you about getting rid of the iguanas you catch. I assume you have a good system that works for you?"

"Yes. There's a good market for meat and skin here in Texas.

Many people love cowboy boots and Mexican food." Zorin chuckled.

Sparky nodded. *"Right. That's terrific. We don't a have our distribution set up for dispositioning the iguanas. Right now, some guy in Houston takes them all, but that won't work as the volume goes up."*

"And it's a long way to Houston."

"Would you be interested in taking the iguanas we catch?" Sparky said. "*We'd pay you a small flat fee per lizard, and you'd keep whatever you sell them for. It's a part of the business we're not keen to get into."*

Zorin crossed his arms. *"Ah, but that's not good economics for us. I make most of the money from catching iguanas, not selling them. So why would I want to do that?"*

"Sure, sure, I see," Sparky said. *"Well, for the iguanas we trap, it'd be our catch fee, so isn't the additional revenue like gravy for you?"*

"That's one way to look at it. You, my friend, assume you will get most of the clients. We're faster and more efficient, and this is all we do. We expect to grow a lot." Zorin gave Sparky a half smile as if to say no offense, but we intend to crush your business.

"I think it's time you wind this up so we can come back to him again if needed," I said to Sparky.

"Fair point. But will you think about it? Maybe you have a business partner you'd want to share this idea with?"

"Great question," I said

"I'll tell them what you proposed," Zorin said.

Sparky got up and moved to the door while scanning the

room again. There was a small living room with a television in a wall unit of shelves. Art trinkets, books, and pictures were arranged in a tidy fashion.

Sparky opened the door and turned back to Zorin. *"Thanks, I hope we can partner in some way. Losing Rodent Roger has been tragic for Mrs. Roger, but she's committed to seeing her husband's business continue."*

Zorin stood and bowed a bit. *"Please give the widow my condolences?"*

Sparky nodded and moved into the doorway. *"I'm sure she'll appreciate that. And Zorin, when you talk to your business partners, please let them know that the more we can partner, the less inclined we'll be to make a stink about how you're dumping half the iguanas back on the island every night."*

Zorin took a few steps toward Sparky. *"What do you mean, man? We don't do that. Our business is proper."*

Sparky nodded, smiled, and waved. *"Bye now!"*

And that, dear readers, is how you bait a hook.

I bit my nails until I saw Sparky get in his car and drive away. I drove past the house to confirm Zorin didn't follow him. He was standing by the front window.

Phew. For now.

Still jacked up on adrenaline, Sparky said he'd take the van back to the spy shop and start processing and watching the video footage. After telling Sparky how well he'd done, I said I needed to go home and beat the crap out of my punching bag, Betty 2. It had been a weird and long day. I got fired, caught a gigolo, and watched my employee go undercover with one of our prime suspects in Rodent's murder.

Chapter 38

11:15 p.m.

Investigator Report—Sunday, March 11
Investigator: Dora Baker

It was an overcast day, high 60s, or maybe it was just me. I'd be lying if I said I woke up full of vim and vigor. How do young people do it? Filo brought me the chef's hangover special, which included a green-chile owl-egg omelet, Vegemite toast, an antioxidant smoothie, and a triple espresso. I drank the smoothie and coffee and gave the rest to Filo. No offense to the Australian or New Mexican people. Or owls, poor things; I had no idea rich people ate owl eggs. That doesn't seem right.

The highlight of my day was talking with you, Xena. I know you said I didn't need to file a report because we have the video, but here's a rundown of the other parts of my day. I'm sending it much earlier in the evening because I'm not welcome in the Audacious Club anymore. Ant said Rascal would sing tonight like nothing happened. Except that he won't be flirting with any rich biddies; you made sure of that. Did I tell you how effective you were today? You sliced right through Rascal with your words. I'm proud to be your operations manager.

I offered to move into a smaller stateroom, but Ant insisted I stay here in the Volcano Suite. He said I'd earned it! How about that? Ant said your chat with Rascal impressed him and that his prodigal lounge singer came by his office to reinforce his commitment to becoming a model employee.

After breakfast, I walked around the pool deck. Twenty-five times around is a mile, I went thirteen laps to get the cobwebs out of my head. I saw Beauregard, who was finishing his work assignment of feeding Dr. Q's iguanas and then walking the miniature Pomeranians. The tiny dogs perform in another show; Quintana isn't feeding them to her iguanas, or vice versa.

Note to self. Which creatures eat iguanas?

You and I talked on the phone and tested the Zoom connection. We moved things around so the video feed would capture everything that went down. I'll not reiterate what happened on the video, but I was nervous when I heard Rascal tap on my door. It was surprising to see him dressed as a food server, but then with one pull, the Velcro holding it all on gave way and there he stood in his leopard undies. I would've guessed those were his undies had he been in the competition I'd won. So showy! I was thankful you fed me lines into my earpiece because my mind went blank. It had been a while since I'd seen anyone, let alone an aroused man who was—how do they say it...?—hung.

You couldn't see it on the Zoom camera, but Ant scowled at Rascal when he saw what he was wearing (and what he was NOT wearing).

The look on Rascal's face when he saw his boss was priceless. It took less than thirty seconds for him to deflate down there.

I've attached the video *Xena busts Rascal*.

After your masterful work and Rascal's awkward redressing, I craved a normal conversation, so I asked Beauregard to dinner. I hope that didn't break the rules since this is a work trip. He seemed like such an interesting man, and you know I've a soft spot for educators.

Dinner was delightful. The maître d' sat us at a table with Dr. Flores. Did you know she almost made the British Olympic team in archery? Used to shoot iguana-eating cats out of the trees. So much moxie!

But not as much moxie as you have, Xena.

Quintana asked me about my charity work, and I lied and said my portfolio of philanthropic grants included the Nature Conservancy, National Audubon Society, and Doctors Without Borders. It is true, though, that I donate small amounts to these organizations every year, because they do important work.

They based dinner on our astrological signs this evening. My Virgo entrée of forty-clove garlic chicken and five hundred mushy English peas was delicious and satisfying. And the root beer Tootsie Roll Pop was a surprising winner of a dessert. Three hundred twelve licks. Beauregard seemed to enjoy his mystery meat potpie, sautéed fiddlehead ferns, and molten Cake of the Gods. He's a Sagittarius and says he loves adventure. Dr. Q's dinner included emu roasted in habanero and dark chocolate mole with preserved lemon sorbet topped with Green Chartreuse. She's an Aries. I was glad I'm not a Gemini. They had to make this-or-that food decisions without hesitation, or they got nothing for that course. A Gemini at our table ate just a dinner roll another passenger gave her.

I went to bed early because playing a rich lady who confronts a gigolo with a big hard-on—pardon my French—had been exhausting.

Maybe you can give me some pointers about how you keep all your lies straight when you work undercover. I recorded everything in my small Moleskine pad but was afraid to look at it too often because I worried doing so might draw attention.

I didn't try to set off the lava bed tonight and collapsed into its ninety-nine-degree warmth and pillowy softness.

End of report.

Chapter 39

Day 13, Monday, March 12
9:00 a.m.

"Xena, Xena, Xena!" Ned sauntered toward me and opened his long arms to envelop me in a warm embrace. He smelled like one of those fancy perfumes they sprayed on men in the shopping mall. I must've caught him post-shower but pre-necropsy. He released the hug and moved back a step. "I've been thinking about Rodent's case."

"I'm glad you called me this morning. I want to show you something." I tapped on a folder I was carrying with my notepad. "I'll need you to keep this just between us."

"No problem, but first some coffee, right?" Ned led the way to his the lobby area for his lab. We grabbed a coffee (my third) and sat next to each other on the sofa.

My goal for this visit was to create a working theory on where Rodent's body went into the water and when, so I could look for more evidence. I knew Ned could help interpret the ME's preliminary report and the tide data that both he and Sparky had been compiling. I'd also brought surveillance information we'd collected that told us Zorin's favorite evening dump sites. I handed Ned a copy of Melissa's report and sipped my coffee as he read it.

"What was Rodent wearing when they found his body?" Ned asked.

"Dark blue overalls." I looked at Ned to see if I could pick up on why he'd asked that question because it didn't have anything to do with the autopsy.

"Maybe then..." Ned adjusted his position to turn toward me and drink some of his coffee. "I wondered how a six-foot man could float for two days in West Bay without being spotted until he hit the bridge at the pass. The dark blue jumpsuit might've blended in with the water's colors. There were off and on storms during that time, too, so the fishing conditions weren't good."

"Less boat traffic," I said.

"Perhaps," Ned said. "I reviewed the video Sparky sent over, the tide charts, and the weather. It was from Thursday night. But time of death isn't until Friday sometime."

I'd assumed he'd died the night before, too. "With him being in the water, would Melissa be able to tell the difference between TOD Friday during the day and late Thursday night, like around midnight?"

"Yes," Ned said. "For a recently deceased body, a lot of changes occur in twelve hours. Decomposition, rigor mortis, algor mortis, and vitreous potassium measurements differ if the body was submerged in water. But after taking the conditions into account, these measures can provide a reasonable indication of time of death. If I'm reading this correctly, it looks like he died Friday between mid-morning and early afternoon."

"That throws a wrench in my working theory."

Ned ran his hand across his bald head. "Let's talk through everything and see what we can come up with. I'm going to guess he died Friday morning based on the time he'd need to be moving in the water to be at the pass early evening Saturday."

I told Ned we believed Rodent had been watching Zorin's movements and followed him to the end of Indian Beach Drive, where he caught Zorin dumping live iguanas. Rodent confronted Zorin. There was conflict, maybe a fight, Zorin hit Rodent on the head and knocked him out. Rodent would've left his van at the circle, but Zorin drove it behind the trees so no one would see it. He used materials inside Rodent's van to tie up Rodent and suffocate him. Zorin then dumped Rodent's body in the water and covered the van with one of Rodent's exterminator's tarps. This wasn't something Zorin planned. That's why he used items from Rodent's van versus supplies he carried. Zorin then cut the zip-tie off Rodent's wrists and threw it into the water.

"I was going to look around on a kayak or from land later this morning," I said. "Except that this doesn't work if TOD isn't until Friday. Zorin would've been with his crew capturing iguanas."

"Maybe he, or someone, came back," Ned said. "I see the screen for toxins is still pending. What if they drugged him until they came up with a plan?"

I stared forward and felt discouraged. I was missing something.

"Let's take my boat out there." Ned tapped my lap and stood. "It's low draft and can go anywhere a kayak can but would be much faster."

I rose as well. "Why not? I could use a shot of fresh air and thinking."

I checked my e-mails and returned a text from Agatha regarding where we'd be meeting in a few hours. It disappointed me that Ethan hadn't yet returned my call. I made a mental note to call him after I left Ned's place.

Ned secured his lab and house and readied the boat. The Pelican Man's red-and-white boat was small and maneuverable; perfect for exploring the shallow waters on the north side of Galveston Island. We went west and found the marshy area at the end of Indian Beach Drive. Ned drove very slowly while I looked in the water. He used a pole to get into the shallowest areas and then to beach the boat. We got out and looked around. Nothing.

"Xena...I don't think the killer dumped Rodent's body here." Ned looked around and across the bay. "It's too shallow."

My entire theory of what had happened was falling apart. "Shit." I walked around a bit more, and then remembered I'd brought the map showing where Zorin had been dumping iguanas. I pulled the map out of my folder and showed it to Ned. "Do any of these places look like better places to dump the body?"

Ned looked at the map. "Here. This dirt road off Camino Street. I've been down it with an old birding friend of mine. Nothing there, but good access to West Bay and much closer to the pass. Housing developments to the west and east, but still hidden."

"Can we go there?" I asked.

"Sure!" Ned said. "That location would make more sense in terms of the tides and time they found him."

We got back in Ned's boat and went west for nearly forty minutes. He slowed down as we approached the site. The thumb of marshy land stuck out into the water. It looked dry enough to drive on, and several vehicle tracks were visible from the water. We trolled the three sides bordered by water. A dirt road along the west side seemed like the best spot to drive and dump a body. Thankfully, the water there was mostly clear. Fluttering fish and swimming turtles caused silt and sand to kick up for a moment.

"There!" I pointed to something light in the water.

Ned pushed the boat closer to the object with his long pole and then used a net to pull it out of the water. It was a gray zip-tie that had been cut with a dull knife or scissors.

I dialed Ethan's cell phone.

He answered. *"Sorry I didn't call you back yesterday. Had a long deposition."*

"No problem." I cut in. "Do you have pictures of the items inside Rodent's van?"

"Yes," Ethan said.

"Tell me if there are any zip-ties, and if so, what color they are."

I heard Ethan clicking his keyboard. *"He had small whites ones, medium black ones, and larger gray zip-ties."*

The hairs on the back of my neck felt tingly and cool. "I

think I found where they dumped Rodent's body. We have a second crime scene."

I could hear movement, like Ethan was getting up and walking. *"Where are you? Touch nothing."*

"Don't worry, I'm in Ned Quinn's boat. I'm looking at the dump site but haven't set foot on land and won't. We just pulled a large gray zip-tie from the water. Looks like it was holding something about the size of two wrists."

A door slammed, and I heard fast footsteps. *"Xena, this might be the break in the case we've been looking for."*

Chapter 40

3:00 p.m.

Finding the place where Rodent's killers had dumped him into the water complicated things for me with Ethan because I needed to reveal why we'd looked there in the first place. But I didn't want to tell him about Zorin's nighttime iguana dumps and compromise what we'd set up with Sparky as undercover William Wiley. Thankfully, he didn't have time to critique my partial answer.

Don't worry, I didn't lie to law enforcement and was fully prepared to provide more information if Ethan had asked for it, which he did not. It seemed to make sense to Ethan that an analysis of tides and weather would make it unlikely that Rodent went into the water where his van was left. Ethan said the forensics captain had raised the same question. It also seemed reasonable to Ethan that a guy like Ned Quinn could look at a detailed map and make an educated guess for where we should look.

I still had issues with Zorin as the perp unless he had help, but I had some time to think things through and regroup. Ethan's team and forensics were processing the second site and would be working on that for the rest of the day. Sparky was manning the spy shop and Dora was enjoying a well-earned day off on her cruise. I leaned back and rocked as the cool breeze blew through my porch. I heard a car door shut and got up to look outside. It was Agatha.

I invited her to my home. A big step on the *how to make a new friend* scale but it felt right. She already knew where it was (because she'd tailed me before beating me up, but that's water under the bridge now, isn't it?) and there was no better place to be on a lovely spring afternoon.

I walked outside to greet her. Agatha radiated casual and fun versus the tough and mysterious looks I'd seen her in before, and wore a blue sweater, blue jeans, red boots, and had her long, straightened hair up in a tussled bun. She had two bottles of wine and a bag of groceries with her. "I brought happy hour fixings," she said. "We have reason to celebrate!"

And we did. Agatha had sent me an e-mail last night saying my tease to the executives worked and they'd agreed to my deal. I replied and said that she didn't need to worry about Ginger's intentions. I wanted to save the detailed explanation for our in-person meeting, because it was too juicy a story to share in an e-mail.

Agatha opened and poured the wine while I put the cheeses, salami, crackers, pickles, and grapes on a platter. We brought everything out onto the porch and sat in my side-by-side teak rockers.

"I love your house, Xena. It has so much personality and feels comfortable."

"Thank you," I said. "I love it even if it's not at all practical."

I told Agatha about the engineer who'd built this house from concrete and steel construction, and that while it was hurricane-proof, it was also high-maintenance in this humid Gulf island climate. That's why the first floor is mostly garage; less to worry about if the area floods.

"Please don't make me wait any longer." Agatha said as she popped a grape into her mouth.

I knew what she was asking for. "First, a couple of questions. Do Ginger and Ward have a vacation planned?"

"Yes, somewhere in Mexico. Cancun, I think."

"And has their love life been a little flat?" I asked.

"You think I know that about my brother?" She smiled. "Yes. He thinks Ginger's sad because her dog died."

"Oh no. When did that happen?"

"Three years ago." Agatha busted out laughing.

I made a perfect stack of cracker, brie, salami, and pickle and ate it. "Ginger is spending time on the Bolivar Peninsula to breathe new zest into her marital sex life."

I told Agatha about Ida and Dylan, their course, and how I got to hear them each read their poems. I gave her the trifold brochure for the course.

"*Write Erotic Love Poems for Your Real Man*, three-month program only $3,200. I had no idea courses like this existed." Agatha fanned herself. "I would've loved to have heard Ginger's poem."

"Are you sure?" I asked. "It was a filthy poem about your brother's body parts and sexual practices."

She nodded without hesitation. "Even so. I would, absolutely."

"Well, all right." I picked up my phone and opened the recorder app.

Surely you didn't think, dear readers, I would've missed the opportunity to record the X-rated poetry readers, did you? For the case file, because I'm a stickler for complete documentation. And I wanted evidence in case Agatha questioned my eyewitness account.

"No!" Agatha sat straight and almost spilled her wine. "You recorded it?"

I nodded. "Just Ginger's," I lied. I'd recorded all the readings. For the case file. "Wanna hear it? Her poem is called 'In Ward,' and that's two words."

"More than anything in the world," she said in a soft, sexy voice.

We topped off our wines, and I played Ginger's reading. Agatha asked me to replay it two more times. Her nonverbal expressions ranged from wide eyes, to a gaping mouth, into full-body cringes, and ended with her hand on her mouth and laughing so hard she cried.

"That was…an awful poem," Agatha held onto my forearm for balance. "And what I'd expect from my dear friend Ginger. Ward will love it, because that boy is shallow. She's made an entire book of dirty poems?"

I nodded and ate a slice of sharp cheddar. "And Dylan, pen name Rod Erogenous, said 'In Ward' was her best poem."

"I'm thrilled," Agatha said. "A huge weight has lifted from my heart."

Agatha and I talked for another two hours. About work, our childhoods, ex-boyfriends, and exercise. I applied Dale Carnegie lessons whenever I remembered, and we had a lovely time. I showed her my workout garage, and we competed to see whose punch would make the punching bag move the most.

Agatha's punch was stronger, and she'd put her whole body into it. She stood a good five inches higher than me—including three inches of her and the two-inch heels on her boots.

"Great form," I said. "Perhaps you can come by one day when we're not already drinking and coach me."

"Anytime." She kicked the bag for good measure and smiled. "This space is impressive."

"How about I pick us up some dinner? Can you stay? My favorite seafood restaurant is three blocks away."

Agatha accepted my dinner invitation, and we argued for the next ten minutes about who would pick up the tab. I won after pointing out that she'd driven an hour to meet with me and would have to do the same to get back home.

We walked to BLVD Seafood and picked up our takeout order. Agatha enjoyed the grouper, and I devoured my seafood stew. The evening was tops and it was nice to think about something other than murderers for a short time.

"Would you like an after-dinner Scotch?" I asked.

"I've never gotten into it, but I'm willing to try if you show me how to best enjoy it."

Challenge accepted, Ms. Reacher.

I poured two glasses of my oldest Edradour.

Sixteen years; I know you were wondering.

It had been finished in a sherry cask and tasted silky and strong. I showed Agatha how I breathe in the spirit, then let the first sip wave around in my mouth before swallowing it. And how doing so made each sip sweeter and more penetrating than the last. Agatha loved my Edradour.

Chapter 41

Day 14, Tuesday, March 13
6:15 a.m.

Investigator Report—Monday, March 12
Investigator: Dora Baker

I'm sorry this last report is later than the others. As you will read below, this was an otherworldly ending to an unusual cruise. After a refreshing thirty times around the outside deck of the ship, I lounged on my cashmere sectional with my first cup of coffee. It was a cool 52 degrees, with wispy clouds floating through the sky as the nimble *Twisted Ambition* cruised across the Gulf of Mexico. I had two choices for breakfast: make your own crepes and pancakes (coaching provided by the cooking staff), or a five-course brunch inspired by the dystopian novel *Brave New World*. You might remember that the government kept most of the citizens in a state of chemically induced happiness and they engineered the synthetic food to be delicious.

I was tempted to attempt my own Nutella and banana crepes, but Beauregard texted me just as I was about to leave and recommended the BNW Brunch. It would be a life-changer, he said, and offered to go with me. He suggested I wear comfortable shoes.

I met up with Beauregard just outside the main dining room. He looked suave in a houndstooth jacket, black turtleneck and slacks, and tan leather shoes. I wore a pumpkin pantsuit with a red button-down shirt and red loafers.

We had thirty minutes before our brunch reservation, so I asked Beauregard to tell me more about the Audacious Stowaway program. I think I'd like to try being a Stowaway one day to enliven my sense of adventure. You know how I'm methodical most of the time, but maybe I should shake things up a bit…or a lot.

Beauregard offered to show me his cabinette because he said it was important that Stowaways learned to love their tiny accommodations to ensure it's a positive experience. The *Twisted Ambition* has 25 cabinettes that book up fast, often by seniors like Beauregard, who I learned is one year younger than me. Cabinettes are five feet wide and eleven feet long. As you first enter, there's a small loveseat and an end table with a TV mounted on the opposite wall. Just beyond the sofa are floor-to-ceiling open cubbies for belongings, although Beauregard said most Stowaways traveled light. At the end of the room was a door that led to the small wash station and toilet (no shower stall). Stowaways were encouraged to use the exercise room to shower. There were two sets of large wall hooks that held the hammocks Stowaways used for sleeping. Each cabinette could hold up to two people, though most travel alone.

Beauregard said Stowaways often needed help getting out of their hammocks, but the Audacious Cruise Lines installed ingenious automatic mechanical tethers that pulled one side of the hammock toward the ceiling to spill out the occupant every morning. There was an illustrated infographic on the wall with instructions for setting the desired tipping time and information about the preferred technique for landing on one's feet by holding onto the ropes as the discharge commences. The cabinette was darling.

Because of my status as a guest in one of the larger suites, the brunch organizers assigned us to the Alpha experience. Beauregard grinned and rubbed his hands together when we got to our plush picnic blanket that was surrounded by a frame of billowing sheer curtains. A hippie fort just for us.

Have you ever done psychedelics? What goes on in international waters, they say... This was my first time, and it was transformational. I remember we started with an earthy tea. Groovy music played in the background. Then we gorged on warm brownies (like Sparky's on steroids) and buttons of some kind. Servers dressed in flowing tie-dyed outfits offered trays of meats and cheeses. I think there was a six-foot rabbit orchestrating everything.

Beauregard suggested we go into one of the "feelie booths." They're the size of a photo booth but show movies. In *Brave New World*, feelies were like virtual reality movies where people could grab onto knobs and experience what the characters were feeling. I chose the feelie entitled *Inside Audubon's Birds.* I became a flamingo, and it was astonishing.

Beauregard preened and then kissed me in the booth. I know this is a business trip and case report but I must let you know what happened so I can process through my guilt.

When brunch was over, they gave us a to-go box with extra brownies and some fruits and cheeses. I didn't want this afternoon to end. I invited Beauregard back to my suite so he could help me finish the Pappy Van Winkle I hadn't consumed in the Audacious Club. He'd never had the elusive bourbon, so it was a treat for both of us.

After everything—the brownies, the flamingos, and the Pappy—I was feeling lightheaded, and blissful, and I told Beauregard that I wasn't rich. I blew my cover, Xena, I'm so sorry. I liked Beauregard and wanted to see him after the cruise if he was interested. He lives just down the coast in Freeport. I'd need to tell him the truth.

It's been fifteen years since my husband died and spending time with Beauregard has felt like a breath of fresh air. Beauregard promised he wouldn't say anything about my true identity and that the real Dora was much more interesting than the rich lady I'd played. Isn't that wonderful? We've agreed to connect in a couple of weeks. I told him we were working on an important case that would be my top priority. I understand that my indiscretion might affect my job status. I've made my bed and will rest in it.

I wanted you to know before you heard from Ant. I think he'll mention my date with Beauregard because…my Stowaway took me on a fascinating birding tour that made the volcano model blow. A few times. So much that it was mentioned in Captain CC's final address to the passengers.

Please don't mention my birding tour to Sparky.

This will be my final daily report since I'll be getting off the ship in about three hours. Ant has arranged for me to leave as soon as security gets set up to process passengers at 9:00 a.m.

End of report.

Chapter 42

7:30 a.m.

If you go to the Starbucks on Harborside before incoming cruise ships have docked, you might see how they back down the channel, so they'll be parked in the right direction to leave while going forward. Before sunrise, it looks like a city is floating down the street. The *Twisted Ambition* had arrived long before I got there at 7:30 a.m. I parked and jogged across the street to find Ant waiting for me at the bench.

"Sorry I'm late." I gave Ant a vigorous handshake. He hugged me because he was a hugger. I'm not a hugger but acquiesced for a polite amount of time.

"No problem, I just got here myself," he said. "Thank you for meeting me here. It's the best way." He lowered his voice. "You know, to keep things off the books."

I felt something hit my stomach and looked down to see he was trying to hand me a big wad of cash that he'd wrapped in brown paper. "Oh!" I accepted the package and slipped it into my bag. I hoped no one was watching us on the security cams because this would've looked like a drug deal between idiots. "Thank you."

"No… thank you," Ant gushed. "The investigation and sting operation"—he smiled when he said *sting*—"went better than I could've imagined. You and Dora blew my mind with your expertise and research. Ercole means a gift from God? Magnifico!" Ant kissed his fingertips and then held my elbow to pull me closer to him. "And I put in a little extra for saving me from embarrassment with your talk of headquarters hiring you." He pushed away and let go of my arm. "That was just talk, right?"

"Relax, you're the only person I've spoken with at Audacious, Ant."

Ant sighed. "Yes, of course. I watched Rascal perform last night, and he was luminous, as if nothing had happened. He told me several times of his intentions to earn our employee of the month award."

I offered my hand to Ant again. "I'm glad there'll be one less gigolo on the high seas." I smiled.

Ant stood straight and saluted me. "I hope you'll sail with us one day. I think Dora had an enjoyable time." He winked as he turned to walk back to the ship.

I returned to my car and looked at the ship. I laughed because one thing I knew about myself is that I was a control freak and I'd never subject myself to the *Twisted Ambition*'s level of chaotic adventure.

Dora said Beauregard would drop her off at home and that she'd come into the spy shop around midday. As I pulled out of the parking lot, I saw Quintana wave down and get into a car, likely an Uber. I followed Q to see where she was going and because I thought it would be fun to run into her, as if it was a coincidence, and ask her for coffee. I was keen to practice my Dale Carnegie and ask her for iguana handling tips.

Q's driver went down Twenty-Fifth Street all the way to Seawall Boulevard and then turned right. I assumed he'd be dropping her off at one of the businesses along the seawall, but the car continued past the tourist area and then turned up Sixty-Ninth Street. About a half a mile up, Q's driver pulled into an apartment complex parking lot. I slowed so I could see where she went before passing and looping back. Quintana walked into a building and the driver left.

I turned around and then parked between two cars at the far side of the lot and thought about the likely explanations. One: Q's friend lives there. Two: Q keeps an apartment in Galveston. But if she wanted a pied-à-terre, there were many apartment communities closer to the cruise terminal. Three: Q has a lover in Galveston. Four: Some other connection?

The apartment complex looked old and, based on the lack of signage and neon-colored flags, catered to regular working people. Not a dumpy area, but lower rent. I put my windows down, reclined my car seat, ate a MoonPie from my ditty bag, and answered e-mails while I decided how long I was going to sit there.

Ethan texted to give me what he called a courtesy heads-up that he'd asked Zorin and his two employees to answer some questions at the GPD. I'd expected he'd be talking to them if he hadn't already to determine their whereabouts when Rodent was likely killed. I wondered if they'd be able to establish alibis for the entire time in question—Thursday evening through Friday afternoon.

I texted back, *Ask Zorin what he does with all the iguanas he catches. And ask him to identify the first customer that asked him to come to Galveston. His origin story is a bit fuzzy.*

Sure. Will call you later.

After about thirty minutes, I heard Q talking and looked up to see her flagging down another car that had pulled in. It sounded like she was having an argument with someone and she was buttoning up her shirt. Her hair, which had been in an updo, was down and messy like a rock star's. Q had just hooked up with someone.

Quintana climbed into the car and the Uber driver then took her back to the *Twisted Ambition*. She'd been gone less than an hour. *Wham, bam, thank you, ma'am.*

I sat in the Starbucks for a few minutes to make sure Q wasn't coming back out. My phone pinged with a text from Steve.

I asked Sasha to share a story she's working on about iguanas falling from the trees tomorrow. Thought you'd be interested in what the County is doing. Only on the island!

That was quite the tease.

Look forward to hearing from her. (shrugging shoulders emoji)

Chapter 43

11:00 a.m.

I galloped into the spy shop because I saw Dora's car in our small lot. It took three leaps over lizard droppings to reach our back door. An increasing number of iguanas had apparently decided our overhead light was the warmest in the neighborhood. I flung open the door. "She's back!"

No one was in the meeting room, but I could hear voices in the front retail space. I walked to the front and tried again. "Dora's back!"

Dora looked full of color even though she was wearing black. Must've been the lava bed. He-he-he.

"I survived the *Twisted Ambition* and Rascal Romano," she said, and winked at me.

I'd e-mailed Dora after her last update to say that I wouldn't share it with Sparky. As far as he knew, she didn't file a report on the last day aboard.

Sparky was sitting behind the sales counter with his laptop. "I'll help Dora get her pictures, video, and audio uploaded to our case folder on the shared drive so we can all access them."

Dora rubbed her hands together. "I took lots of pictures!"

The front door clanged as Sasha walked in with her salad-plate-size sunglasses. She was a lovely young woman, but I just didn't understand some fashion fads like oversize spectacles. They made her look like something from a Kafka movie.

"Hey, Sasha!" I said.

I got surprised looks from Sasha, Dora, and Sparky. Did I tell them Steve had just given me a head's-up that Sasha would stop by? No, I did not.

I introduced Sasha to Sparky and Dora and told them she and I had met at the *Galveston Post Intelligencer.*

Sasha bounced on her heels. "I'm not the receptionist any longer. They promoted me to Reporter-1!"

"Congratulations," Dora said.

Sasha nodded and opened her pad folio. "I'm here on official business. I just posted a story online that Steve said you needed to know about."

Sasha shared that she and Steve are partnering on a larger piece about iguanas and invasive species and that while doing research—a lot of which comes from Florida for obvious reasons—she found several articles about iguanas going into torpor and falling out of trees when nighttime temperatures dipped below forty.

"And you know how they've been talking about the cold front coming?" Sasha asked.

We all looked at her but said nothing.

"I talked to the chief meteorologist from KPRC Houston who's well-known here on the island, Frank Billingsley, and he said the cold front will come in stronger than they first thought. We'll be getting down to mid-thirties tonight. And that means the iguanas will fall like snow in the Sierras. I added that last part."

"Fascinating," I said.

"There's more," Sasha said. "I called the Jamaica Beach City Manager for comment. They've got a lot of iguana problems, more than most places. He seemed unaware that lizards went into torpor, asked me what torpor meant, and said he'd call me back." She stopped for a moment, I think to catch her breath.

Sparky and I were likely thinking the same thing, that Jamaica Beach had all the iguanas because Zorin keeps dumping them there. Their residents must pay faster.

"But here's the kicker. They had an emergency city meeting and hired Southwest Exterminators—"

"Skeeter," Sparky and I said in unison.

"You know him?" Sasha said. "They hired him and his team, I heard because they're affiliated with the Rodent Roger firm, which most people know and trust, to come by tomorrow and scoop up all the iguanas. Jamaica Beach is paying one flat fee for them to rid the area of as many iguanas as possible. I guess the guy, Skeeter, is renting a couple of vans so they'll have several." She then held up her pen. "And guess what?"

"What?" we all said at the same time.

"I'll be doing a Facebook live broadcast tomorrow morning as I follow Southwest Exterminators around. It's going to be great."

Sasha explained that the Jamaica Beach City Manager asked its homeowners and property managers to bring all the stiff lizards to the curb for collection so they could get more off the island. They put flyers in everyone's mailboxes.

"They want the residents to handle the iguanas?" Dora asked.

"Yes, ma'am. Their flyer offers tips." Sasha handed us each a flyer.

"They're telling people to use oven mitts," Sparky said.

"Or barbeque tongs," Dora said.

"Or put the big ones in baby strollers," Sasha said. "Because they can weigh twenty-five pounds."

"This event has delightful disaster written all over it." I smiled. "I bet your live show will go viral, Sasha."

She nodded. "There's more. Steve also wanted me to tell you that residents in the Sea Isle neighborhood heard about what Jamaica Beach was doing and have contracted with the Lizard Liquidators to pick up their frozen iguanas. We'll have a social media intern covering that story. She's not yet Reporter-1."

Sea Isle was a large Galveston neighborhood three miles west of Jamaica Beach and close to two of Zorin's favorite iguana dumping sites (including the one we believed was used to dump Rodent's body). I didn't know whether to feel concerned, thrilled, pissed, jealous, or on heightened alert. "Is there more, Sasha?" I asked.

She looked through her notes. "No, I think that's about it. The collection will begin at seven in the morning. I've one question related to your professional expertise. Does pepper spray work on iguanas?"

I chuckled. "Probably, but you won't need it. Frozen iguanas won't attack, and alert ones will run from you."

"Oh," Sasha said. "Because Steve mentioned one attacked you and that you were bleeding from multiple places."

Sparky cackled.

"Just don't leap on one from behind." I mimicked my flawed moves and then laughed.

After Sasha left, I looked at Sparky and Dora. "This could be a catastrophe. Two competing companies—one that may've murdered the other's leader—will participate in an iguana collection event that'll test Zorin's desire for market dominance. Will he dump half of them back and risk being caught? Has this scheme exposed the reality that William Wiley has no influence on Skeeter or Ultima? And how will today's grilling from Ethan affect Zorin's demeanor and motivations for mischief? I also question whether Skeeter, his son, and the other guy know how to catch and store so many stiff lizards. And what will Ultima Penelope Roger be doing tomorrow? Staying in the background or asserting herself as a community hero?"

I looked at my watch.

"Let's meet in thirty minutes to update our charts and discuss whether this cold front will chill our progress or provide the chaos we need to reveal those with criminal intent."

Chapter 44

Day 15, Wednesday, March 14
7:00 a.m.

We picked up coffee, beignets, cinnamon rolls, and breakfast burritos and invited Steve to join us at the spy shop while we monitored GPI's Facebook Page. We also had cleaned off the white boards so we could make note of anything we wanted to follow up on. Steve had told us Sasha and the intern, Jenny, would go live several times through the morning and that he'd be coaching them by text as needed.

Steve staged his food, beverage, laptop, and phone on the corner of our meeting room table for perfect access. "The Liquidator people are still on your POTENTIAL SUSPECT list, right? Does this Operation Stiff Lizard help or hurt your case?"

"While we're not sure, we think it could muck it up by disrupting their regular flow and inventory," I said. "They're suspects who might have an alibi. I'll be talking to Ethan later. Anything I say related to that is off the record."

Steve nodded. "Sasha has gone live."

GPI FB Live Feed—Reporter Sasha Barlow

Good morning, Galveston. I'm Sasha Barlow, reporter with the *Galveston Post Intelligencer* at the Jamaica Beach Circle K. I'll be live streaming here on Facebook several times this morning during what we're calling "Operation Stiff Lizard." The green iguanas that have been increasing in number over the last few weeks are cold intolerant, and last night's cold front has left many of them in a hibernation-like state called torpor. They may look dead, but they're just stiff. The City of Jamaica Beach hired Southwest Exterminators to collect and disposition as many iguanas as they can before the iguanas start re-awakening when the temperature goes above forty. Behind me are their three vans. Let's say hello before they head into the neighborhood.

Hey, I'm Skeeter, owner of Southwest Exterminators, and this here is my son, Andy, and team member Mike.

Best of luck to you! I'll be following each of these vans at different times in the morning and will show you how these trained professionals are helping the community of Jamaica Beach reduce the number of green iguanas, which are an invasive and unwanted species. Sasha Barlow signing off for now.

"She did great!" I said.

"It was nice to see the three trucks at the start," Dora said. "They can hold a lot of iguanas in those cages."

"I hope we get to see what it looks like when they're full at the end, too." Sparky cracked his knuckles and powered up his laptop.

"I'm pleased," Steve said.

"You might tell Sasha that Andy will provide the best video. Best meaning most cringeworthy." I poured hot sauce on my burrito, topped it with a cinnamon roll, and sat down. "He's the greenest on Skeeter's crew, and what we saw from him looked a bit... awkward."

"Good tip." Steve texted for a few minutes. "Looks like Jenny's going live now."

GPI FB Live Feed—Reporter Jenny Becker

Hey, I'm Jenny Becker, for the *Galveston Post Intelligencer*. You just saw Sasha Barlow's live video from Jamaica Beach. I'm a few miles west at the Sea Isle Supermarket. Sea Isle residents have pooled together to hire the Lizard Liquidators to pick up and dispose of any frozen iguanas they can find. I talked to the Lizard team of Zorin, Seth, and Fatty a few minutes ago. They'll be operating one van. When the van is full, they'll transfer the iguanas to a refrigerated truck they've parked here at the supermarket. Like

Sasha, I'll be going live on Facebook a few times this morning during Operation Stiff Lizard.

"Interesting," I said. "What that means is that the iguanas picked up today by the Lizard Liquidators won't ever wake up."

Dora covered her ears. "I know that's what happens to them. I just hate to think about them all dying."

"Most humane way to go, all options considered. They shot a few with an air gun the other day." Sparky passed around a box of beignets.

"Aren't they all killed?" Steve asked.

"Mostly." I regretted the word as soon I said it. This was Steve I was talking to.

"Mostly?" Steve asked. "What does that mean? Do some have a different fate?"

Sparky and Dora looked stiff like the iguanas. They knew I'd be weighing how much to tell Steve. "We're looking into whether any of the smaller iguanas get dumped back on the island. Seth, who works for Zorin, mentioned in an offhand comment that they might return the younger ones. But that could've been his libido blathering on. I'll let you know what we confirm. That's way off the record."

Steve again nodded. "And a potential game-changer in terms of motive, I would assume."

I nodded in the same flat way he just had.

"Look alive, folks, Sasha is streaming again," Sparky said.

Sasha was standing beside Skeeter, who was holding a

large, rigid iguana. Skeeter turned the iguana around and upside down to show the camera, then he placed it in a cage in the van. Her camera then panned down the street to show homeowners bringing iguanas to their curb.

"Oh, my goodness," Dora said. "Look at them all!"

Sparky pointed. "The guy three houses down has several in a wheelbarrow."

"This number doesn't seem possible," I said. "Especially of the bigger ones. This has been happening for…what, two months?"

Steve leaned back and tapped his head with his pen. "Can't be longer. It was too cold."

Jenny went live on Facebook again. Zorin was driving the van while Seth and Fatty walked alongside picking up iguanas and putting them in the van.

"They don't have cages," Dora said. "Won't the iguanas wake up and escape?"

"Brilliant." I walked up closer to the monitor to look inside Zorin's van. "That's why their large refrigerated truck is so close. They'll outpace Skeeter's three trucks, I'd bet."

Steve was texting. "I'm asking Jenny to show us more of how they're stacking the iguanas."

Sparky had been staring at the screen. "It almost looks choreographed. Seth and Fatty are in total synch. They've done this before."

"In Florida," Dora said. "I remember at least one article that mentioned they'd scoop up large numbers of iguanas after frosty nights."

Jenny and her driver passed Zorin's van and then stopped

and videotaped as they went by. Zorin's van had industrial wire shelving along the perimeter of its inside so they could load it up without placing iguanas on top of one another.

"Have they always had those shelves?" Dora asked.

"Nope," Sparky said. "They had it stacked with cages before."

"Where'd they get shelving on such short notice?" Steve asked.

I sat down and leaned back. "That set up doesn't look like an afterthought. They already had it."

"In the warehouse?" Sparky said. "We've not seen them moving shelving in and out."

I gave Sparky the look to not say anymore. "Tell Jenny we'd like to see inside the refrigerated truck when they go to empty the van."

"Roger that." Steve glanced at me. "I know that look. What're you thinking?"

I gave Steve a slight grin and lifted my finger. "It's percolating." I then looked at Dora. "I know we've got this somewhere, but will you remind me how long it takes an iguana to reach maturity?"

"Sure," Dora said.

Over the next hour, Sasha and Jenny posted dueling live videos showing the two teams of exterminators picking up iguanas by the roadside. By 8:30 a.m., the temperature had risen to thirty-eight degrees.

I made a fresh pot of coffee and passed around the bottle of Tums. "I ate too much, but it was good."

Steve took a Tums and nodded. "Me, too. Sasha just

texted me. Things are winding down. Skeeter's son said their vans were full and his dad told him to wrap things up and meet at the Home Depot parking lot."

That's where the Bike Around the Bay two-day, 190-mile ride began its second day. The Home Depot parking lot was a common starting point for charity runs and bike rides because it was at the base of the Galveston causeway.

"Sasha also said that Andy ran out of cage space and has been putting the frozen iguanas on top of each other in the van."

"What is he thinking?" Sparky asked.

"Maybe he believes they're dead." Dora said.

"This could get messy," I said. "Is Sasha going to follow him?"

"I don't think so," Steve said. "I asked her to interview some residents."

"Can she come back to do that?" I looked up the temperature on my phone. It was forty degrees. "We need to monitor young Andy."

Steve texted Sasha. "All right. She's going to follow him to Home Depot and then circle back to talk to homeowners."

Jenny's last live stream showed that the inside of the larger truck Zorin had waiting at the Sea Isle Supermarket contained similar industrial shelving as what they'd put into the van, with many shorter shelves so they could store more iguanas without them touching and warming up one another. Fatty stood in the truck's open the doorway while Seth tossed him iguana after iguana.

"That's quite the operation," I said. "Did anyone else notice the lettering on the truck's door?"

"I just got a text from Sasha. She's going live, says something's wrong." Steve stood and waited for her video to begin on Facebook.

GPI FB Live Feed—Reporter Sasha Barlow

I'm Sasha Barlow, reporter with the *Galveston Post Intelligencer*. Operation Stiff Lizard is coming to a close and I'm following a van from Southwest Exterminators, where something's happening to the iguanas. We're on Sixty-First Street right now, heading to the Home Depot parking lot. My driver is going to get as close to the van as possible, and I'll turn the camera so you can see what I see. If you look at the back windows of the van, you can see there's a tail moving across the window. I think an iguana is coming out of torpor. And there's a head that just popped up. It looks like the van is rocking. Whoa! An iguana just slammed against the back window. They're all coming to! I can see several iguanas jumping around inside. The van has slowed way down. It's rocking more now; looks like it might tip. His brake lights are on and the van has stopped. It's an explosion of reptiles inside that van! The front door just flung open and Andy has tumbled out of the van. He's bleeding all over—someone call 911! Iguanas are leaping out of the van and running through traffic. One just got squashed by a truck going the other direction. Crap! An iguana just jumped on our car! Go away! Another one's on our hood now. Andy's standing. Now he's jumping, trying to catch the iguanas soaring out of the van. Poor Andy, he keeps reaching for them and the iguanas are slicing him open. I need to help him. This is Sasha Barlow signing off for now.

Sparky had both his hands on his head. "Stop, Andy, stop."

Dora sat staring at the screen and rocking in her chair. "Let that be the last one. Let that be the last one. Let that be the last one."

I was gripping Steve's forearm, remembering what it felt like to have an iguana slash me all to hell. "Andy, you can't win this battle!"

Steve held up his phone. "Abort, abort, abort!"

Chapter 45

5:30 p.m.

I asked Ethan to my house for a meeting regarding our separate Rodent Roger murder investigations. I acknowledged it was an unusual request, but I wanted us to talk someplace quiet and comfortable because we would need to cover a lot of ground and it could take some time. My office would be too chaotic. His office too formal. A coffee shop wouldn't be secure. My living room was just right. Even so, I was surprised when Ethan accepted my invitation. Perhaps it had something to do with him feeling frustrated about their lack of progress in finding Rodent's killer.

My living room had four comfortable armchairs, each with its own side table and a small footstool. It was a perfect setup for someone like me who values personal space more than almost anything else. There was no television or other distractions because I'd designed it to be a conversation pit. Ethan chose the chair that looked out over the porch and down the staircase. I put my phone as a placeholder on the chair to his left, back against the living room wall.

"I have wine, whiskey, or water," I said.

"Whiskey, please."

"Scotch or bourbon?"

"Bourbon, definitely," Ethan said.

"Neat, splash, rocks, or ginger ale?"

"Splash," Ethan said.

I poured a bourbon and a Scotch, added a small splash to both, and joined Ethan. "Hope you like Weller."

"Very much, thanks." Ethan took a sip of the drink and nodded. "Where shall we start, or do you have this conversation planned out like your Perry Mason meeting during the birder murder?"

He was referring to the meeting I held at my spy shop with the entire GPD major case team to unfold, with dramatic flair, the evidence my team had collected and reveal who we thought the killers were and how we'd catch them.

"I wish," I said.

"Me, too," Ethan said. "You were impressive, and we got the bastard."

That felt nice to hear, but also like pressure. Had Ethan only accepted my invite because he thought I'd solved the case? "Let's just say I'm getting close. That's why I wanted to meet with you, to put our heads together. But if you're OK with it, I'd like to start with a few questions."

"All right."

"What did Zorin tell you was the impetus for him setting up shop on the island?"

Ethan shrugged. "He struggled with that question. Said

it was one of his Florida customers but couldn't remember who. I followed up and asked Mr. Montaño how he knew there'd be more than one iguana to catch, that there would be enough work to establish a business."

"Good question," I said.

"Mr. Montaño's response was that there's never one iguana. And that he'd seen how they proliferated in Mexico and Florida. It was only a matter of time until they got to Texas."

"We heard that from others." I looked at Ethan to see if he was ready for me to keep rolling out the questions. "We know where Zorin lives on Miramar Drive and about the warehouse they have on 12 Mile Road. Do you remember the street names for Seth and Fatty?"

Ethan took a sip of his drink and held up one finger. He looked through a small briefcase he'd brought and pulled out his flip notebook. He turned several pages. "Mr. Seth Judge lives on Cedar Lane." He flipped more pages. "And Mr. Richard Platt, who goes by Fatty, listed a home address on Sixty-Ninth Street."

"3291 Sixty-Ninth Street?"

"Yes..."

I held up a fist and shook it. "That conniving bitch with the emphasis on *con*."

Ethan sat up. "I've played along with your rapid-fire questions. How about you tell me a few things I don't know?"

"Absolutely, but one more question."

"What is it?" Ethan had a bit more bristle in his voice.

"Were the Lizard Liquidators team able to establish they had alibis?"

"Mostly yes," he said. "We even checked with the customers they serviced and can say with high confidence that they were not in the neighborhood of the suspected dumpsite from 8:00 a.m. to 3:30 p.m. the Friday we believe the perps killed Rodent." Ethan slapped his thigh. "Your turn."

I stood and got a plate of cheese and crackers from my kitchen. I'd hoped to have more ready, but our meeting at the spy shop had gone overtime because of several new leads we hurried to validate.

"Did you see the footage from this morning's iguana sweep?" I had my laptop ready in case he hadn't.

"Hard to miss." Ethan rolled his eyes. "One of my guys assisted with the Sixty-First Street fiasco because several of the other officers were on the West End."

"Were you surprised, as we were, by the number and size of some of these iguanas?"

"I was."

I told Ethan that female iguanas started breeding around two years old and their eggs hatch after sixty to eighty days. Green iguanas over four feet long are likely five years or more old.

"And here's the kicker," I said. "We had a real cold snap from January 16 through the 19th. Remember how we had problems with icy roads?"

"I almost slid into the gulf."

"Iguanas are intolerant of cold; that's why this morning's

scene was predictable. They go into a torpor state and will survive as long as it's not too cold for too long. If there were iguanas on this island during our January cold spell, most didn't survive. In other words, most of the iguanas we have here today have been on the island a maximum of two months."

"Meaning someone dumped them here." Ethan said.

"Exactly. It took us a while to figure this out, because the herpetologist we've been talking to said that it was a matter of when, not if, green iguanas would come to the island. That it was inevitable."

"Like what Montaño said." Ethan grabbed a piece of cheese. "Interesting, but I assume there's more."

"Much." I looked down at my notes and checked off a couple of items. "This timing also fits when we consider that Rodent started getting calls about iguanas in February and Lizard Liquidators registered as a business in Galveston County early February. My first key point is that we know someone intentionally flooded the island with invasive green iguanas, which is against the law."

Ethan sat up. I'd gotten his full attention. "Who'd want to do that?"

I took a warming sip of my Edradour. "I'll get to that question, but first let's consider where the iguanas came from."

"Pet store warehouse?" Ethan tossed out.

I shook my head. "The number and size of the lizards suggest that these iguanas came from another place where they're abundant. Mexico or Florida."

I made my case for why we believed the iguanas came from Florida. Although farther, it would be easier to drive iguanas to Galveston than try to smuggle hundreds of iguanas through the border. And Montaño told the City Council their parent company was in Florida, although we don't think that's true.

"But it was this morning's iguana collection event that gave us the additional leads we needed to confirm that the Lizard Liquidators brought the iguanas to the island." I held up a finger. "First, the way Zorin's team operated told us they'd done this kind of thing before. That alone didn't surprise us, because we'd read that similar mass catches happened in Florida when the weather turned cold. In fact, the weather on January 25 went down to thirty-eight degrees in the southern half of the state. There was a large iguana catch the next morning, where dozens of companies and individuals picked up frozen iguanas for fifty dollars per head paid by the government."

"Interesting. Were our guys there?"

"Well, they weren't in Galveston yet." I held up two fingers. "When we watched the live feed today, we noticed they'd outfitted the inside of their van and refrigerator truck for storing hundreds of stiff lizards." I held up three fingers and smiled. "Although the license plate on the large truck was from Texas, that's likely stolen. The USDOT number and lettering on the cab door suggested the truck came from Florida. We believe that Zorin and his team drove two trucks and a van full of iguanas from Florida to Galveston and then dumped them and set up shop to pick them back up for a fee of $125 each that any vacation homeowner would gladly pay. As a bonus, they won't have to compete in Florida's saturated business climate where anyone with a snare or air gun can become an iguana hunter. So key point number two is that the Lizard Liquidators drove the iguanas to Galveston. Do you need to stretch or take a break?"

"Nope, this is just getting good. Keep going, assuming this all leads to Rodent."

I nodded. "Of course. The next logical question is why did they come to Galveston Island?"

"I wondered that myself."

"The gulf shore of Texas would be on anyone's short list because of climate. It's not ideal, however, because our winters can get too cold for iguanas and for long stretches."

"Like January 16 through the 19th," Ethan said.

"Right," I said. "We believe they gave the island a shot because they have a connection here who knew that the open West End would be a good place to get a new population of iguanas going. The January 25 freeze event in Florida offered them the opportunity to bring animals here early in the year so the number of iguanas would double or triple by late summer."

"Who's their local contact?" Ethan asked.

He was getting a bit antsy, but I'd need to get through everything, or he'd never go along with my plan.

"Getting there." I got up to refresh our drinks and grabbed two paper menus from BLVD Seafood and handed one to Ethan. "They're three blocks away and will deliver. I think this'll take another couple of hours."

"That long?" Ethan opened his eyes wide and paused like he was deciding whether to play along. He looked at his watch. It was 6:30 p.m. "Crab cakes. GPD will pay for us both."

"Fine by me." I called in the order and sat back down. "We've been following Zorin and his team around and have estimated the number of iguanas they're trapping and how much money they're bringing in. We felt we needed to follow the money to determine if it could be enough to justify murder."

"Excellent. And…?" Ethan asked.

I took the next fifteen minutes to share our initial financial worksheet based on numbers of iguanas per day and some assumptions about revenue from iguana hides and meat. I told him that Seth had confirmed these streams of revenue and that our research told us it was typical for these businesses.

We moved to the dining table and Ethan looked over our worksheets and pictures of Zorin's team in action. BLVD delivered our meals, and we continued to talk as we ate.

"This is outstanding work," Ethan said. "We've been wondering about the economics of Montaño's outfit. I don't need to tell you that money is a common motivator for crime."

"Love, money, or fame. How about greed?" I smiled. "We determined that Zorin was returning to the warehouse each evening to pick up the smaller, less salable, iguanas and dump them back into the West End."

"No!" Ethan said and wiped his mouth. "That's double-dipping."

"Who knows how many times they'll catch and release some of these animals? Could be dozens of dips and thousands of dollars." I pointed to Ethan. "And remember, this is illegal besides being unethical."

Ethan nodded. "Do we think Rodent figured that out?"

"We do—both that they dumped the initial population of iguanas and were releasing some after trapping them." I put a still shot from the drone footage that showed Rodent's van covered by the tarp. "And we think this marsh was one of Zorin's favorite places to release the iguanas they'd caught earlier in the day."

"Rodent followed him in his van? No way they wouldn't notice him."

"To be clear"—I ate my last shrimp, set my plate aside, and pulled my notebook and folder in front of me—"there's no *they* during this nighttime operation. Our surveillance shows Zorin picking up and releasing the iguanas. Rodent would've seen that and felt like he could handle confronting one old man."

"Good clarification. So Zorin and Rodent got into an argument, and one thing led to another?"

"That's correct, but doesn't tell the complete story. And after watching the Lizard Liquidators this morning, we've changed a few of our initial assumptions."

"You're killing me here, Xena." Ethan pushed his plate to the side. "This is fun and all, but please tell me we're getting close to who killed Rodent and why they did it."

"Extremely." I put our food containers in the garbage and wiped off the table so I could spread out more examples.

"We agree that Rodent's apprehension and killing appears to be a crime of convenience. One thing led to another. But it still doesn't answer why they didn't kill him until the next day and how they killed him the next day when they appear to have alibis."

"Right," Ethan said. "Cue the local contact?"

"Let's stick with Rodent for a moment. We believe he was the nuisance they didn't expect. In Florida, and we assume elsewhere, pest control companies often draw the line at trapping wildlife, especially invasive species like pythons, pigs, and iguanas. The Lizard Liquidators didn't know or care about Rodent Roger Pest Control and assumed he'd not care about them or the iguanas. But Rodent wasn't an average exterminator."

"That seems clear."

"And he was smart. Rodent told us that something didn't seem right, and he believed the uptick in iguana sightings was the tip of a crappy iceberg. When he confronted Zorin, we believe Zorin hit Rodent on the head and then bound him with zip-ties from his van. Zorin drove the rat mobile behind the bushes and then covered it with one of Rodent's tarps."

Ethan was tracking with me and nodding.

"But here's my third key point. We don't think Zorin could be the leader of this criminal enterprise. Sparky talked with Zorin, who acknowledged he had a partner or partners. And we think that Zorin isn't the 'boss' that Seth was referring to when I talked with him."

I looked down at my notes. It was time for Ethan's plot

twist. "Yesterday I followed our iguana expert, Dr. Quintana Flores, as she got off the ship. I was hoping to chat with her a bit more about iguana handling and our issue here on the island. Her Uber driver took her to an apartment complex on Sixty-Ninth Street."

"Wait," Ethan said. "What?"

"You heard me correctly. Dr. Quintana Flores went to see Fatty while her ship was in port. She was there for under an hour and left looking upset. She went back to the *Twisted Ambition.*"

"How did you find her in the first place?"

"We called Moody Gardens looking for someone to talk with about iguanas. They recommended Quintana. She'd done a talk on reptiles there. We don't think Moody Gardens had any involvement. Just a weird confluence of events."

Ethan was scrunching his brow. "I don't get it. Based on what you've said, she's a well-regarded scientist and environmentalist. What was her motive?"

"Here's what we've learned about Dr. Flores. She's passionate about supporting the Blue Iguana Foundation and research to help save endangered Grand Cayman blue iguanas. We'd guess that's why she started doing the cruise ship shows and tours. Donations from passengers have buoyed the foundation's bank account and likely increased her standing and influence with her older colleagues. We also know that Q blames American tourism and Western imperialism for the blue iguana's decline. She told Steve Heart that she worked with iguana hunters in Mexico when she was younger. We believe that the person she worked for was her uncle, Zorin Montaño."

"She his niece?"

I placed two photos in front of Ethan and tapped on the one on his left. "This is a picture of Quintana's childhood home on Grand Cayman. She shows this to her tour participants as part of her story she hopes will lead to a donation to her foundation." I tapped on the other photo. "This is a picture that Zorin has on his bookshelf."

"Same house," Ethan said. "How do you know Dr. Flores shows this house to people on the tour?"

"We got lucky," I said. "One of my team members was onboard the *Twisted Ambition* working an unrelated case and attended Q's tour. Dr. Flores also told tour attendees she learned street smarts from her uncle because her dad had been gone a lot."

"Was Dr. Flores in Galveston the day Rodent died?"

"The *Twisted Ambition* was in the middle of the Gulf of Mexico."

"Ugh!" Ethan leaned on his elbows. "I'm looking for a murderer, not a mystery novel."

"I'm looking for the same thing you are, Ethan. Quintana is smart, headstrong, and driven. She would've been able to coach Zorin and his team on how long they can keep iguanas in torpor without killing them. We suspect that Quintana convinced her uncle to go to Florida and that proceeds from his work have been supporting the Blue Iguana Foundation for some time. It's a version of the Robin Hood story. Quintana is giving us invasive iguanas she feels we deserve, charging us to get rid of them, and using the money to save her beloved blue iguanas."

Ethan stood and walked around. He went out to the porch and back to the dining table. He sat down. "Let's say that for the moment I concur with your version of events. We've been thinking Montaño was connected and don't have a stronger theory at the moment. Although quirky as hell, we don't think Rodent's widow had anything to do with it."

"I agree, although she pissed me off a lot."

"Mrs. Roger told us she fired you. And yet, here you are, still investigating."

"Rodent is my client. He came to me and asked me to help him."

"All right. I'd like to hear your recommendations—I know you have some—for how to determine who killed Rodent."

"This is the reason I asked you here tonight. There are some outstanding items that, once understood, will help clarify who killed Rodent and who you can hold accountable. But I need your help."

I walked Ethan through my list.

1. Confirm with the local Minuteman Press that they printed the flyers for Lizard Liquidators before any clients booked them to trap iguanas.

2. Double-check alibis for Zorin, Seth, and Fatty for Thursday night and Friday.

3. Process Fatty's car for evidence.

4. Stakeout Zorin to catch him releasing iguanas.

5. Use potential charges for illegal dumping as leverage to get them to talk about the Thursday night encounter with Rodent.

6. Ask Montaño who his partners are and whether Quintana Flores is any relation.

7. Ask Fatty who Quintana is and whether she's the ringleader.

8. Ask Seth if Quintana is the boss.

9. Follow the money. Determine if the Blue Iguana Foundation is getting donations from Zorin's business.

"Those things would all be helpful to know," Ethan said. He underlined a few items and added to my list. "I'd also like to get copies of e-mail communication from the ship and cell records for Zorin and Fatty. And get my forensic accountant looking at the Lizard Liquidators' bank account, although I think we're going to need to establish the initial dumping charge and evidence of an altercation with Rodent to get a judge to buy off on that. And we've got the complexities of dealing with a foreign-flagged ship and a British subject, but thankfully the US has good extradition treaties and information sharing practices with the UK."

"Quintana will be back in port on Sunday and then not again for five days."

Ethan looked down at his watch. It was 9:15 p.m. He sighed and then chuckled. "You know, Xena, this isn't the way these cases are supposed to work. Private investigators catch cheaters with risqué photos and compromising sex tapes. They don't bust wide open major murder investigations. Who do you think you are?"

I smiled so wide I thought my lips would crack. "Oh, I catch cheaters, I assure you of that. In fact, the unrelated case we just closed on the *Twisted Ambition* involved an onboard lounge singer named Rascal who was moonlighting as a gigolo for rich, older women."

"Rascal," Ethan said.

"*Rrr*ascal. And it was a fine piece of work." I annunciated each word with a tilt of my head.

"You're not taking my comment seriously," Ethan said. "Good."

Chapter 46

Day 16, Thursday, March 15
6:00 a.m.

It was the second of the two-morning cold spell and we were halfway through tagging iguanas that had fallen from a group of trees Ned had on his property. The stiff iguana in my hand was three feet long and weighed 5.2 pounds. I know, because I weighed him myself as I played Ned Quinn's lab assistant. Our strategy was to tag the animals that were two to three feet long. Big enough to conceal the transmitter and small enough to be selected for the nighttime dumping ritual.

"How long did it take you to modify and paint the trackers?" I lifted the lizard above my head and used it to do a few chest presses before handing it to Ned.

When iguanas were in a hypothermic state, their skin looked lighter and dull. Ned had painted the tiny tracking devices khaki, brown, and gray so they'd blend in better. He painted the antennae beige at the base and then medium orange to match the way most of these iguanas' spikes looked.

"All damn night, I'll have you know." Ned applied the tracker using marine-grade pharmaceutical glue. "I've got three color schemes and spine lengths to choose from to better fit each iguana. Most fun I've had in a while." He aimed his headlamp at me and smiled.

Headlamp, because we were working within the tree canopy, and the sun was just about to rise. It was a cold thirty-seven degrees, damp, and dark. The Lizard Liquidators had told Ned the only way they could work him into their schedule was if they got there right at 7:00 a.m. and picked up the iguanas already on the ground. They wouldn't have time to search in burrows or get them out of trees. Zorin told Ned that yesterday's Operation Stiff Lizard coverage had heightened awareness about whom to call to get rid of nuisance iguanas. They were booked solid for several days.

At 6:50 a.m., we packed everything up and returned to Ned's lab. I watched and took pictures from inside as Ned greeted the team and showed them the stand of trees where they'd find several iguanas. I watched how Fatty moved as they prepared the cages and walked to the trees. He was skinnier than Seth and had long black hair pulled into a braid. His thick eyebrows and strong nose framed his two enormous dark eyes. He was attractive in an Al Pacino, dark stallion kind of way. I could imagine why Quintana found Fatty appealing.

The Lizard Liquidators team did their work and left within fifteen minutes. As they were packing up, I watched how they interacted with one another to get a sense for the informal pecking order. My boy, Seth, seemed like the junior member, with Fatty and Zorin issuing directions for him to follow. I wondered how Quintana affected their group dynamic.

Ned joined me in his office and made us both an espresso. I inhaled the steam that was rising from the tiny cup. I loved excellent coffee. "How many iguanas did they get?" I asked.

"About twenty." Ned sat at his desk and typed like a wild man. He turned his screen so I could see it. "Looks like at least ten were tagged."

The screen was mostly black. There was a tight cluster of green dots moving in unison and others that seemed stationary. "I have cool gadgets, but this is amazing. Tell me what I'm seeing."

Ned pointed to the cluster moving. "Here are the tagged iguanas they caught and took with them. They'll eventually move out of range of my receivers." He tapped on the other side of the screen. "And these are out there where we tagged them still in a state of torpor. It'll be fun to track their movements, too."

I'd called Ned yesterday afternoon to ask if he had a gadget that could track the movement of individual iguanas. After spirited brainstorming, Ned had fashioned an elegant solution. Something to do with hybrid Doppler, radio transmitters, and something, something, something. He then called the Lizard Liquidators to request an appointment for them to take away stiff iguanas this morning.

What could go wrong?

It was a calculated risk in two ways. One of the Lizard Liquidators might discover the devices. But Ned had reduced the size of the trackers to something the size of two grains of rice with an inch-long spike that he'd painted to blend in. He placed each tracker along the animal's spine and above its lower hips. It was a spot most handlers wouldn't touch while moving them around.

The second risk was that Operation Iguana Tracker assumed that Ethan was going to go along with my plan, which he did. My team was going to focus on getting photographic or video proof that Lizard Liquidators was still releasing iguanas. Being able to show individual iguanas going in and out of captivity would be a delightful bonus.

Ned helped me load a few receivers and antennas into my car. "I'll have Sparky install these tonight," I said.

Ned patted me on the back as I closed my car's hatch. "We might not need them, I already have receivers throughout the west side for my bird rehab work, but this will ensure we have better coverage at their warehouse on 12 Mile Road and the areas where Zorin has been releasing the iguanas, including where we found the zip-tie in the water."

"Thanks." I grabbed my camera and bag and put them in my back seat.

Ned took a couple of steps toward his house and waved me to follow him. "Let's have a proper breakfast and watch the iguanas in those trees get lively with the sunrise."

I looked at my watch; it was almost 8:00 a.m. "Why not," I said. "Ethan told me not to do anything until he called later today."

"A request I'm sure you'll ignore." Ned cackled like a hyena.

He made me laugh. "True, but even a spy girl's got to eat."

"Now you're talking!"

Chapter 47

11:00 a.m.

Common loons winter on Galveston Island, and many prefer to dive for food in the protected waters of Offatts Bayou. Their haunting calls echo and evoke fear, reflection, loneliness, and wailing. Or maybe that was just what was going on inside my head as I watched them from my car. I felt stuck in a holding pattern and like I was plunging toward concrete at the same time. The loons' eerie trills reverbed on top of one another in a complex dance of hollow sound.

I looked down at my daily list, hoping it would help calm the reverb going on in my brain. The top of the page said TODAY.

Focus on today, Xena, on what you can control or affect.

And therein was the challenge with this case; there was so much I couldn't, perhaps shouldn't, control. Tough medicine for a self-proclaimed recovering control freak. Today's theme was transitions. Many of the next steps in this case had transitioned to Ethan and his team. Quintana Flores changed in my mind from curiosity to suspicion. Ultima Penelope

Roger was moving to Los Angeles. Rodent's business had transitioned to Skeeter and his bumbling son, Andy.

After his disastrous drive down Sixty-First Street with the zombie iguanas, Andy needed a dozen stitches and a lot of skin glue but was going to be all right. I know you were wondering.

There were promising transitions, too, like my productive partnership with Ethan and budding friendship with Agatha. First on my list for today was to update Gregory on my meetings with Agatha and give him my wholehearted blessing to hire Agatha for contract gigs. That conversation went well, and Gregory was glad to hear that my disputes with the Houston executives would soon be resolved. I then texted Agatha to say hello and thank her for a lovely and productive time Monday night. She texted me a picture of the poetry collection she'd ordered from Amazon. It was a chapbook written by Rod Erogenous titled *Horses.*

I sent Sasha an e-mail congratulating her on her terrific live coverage and follow-up of Operation Stiff Lizard. I wished her well in her new role as Reporter-1. Why? Because that's what caring people do, right? They write thank-you notes and send good wishes. I was learning how to people… Another transition.

Ant was happy to hear from me but unable to speak right then. Said he would call me later, after the *Twisted Ambition* pulled away from Grand Cayman, because there was too much to do before then. I looked forward to checking with him and planting a little seed in case we needed to interview, or worse, apprehend Quintana.

Ethan suggested that, had Dora not contacted Moody

Gardens looking for a herpetologist and Ant not asked us to bust his gigolo, neither he nor I would fathom what was going on regarding who killed Rodent Roger. My philosophy has always been that deliberate actions drive our successes. And while that's true in part, it's clear some of it is just reverb.

Chapter 48

10:15 p.m.

Rock opera music from the band Muse blared in my noise-canceling earphones while I poured a Scotch and made up a plate of leftover cheese and crackers. I'd gotten a text from Sparky saying he'd installed and tested all but one transmitter and was going to go home after he finished. He'd not seen Zorin or any of the Lizard Liquidators. Ant had texted me, too, to let me know he'd be calling in twenty minutes.

I sat in my home office and googled *Richard Platt*, aka Fatty. Ugh! Such a common name. He could be a wrestling coach, a Hollywood agent, or a million other people. Then I tried *Fatty* and *Iguanas*. Better. Besides Jenny's Facebook posts for Operation Stiff Lizard, I found a link to the website BeAnIguanaHunter.com. Fatty apparently taught people how to make money catching and dispositioning green iguanas.

The music cut off in my headphones for an incoming call. "This is Xena."

"I'm so sorry," Ant said. *"What a day we've had on Grand Cayman today. Beach conditions were dreadful, and they canceled a lot of the shore excursions."*

"Oh no!" I said, faking an interest. Because that's what people do, right?

"It's not the first time and one reason we'll be shifting over to Jamaica for this five-day itinerary next season."

I grabbed my pen. "You won't go to Grand Cayman?"

"People prefer Jamaica for a lot of reasons. It's the right thing to do, even if it means we'll part ways with Quintana."

"That's a big change," I said with genuine interest. "Does she know this yet?"

"Of course. We plan at least two seasons ahead. She knew three months ago. What a lovely human being. She tells me she's got something else cooking, and I've no doubt. That woman is always thinking of novel ways to get donations for her foundation."

That must've been what triggered her to dream up the idea to infect Galveston with an invasive species that only she and her minions could handle. For a fee.

Sorry. Do I sound bitter? I rebel hell am.

Did I tell Ant that his sparkplug of a performer likely played a role in killing my friend? No, I did not.

"Business is business, eh?" I said, faking my calm. "I'm so glad she'll be fine."

"I wish all my entertainers were as easy to deal with as Dr. Q." Ant sighed again. *"Everyone on the ship is happy, now, with free drinks and dollar oysters, so I'm all yours. Anyone who gets a pearl wins a thousand dollars."* Ant lowered his voice. *"There are no pearls."*

I asked Ant how things were going with Rascal and he said all was well and that Rascal had made up a story of a new fiancée back home to explain to his co-workers why he's no longer hitting on rich passengers.

"Terrific," I said. "Let me know if you need a booster shot of tough love; I'd be happy to do that."

"Wonderful. What luck that Quintana told me about you."

"I agree. Speaking of Quintana again, I'd love to talk with her about meeting when the ship comes back to Galveston on Sunday. Perhaps you can transfer me to her room once our conversation has concluded."

"Xena, I would if I could, but Quintana isn't onboard."

I stopped doodling and turned up my headphones. "What do you mean?"

"She stayed on Grand Cayman and took a flight to Houston this afternoon."

My stomach tightened and my mind went into overdrive wondering why Quintana got off the ship mid-trip. "Was there an emergency? I'd be happy to help her if I can."

Ant chuckled. *"No emergency. She's done this a few times. She takes the same three-hour nonstop flight on United."*

I loaded up the United Airlines website.

"It's not uncommon for our entertainers to hop on and off the ship. One of the staff takes care of her animals."

I could feel sweat on my forehead. I found the United flight but needed to confirm. "Do you remember when she landed in Houston?"

"Sure, because I booked a driver for her. She landed at 6:45 p.m. your time. She's probably already on the island. Send her

an e-mail. I'm sure she'd be happy to meet with you."

I panicked as I looked at my calendar to find the date I met Ant and Q the first time. It was Saturday, March 3.

"I will, thanks," I said, faking that I wasn't about to explode. "You mentioned that it's pretty common for entertainers to hop on and off. That first day we met…I think it was a Saturday. Was Q just getting off the ship or coming back on?"

Ant chuckled. *"On. That's why she was a few minutes late. She'd gone through security to get her luggage back on the ship, then turned around and went back through security to meet with you."*

Bile rose in my throat and the ramifications of this shocking information were hitting me like a Mack truck. "She took that same flight to Houston?"

"I think so," Ant said.

I muted my headphone and took a deep breath and looked at the time. "Thanks for filling in for her. It ended up a win-win situation."

"Absolutely."

I tapped my pen several times. "Ant, I'm sorry, but I really need to go. Let's catch up again soon, OK?"

"I'm hoping you'll sail with us, Xena."

"You never know!"

I texted Sparky. *Abandon operation. If you're still out in the field, pack up quickly and meet me at the spy shop.*

I texted Ethan. *911: Call me now.*

My cell phone rang.

"Xena, I know Sparky's been shot. I'm on my way. I'll see you when I arrive."

"WHAT!!??"

Chapter 49

10:55 p.m.

"Sparky's been shot?!" I ran around my house getting shoes on, grabbing my purse, running down the stairs. Took my keys off the hook and locked the door.

"Isn't that why you're calling?" Ethan sounded amped up now, too.

I started my car, but then realized I didn't know where I was going. "Ethan, I know nothing about this. I'm in my car. What's happened and where's Sparky?"

"Shit. It happened about an hour ago. All I know is shots were fired, one person hit. The neighbor who called 911 on their phone said the victim says his name is Sparky. I'll text you the address, ambulance is in route."

I put my phone in hands-free. "I'm already driving west, tell me where to go."

"Eckert Drive. Take San Luis, then a right on 11 Mile Road, left on Stewart, right on Eckert, follow the lights. He was parked along Lafitte's Cove Nature Preserve."

I was gripping the steering wheel as if my life depended

on it. "I know where that is. At least he's talking. This can't be happening."

I could hear Ethan's siren on his car and the sound of his engine. He was hauling. *"Right, he could say his name. Now tell me why you texted me."*

I was drumming my thighs and breathing so hard I felt dizzy. "She's here. Quintana Flores is in Galveston."

"Not on the ship?"

I was driving like a maniac, hoping I didn't run into another maniac. *Don't you move into my lane. Turn green, turn green. Nobody do anything stupid.* "She got off in Grand Cayman and flew into IAH this afternoon. Landed at six-thirty."

Ethan swerved. His breathing was elevated. *"Well, that's a whole new wrinkle."*

You know how they say that when you're injured or dying, your whole life flashes in front of you? The same happens when you're worried you might lose someone, except it's moments you spent with them that you see. Visuals of Sparky pushed through the mess in my mind. "There's more. She did the same thing the week Rodent was killed. She was here on the island and unaccounted for."

"We'll talk when you get here. I just parked." Ethan's car door slammed, and the line disconnected.

As much as I wanted to be there in an instant, the Laffite's Cove Nature Preserve was eighteen miles from my house and would take the better part of thirty minutes to reach. I knew the mileage because I often used it as a waypoint during my training rides.

I focused on my breathing and tried to calm down. I pushed for Siri. "Call Dora."

She picked up. *"Hey—"*

"Where are you?" I crossed Sixty-First Street. It should be clear sailing from here with very few traffic lights.

"I'm home. What's wrong?"

"Someone shot Sparky. He was at Lafitte's Cove Nature Preserve. Ethan and the ambulance are there. I'm on my way. That's all I know. Wanted to make sure you're safe. I'm sure they'll take him to UTMB, but I'll text you. Lock your doors and keep your ditty bag close."

"Be careful driving."

"I will. Gotta go."

Diamond Beach. Making good time. I pushed for Siri again. "Call Steve."

Steve answered; he was driving, too. *"You calling about the shooting? I heard it on the police scanner and am on my way."*

Good. I'd need Steve's shoulder. "They shot Sparky!"

His engine revved, and a horn beeped. *"Who? How?"*

"Don't know anything, I just passed the Tipsy Turtle and will be there in seven."

"I'm right behind you," he said.

Chapter 50

11:25 p.m.

As I turned onto Eckert Drive, I saw the lights. Police, fire, and an ambulance heading straight for me. I pulled to the side of the road to let the ambulance pass.

Sparky's in there. I need to turn around. Check in with Ethan, then go.

I pulled up as close as I could and got out. They had police tape around Sparky's car and a larger area in the park. I walked up to the tape and searched for Ethan. "Ethan!"

He waved and came over to me, right up to the tape. But he didn't invite me into the scene. "They just took him to the UTMB trauma center. He's unconscious but still alive. Gunshot to his chest." Ethan was panting, but he seemed calm. "Do you know why he was here?"

"He was attaching a transmitter. To one of those trees or a pole. To pick up signals from iguanas that Ned and I tagged with trackers." The weight of what we'd done hit me and I stumbled. "Quintana wasn't supposed to be here."

"I know. We don't know if she had anything to do with

this or if it this has anything to do with Rodent's case. Not much to go on right now."

I grabbed my head with both hands and looked around. "I need to go to Sparky. I need to warn Ned."

Ethan lowered his gaze to look me in the eye. "Xena, they'll not let you see him or give you any information because you're not family. Give Ned a call so you're sure he's all right, but I think the best thing you can do is help us identify what belongs to Sparky so we might know if the shooter left us any evidence. This place will crawl with media in a few minutes, and I don't want your picture in the papers or on the television. Can you do that?"

Ethan was right. I shouldn't be seen at the crime scene, especially if Quintana had any involvement. I wiped my eyes and nodded.

Ethan walked me over and introduced me to the forensics person processing Sparky's car. He put white booties on my feet, gave me gloves, and asked me to look and tell him if I saw anything that didn't belong to Sparky or was obviously missing. I tiptoed around his car while trying not to lose my composure. I didn't see any blood and wondered if they'd shot him somewhere else. All I could think about was that I'd put him in danger.

"All of this is his," I said. "I'm not sure anything is missing."

Ethan led me back to the other side of the tape. "My guys are talking to neighbors. It'll take time to process the site. You and I both know it's best you go now that Flores is on the island. Stay at home. Do not investigate this. I can't stress this enough—do nothing." Ethan gave my shoulder a friendly push. But it was a push.

I ran to my car and got in. I texted Steve. *When I told you it was Sparky, that was off the record. Not releasing the victim's name yet. Got it?*

Steve's car pulled beside mine. We looked at each other.

I texted. *Steve, this is important. You don't know who they shot and I'm not here. Got it?*

I looked again at Steve, who was still sitting in his car.

OK. For now. He texted.

I backed out and drove away. As I turned left onto San Luis Pass, I screamed in my car so loud it echoed.

Chapter 51

Day 17, Friday, March 16
12:05 a.m.

Ned was sleeping when I called to tell him I was on my way to his house. I was happy to hear his groggy, aggravated voice because it meant he was safe. He'd put on a robe and some coffee by the time I got there and met me outside.

After filling in Ned on what had happened, I could see the pain and guilt on his face. His vibrant smile had turned into a pallid frown and drooping eyes.

I held his shoulders. "This was my idea, my plan. I'm the one responsible."

"I was just as eager as you. If Quintana saw one of those iguanas, she might've noticed the tracker."

"We have no reason to believe that's what happened, but that's why I want to make sure we keep you safe. If they know about the trackers, Zorin will guess they came from you."

We sat for a few minutes and just stared at each other.

Ned sat up. "Do you know if Sparky got the transmitter at Lafitte's Cove installed?"

I shook my head. "I didn't see the transmitter in his car."

Ned ran into his office and started typing on his computer. I knew what he was doing. He was checking to see if the transmitter was operational and had picked up any iguana signals. If Sparky was there when Zorin released a batch of animals, they might've clashed.

I followed and stood behind Ned as he worked. He was looking at long lists of numbers and time stamps and then switched over to the modeling program that showed the green dots.

"Bingo!" Ned turned to me. "The transmitter is working, and it's showing that two tagged iguanas are in Lafitte's Cove right now."

I bent to get a closer look. "You're sure?"

"Yes."

"That's proof that they're releasing the iguanas and were in the area where someone shot Sparky. Can you tell what time they released them?"

"Roughly." Ned typed and went back and forth from the number lists to the black-and-green screen. He explained that he'd programmed the transmitters to scan for pings every thirty minutes. All ten of the captured and tagged iguanas pinged in a cluster near 12 Mile Road until 9:17 p.m. They were in the warehouse. Then, on the next measurement, only half these animals remained.

"We know they left with some iguanas between 9:18 and 9:36 p.m., right?" I asked.

"Right." He went back to the lists of numbers, then copied and pasted a data set and went back to the modeling program. "At 9:50 p.m., the transmitter at Lafitte's Cove started generating data and two of the iguanas with trackers were within range."

"What's the range of these transmitters?"

"About a quarter of a mile." Ned switched to a Google map of the island. We were thinking the same thing.

"And since we know that Lafitte's Cove is just past 11 Mile Road, if the iguanas had escaped, they'd have to have traveled about two-thirds of a mile in…" I looked at all the times I'd written on Ned's notepad. "No more than thirty-two minutes. Damn, that sounds possible."

"But not probable, given the streets and canals between 11 Mile Road and 12 Mile Road. I think that was Zorin's first stop." Ned typed and then pulled up another screen with green dots. "We still have Zorin on releasing iguanas because transmitters picked up the other three tagged animals near where you found Rodent's van at the end of Indian Beach Drive. That's at least five miles west."

I was tapping my finger on my lips and trying to keep track of everything Ned was saying. "At what time did those iguanas ping at Indian Beach Drive?"

"9:10 p.m. But the iguanas might've been there up to twenty-nine minutes earlier."

"Iguanas are fast, but not that fast. This proves they released iguanas tonight." I kissed Ned on the cheek.

"And if they had an encounter with Sparky, they kept going on their route afterward."

"That complicates things, but I'll relish this minor victory."

I dialed Ethan, and he didn't pick up. I texted him. Call me *ASAP. Have proof Zorin dumped iguanas in the area tonight.*

Ethan called back after fifteen minutes and I told him the about the data Ned had collected from the tagged iguanas and what we believed it meant. He gave me the name and e-mail address of the forensics team captain so Ned could send him the number lists and graphs, along with information about the tracking devices and Ned's credentials.

"He'll tell me if we can use it to bring Montaño in for questioning," Ethan explained.

"What about Quintana?" I asked, knowing full well that none of this connected her to any crime.

"In time, perhaps." Ethan's car door dinged. He was going somewhere. *"If this pans out, it'll be a good lead, Xena, which we welcome. The shooter didn't leave us any obvious clues as to their identity or motive. It's early in the investigation, however, and damn early in the morning. Get some rest. I'll call you later, but it might not be until afternoon."*

I sighed. "All right."

Ethan's car door closed. *"I hope Sparky pulls through."*

And with that comment, I plummeted back into the darkness with the realization that Sparky might die. And I'd put him in harm's way.

Chapter 52

2:00 a.m.

Dora insisted she'd wait in the reception area of the UTMB Emergency Department for news from Sparky's parents about his condition. She'd known Dierdre and Walter Wiley for years, and they'd promised to keep her in the loop, knowing we'd not get any information from the hospital. I was glad Dora was there because I knew she'd be safe at the hospital.

I'd thought about calling Gregory, and even Agatha, but knew they'd both say the same things Ned had: don't blame myself, hopefully he'll survive, have patience while Ethan and his team work to arrest those responsible. But I didn't want to hear it.

Instead, I stared at my security camera feeds and sat on the floor in the corner of my office. At 3:00 a.m., I got my gun out of my home safe, loaded it, locked the safety, and placed it in my bag. At 4:00 a.m., I streamed songs from the Amazon playlist called *Music for Sad Times* and drank plain soymilk. Not Scotch. I needed to be alert and strong.

My cellphone ringtone jolted me awake. It was Dora.

"Any word?" I thrashed my head back and forth to wake up and looked at my watch. It was 6:25 a.m.

"He's going to pull through, Xena." Her voice was animated and strong.

My eyes teared up with relief.

"His mother said the doctor thinks he'll make a full recovery. Isn't that wonderful?"

"Yes," I said. "Can we see Sparky? I'd like to talk with him, and I know Ethan does, too."

"Not yet, maybe not today." Dora's voice was more measured. *"He's lost a lot of blood and was in surgery for several hours. They're keeping him sedated."*

"Oh." I felt disappointed. "What's important is that he's getting world-class care and will survive this."

Dora said Sparky's parents were taking shifts being with Sparky at the ICU and would let us know when he was alert. She was going home to take a shower and then open the spy shop at 10:00 a.m.

My stomach tightened because I wasn't sure if that would be safe. I had no reason to believe that Quintana or Zorin had connected Sparky to the spy shop but knew it wouldn't be hard for them to do so. It was a matter of when, not if.

"Maybe we should just close the shop today," I said.

"No, Xena, I'd feel better there than at home. Isn't there something I can research or document for the case? Something I can do to help?"

"Maybe, but —"

"If you're that worried, then join me. There's nothing we can't do together."

"You're right." I got up from where I'd fallen asleep on the floor. "See you at ten."

Chapter 53

12:30 p.m.

Dora had sent links to Ethan about Texas and federal laws that address the importation and release of invasive species. And I'd created an overall timeline for Rodent's disappearance and killing, and the attack on Sparky, that included what we knew of the whereabouts of our suspects: Zorin, Seth, Fatty, and Quintana. We'd downloaded any information we could find about the yearly financials of the Blue Iguana Foundation. We'd updated our case charts. These were the simple tasks, but it felt good to be productive.

Ethan called with mixed news. He was pleased when I told him Sparky's mother said he'd survive and said that the hospital had given him a similar update on Sparky's condition. Forensics green-lighted use of Ned's tracking information, and Ethan felt they had an excellent shot at charging Zorin and company with the release of invasive species. Video captured on a Ring doorbell showed Zorin's white van leaving Eckert Drive minutes before someone shot Sparky. A few other cars entered and left the neighborhood, but nothing suspicious. His team had rounded up the three Lizard Liquidators, brought them to the station, and would question them soon. Quintana hadn't been with any of the men when detectives went to their homes, and there was no sign that she, or any woman, had been staying at Mr. Pratt's apartment. Ethan confirmed that they'd be asking each man if they knew Dr. Flores.

"I wanted you to know that we've not located Dr. Flores, so watch your back," Ethan warned. *"Do not attempt to find her. I repeat, do not try to find Dr. Flores. But if her whereabouts become known to you, I expect you'll let me know."*

Translation? Try to find her.

"I understand," I said.

Dora and I brainstormed ways we could find where Quintana was hiding on the island, if she was on the island. We made a list of hotels that accepted cash and didn't require identification to get a room. We knew she had a driver from Houston International Airport because Ant had set it up. If she rented a car here on the island, there were just a few places to choose from. We listed known or probable contacts she had in Galveston.

My challenge was that I didn't want to leave Dora alone at the spy shop and could do very little to check out any of our leads from the shop. I signed for our lunch delivery of muffalettas from Maceo's and joined Dora in the meeting room.

"Sit and have lunch," I said to Dora. "Let's shift gears from guessing where she might be to what's going on inside Quintana's mind. Let's assume she's heard the GPD have taken in Zorin, Fatty, and Seth for questioning. This news is unnerving her if she's the boss of the operation, which we believe she is. What's she doing right now? What's she thinking? What's motivating her? Who is she calling?"

Dora grabbed a quarter muffaletta and an iced tea and sat next to me. We both looked like a tractor had driven over us, and metaphorically that was true. Tea and food would help.

Dora ate for a few minutes before saying anything. "We know she's supposed to get back on the *Twisted Ambition* tomorrow. I assume she's doing a risk-benefit calculation in her head about that. While reporting for duty would be a risk, it's also her ticket out of the country."

I nodded. "Yes, yes, that's excellent. And her assessment will address concerns about her potential criminal liability and her financial health."

"We know how motivated Quintana is by money," Dora said.

We ate and mulled this over for another few minutes.

"Dora," I began, "where'd the rich Dora Baker leave things with Quintana regarding a donation to her foundation?"

"The last thing I told her was that her blue iguanas were extraordinary and that she should expect to hear from my assistant regarding a sizeable donation."

"She gave you her e-mail address, right?"

Dora nodded.

"What if Dora Baker's assistant sent Q an e-mail saying Ms. Baker has decided to give the Blue Iguana Foundation an initial donation of twenty-five thousand dollars..."

"Ooh, and she's worried about how to best send it so it's secure."

"And that she's willing to have her driver meet up with her at the ship and give her a cashier's check or cash, whichever she prefers. As long as she gets a receipt for accounting purposes."

"I'll take the cash, please," Dora said, imitating Quintana's perky voice.

We both laughed.

"But could that work?" I asked. "And what would we do with her if she arrived? We might not know if Ethan has enough to question her until tomorrow or later."

"Could we try to set up the exchange and abort it if Ethan tells us to?"

"That's a brilliant idea. One thing, though. If we do this, I need you somewhere I know you're safe. Not at home. Not here."

"Don't you know someone at the Galvez?"

I smiled. "Indeed, I do."

Dora and I spent the next hour drafting the perfect e-mail to send Quintana, and at 2:07 p.m. we pressed SEND. Dora then grabbed an overnight case and her ditty bag and checked into the Hotel Galvez under the name Szasz Roderick.

I sat at the spy shop alone with my ditty bag and gun next to me at all times. Diedre Wiley called to say Sparky was doing better than his doctor expected, but they planned to keep him sedated until tomorrow sometime.

At 6:28 p.m. Dora received an e-mail from Quintana, who wrote she'd be "thrilled and honored to bring her significant monetary gift to the foundation." Quintana mentioned that she'd had problems depositing cashier's checks in Grand Cayman and that cash would be safer. She offered a receipt on the foundation's letterhead for Dora's accountant.

We worked together on the response, which we sent at 8:11 p.m. D. Baker's assistant stressed that they'd need her response by 11:00 a.m. so Ms. Baker could withdraw the cash from the bank before it closed, as well as schedule her driver to get the money from Houston to Galveston on Sunday. At 8:13 p.m., Quintana responded and agreed to our timing and plan.

I turned off the lights in the spy shop and opened the blinds, then sat at the sales counter watching people drive and walk by. I tapped my fingers on the glass as I contemplated what I would share with Ethan. Just as I was about to call him, he called me.

Chapter 54

Day 18, Saturday, March 17
11:15 a.m.

I had to wait until 11:00 a.m. to get a cherry pie and key lime pie (Sparky's favorites) from the Old Moon Deli and Pies shop. I then drove to the UTMB building that held the Surgical Intensive Care Unit. I knew they wouldn't let me see Sparky and that doctors still had him sedated. But his mom, Deirdre, said she'd sneak the pies into his room. We'd talked on the phone earlier and agreed that pie smells would give Sparky added motivation to heal and get better. Sparky was a pie-eating machine, and Old Moon Deli and Pies made the best in town. When you visit, plan to go there with an appetite.

"How is he?" I asked Dierdre.

"Better than yesterday, and the doctors seem quite pleased. He had a collapsed lung from the bullet and significant damage. But we're lucky because the bullet missed his heart and major arteries."

"The police are working hard to find the person

responsible." I looked into Dierdre's eyes to tell her the words I couldn't say about how much Sparky meant to me.

She nodded. "I know. They've got an officer guarding his room. You better go before they see us here with pies. I don't think they believe in their therapeutic effect." Dierdre winked at me.

It was true, Ethan and his team were working overtime to close these cases. He'd told me that all three Lizard Liquidators said they knew Quintana when the detective showed each one her photo. Zorin was her uncle, Fatty was her kissing cousin, and Seth said while Quintana wasn't a relative, he'd known her through the other two guys. Seth also copped to copulating with Ms. Flores whenever she was inclined. That sounded like my big libido boy Seth. All three men said Quintana had nothing to do with the business but was a naturally bossy person, so she might think she's in charge. All three said—yes, all three—they didn't know where Quintana was and that she had expensive tastes. In other words, they'd given rehearsed answers, which meant she was staying in a crappy pay-by-the-hour motel. I'd staked out a few of the better fleabags last night, but never saw Quintana. Ethan also told me the two young guys had thrown Zorin under the bus. They said he was the only one releasing the iguanas at night and that they had nothing to do with it.

The status of the Lizard Liquidators: Ethan had charged Zorin with releasing an invasive species and was holding him while they searched his van and truck to determine if he had dumped the initial population of iguanas on the island. We knew he had but lacked enough evidence for a charge. Ethan said he'd have to cut Zorin loose by Monday since all the GPD had right now was a gross misdemeanor charge. Fatty was released but knew he was a person of interest in Rodent's murder because the detective who questioned him said clients didn't see him with the other two guys on the Friday that someone killed Rodent Roger. The police released Seth, who Ethan said didn't possess the brain power or work ethic to be a big player in this case. That sounded like my boy Seth.

I went to the spy shop, even though I'd put a sign on the door saying it was closed for staff vacations. I ate the Rueben sandwich I'd bought at Old Moon and loaded up my ditty bag. Yes, the one with the gun in it; I know you were wondering. Calls to Dora and Ned confirmed they were both safe and being careful.

It was a weird in-between time that I've experienced with many cases. The eerie quiet moments just before everything explodes in chaos. I locked up the shop and got in my car, hopeful that if I drove around enough, I might find Quintana or Fatty, who were surely working to cover their tracks and optimize their crumbling circumstances.

Chapter 55

Day 19, Sunday, March 18
9:15 a.m.

The limo and black cap were loaners from a guy we'd installed a security system for last year. I put on the blonde wig and fake boobs I often used when undercover, then added my latest accessary: plate-size sunglasses. Sasha had told me where to get them on the island for five bucks. The black suit made it official—I looked like a driver. I doused my neck and wrists with half a bottle of cheap musk. I didn't want Quintana getting too close.

The cruise port was bustling as usual. I pulled into one of the VIP spots close to the door. Farther down, a dark sedan had parked illegally. Although I guess it wasn't illegal for the police.

I see you. I texted Ethan.

To be clear, Ethan wasn't thrilled with the little plan that Dora and I had hatched, but it was marginally not illegal as long as all they did was ask Quintana to talk.

At 8:30, Quintana emerged from security. I wondered

how long she'd been on the ship and where she'd been hiding. I must've checked out ten places yesterday with no success. I had a theory she might've had another friend with benefits on the island.

She's here. I texted Ethan.

I rolled down my window just as Quintana walked up to the limo. She took a step back as the musk cloud hit her. "Clementine?" she asked.

"Yes," I said in a made-up raspy voice. I'd learned that eating Doritos fast without water made me sound like Kim Carnes. If that's too obscure a reference for you, readers, you can google her. You might remember her hit song "Bette Davis Eyes." Regular Doritos, by the way, not nacho cheese, which would've made my mouth and everything within five feet neon orange.

"I'm Dr. Flores. You work for Mrs. Baker, right?" Quintana bit her lip.

"Yes," I croaked. "Mrs. Baker asked me to check your ID."

Quintana nodded and started looking inside her purse. I could see Ethan and two of his detectives walking up to her.

"Are you Quintana Flores?" Ethan said.

Quintana spun around and jumped back a step. "Yes. Who are you?"

Ethan introduced himself and his detectives and asked if she would talk with them about her uncle Zorin Montaño.

Quintana nodded and looked back at me, then looked at Ethan. "Sure, but I only have a few minutes. I work on this ship."

Ethan walked Quintana down the sidewalk closer to their car. They talked for several minutes. Quintana checked to ensure I was still there every minute or two. Their conversation got more animated after about ten minutes. Quintana pointed at the ship several times. Ethan shook his head and handed her his business card.

Quintana turned and bounded to and through the door to security.

Ethan talked on his radio, then looked around. The two detectives got into the dark sedan and Ethan walked up to me. "Nice disguise, but what's that smell?"

"Malibu Musk. It was all the rage in the eighties. You let her go."

"Had to," Ethan said. "All we have is suspicions and weak links at this point. She said she loves her uncle but knows nothing about his business. Poor old guy. If we get more evidence against Fatty or Seth, we'll give them an incentive to give her up if we can. We'll chat with her again."

"And there's Sparky. Hopefully he knows who shot him."

"I'll talk with him later today or tomorrow." Ethan tapped on the car limo door. "We'll get her, Xena."

"I hope so."

"You were right about the money," he said. "As much as we knew she wanted it, she was smart enough not to take anything from you while we were watching."

Ethan walked back to his car and left. That was my cue to depart because I wasn't prepared for her to walk back out and expect twenty-five grand in cash from me.

I removed my disguise, took a shower, and then gave the limo an inside-out cleaning to get rid of the musk smell and Dorito crumbs before returning it. After that, I punched the hell out of Betty 2, and it felt good.

Chapter 56

4:30 p.m.

The ship's horn blares as the *Twisted Ambition* pulls away from the dock. With just three hours of sunlight left, I've no time to waste. I suck on the mouthpiece of my hydration backpack and push off down Twenty-Ninth Street. Within ten minutes, I've cleared Sixty-First Street, and it's a smooth ride west.

That's right, readers. You've caught up to where I currently am in this ~~journey~~ ~~triumph~~ ~~investigation~~ ~~shit-show~~ story. As you can imagine, I'm miffed at Ethan because he failed to find some reason to hold Quintana Flores in Galveston. Now our prime murder and assault suspect—never mind the whole debacle of dumping a fast-breeding invasive species on our fair island—is sailing out of US territorial waters.

I put things into perspective. Focus on what I can control. Like preparing for the triathlon I hope to finish in four weeks. That's one week before I turn the big four-oh, if you've been paying attention.

Sunday afternoon is the best time to bike west on San

Luis Pass because all the traffic is going the opposite direction as the weekenders and vacationers head off the island. The wind is light and I go twenty-two miles per hour. My cellphone rings. I look down at the screen and recognize Ant's number. I push the ANSWER button on the one AirPod I've got in my ear (never two while riding; safety first).

I find a break in the eastbound traffic and turn around to head back to the shop. For the next five minutes Ant shouts in my ear. Something about Quintana taking hostages. I tell Ant that Dora will call him in a minute, and then tell Dora to call Ant and meet me ASAP.

Right now, I'm peddling as fast as I can down Twenty-Fifth Street toward my spy shop. With a hop over the trolley tracks, a turn down the alley, a sharp left into the parking lot, and a short swervy skid (for show), I'm eye to eye with my brilliant operations manager who's loading the cargo van we use for stings and stakeouts. I swing my leg over the bicycle seat. "Got my big ditty bag?"

Dora nods and gives me an exuberant thumbs-up. "And the overalls Ant suggested you wear. I threw in the red scarf that was on your desk." She gets in and starts the engine. "We've only got five minutes until they leave to pick up the pilot captain. The name of your boat driver is Barnacle."

"Of course it is." I climb into the back of the van, pull the curtain, peel off my damp swim/run/bike one-piece triathlon suit and rummage through my bag. "Damn!" Forgot to replenish underwear in my ditty bag. I put on my go-to clingy black dress and wrap the scarf around my neck. Then slip on the navy-blue overalls over the dress. The crotch pushes the skirt up over my hips. I pull on black running shoes, no socks, and return to the front seat.

We're nearly there. "Tell me again what Ant said."

Dora pulls the steering wheel hard right to avoid hitting an old lady pushing a shopping cart, or maybe that was Gertie, in the middle of the street. "Our suspect is having a meltdown and has taken the Bearded Lady Barbershop Quartet hostage. She wants the ship to change course. Drug use is likely."

I pulled my hair into a short ponytail. "All that happened since the ship left port? Ethan's brief chat with Quintana must've made her panic."

"Ant thinks it might be a bluff, but he and the captain want us—meaning you—to come fix things so they don't have to get headquarters or the Coasties involved. The security director worries about booby-traps." Dora points to my bag. "I added a few toys from Sparky's secret stash. Video cam glasses; touch the nose bridge for two seconds to record. Tranquilizer blow darts; big ones for humans, smaller for iguanas. Try not to mix them up. And tear gas hidden in a Mountain Dew can. It's voice activated when you yell"—Dora then whispers—"*Yahoo!* Emphasize the *hoo* for best results."

"Thankfully, that's not a word I use often."

"And why Sparky selected it over the more obvious choices of *cowabunga* or *shithole*."

"Smart. You remember what to tell Ethan after I've made it onboard, right?"

"I'll be cocked and loaded," Dora says.

Dora's comment reminds me I have a loaded gun in my ditty bag. "Here, take this. It's loaded, too."

Here we are at the marina and the pilot boat is pulling away from the dock.

"No!" I bolt out of the van, run down the pier, jump onboard, and land with a thud and sloppy somersault. While the boat bounces, I get up and wave like a dork, hoping to be picked for the kickball team. "Barnacle? I'm Xena Cali. The captain made arrange—"

"Stand there." Barnacle's face shows no emotion. He points to the railing that leads to the front of the boat and we head full throttle toward the *Twisted Ambition,* which has cleared the pass between Galveston and the Bolivar Peninsula.

Picture me, with spray from the six-foot waves in my face, staring at the small open doorway on the side of the large, moving cruise ship. Did I mention it's moving? Barnacle says eight or nine knots, which is about ten miles per hour. My baggy overalls flap in the wind and push my dress skirt farther up. I hope I don't get cotton burns in my lady parts.

The opening looks eight feet square and ten feet above the waterline. Two deckhands wearing life vests hold the sides of a rope ladder that runs from the top of the opening to several feet below it. The bottom of the ladder drums the side of the ship in the wind. A third man, maybe the pilot captain, stands behind the ladder.

A deckhand on my boat pushes a life vest into my hands and points for me to get out onto the bow. I freeze.

Barnacle waves me forward and points to the same place. "It's time."

The words take a few seconds to penetrate, and I feel nauseated.

The boat pulls alongside the ship, which is the size of a city, then slows to match its speed. We're just one or two feet away now. The pilot captain steps on the outside of the ladder, climbs down, and extends one leg to the boat. He grabs the railing, releases his hold on the ladder, and pulls himself onto the smaller vessel. He looks at me, nods, and moves aside so I can make the reverse transition.

Honestly, I'm terrified. I can leap from one building rooftop to another without blinking, but this scenario has disaster written all over it. I shake my head and shoulders to snap my mind back into action. There's not much to do but sigh and get this over with. I pull the life vest over my head but can't secure it because my ditty bag is too fat. If I end up in the water, it'll fall off for sure. I'll be shark chum anyway, right?

The boat looks glued to the cruise ship, but I know it's not. I let go of the railing and grab the rope ladder with both hands. The boat bounces in the wake of the larger vessel. My right hand loses grip and I dangle sideways.

"Go!" Barnacle yells.

I re-grasp the ladder rung and place both feet onto the narrow wooden step. The ladder, although being held by the deckhands, slides back and forth. One deckhand, who looks twelve years old, motions for me to climb.

My hands start near the bottom of the opening. I climb

four steps and then accept their help to get inside. The pilot boat pulls away from the ship.

A short hallway leads to what looks like a supply room with floor-to-ceiling steel shelving packed with boxes. Ant and two security guards are waiting for me. Ant puffs out a big breath and nods. "You made it. I assume this was your first time?"

"First and last. The pilot boat driver didn't seem very happy to pick me up."

Ant moves closer. "I had to tell him you were a critical crew member who'd missed the ship and had been trained for vessel-to-vessel transfers. He wouldn't have allowed you onboard otherwise. That's why I suggested overalls."

Vessel-to-vessel transfers? This is a regular thing? I consider throwing Ant overboard but know I might need his help to neutralize the situation. "Let's do this. Where are we going?"

"The Audacious Club lounge on the Platinum deck." Ant looks at me and runs a hand down his chin. "We'll have to find you something in the costume cabin, first. You can't go in there dressed like that; the passengers don't know what's going down. Just that their lounge is being used for a private gathering."

"No time." I yank off the life preserver and backpack, unzip the overalls and remember that my dress is bunched up at my waist and I'm not wearing underwear. I continue zipping and lift one leg, then the other, out of the overalls. I stand, extend my arms up and then bow. The guards stare at me and my black mamba tattoo. Ant's cheeks turn pink as he turns his head away.

I shrug, thankful I didn't blow off my waxing appointment, then pull down the tight skirt of my dress, kick off my tennies, slip on the black flats I had in my ditty bag, and re-wrap the red scarf around my neck. It matches nicely with the shiny lipstick I apply while repacking my bag.

"This good enough?"

Chapter 57

5:30 p.m.

Here's the situation. Quintana has hostages and some number of weapons. She wants Captain CC to drop her off at the Port of Havana, which logistically would be easy-peasy because the ship sails between Cuba and Cancun on its regular route. The problem is there'd be no way CC could do this without alerting the Audacious Cruise Line's home office and the US Coast Guard. The captain is highly motivated to keep both overseers at bay and unaware. Her year-end bonus will be kaput if Quintana gets her way. And while they want Quintana stopped, the captain is worried that if they sic their trigger-happy, ex-military security team on Q that she, and maybe others, will end up dead. Shots fired, pandemonium on the ship, etcetera, etcetera.

I tell Ant to prepare the captain to reverse course, but that she shouldn't turn around until I give the green light that I've neutralized Quintana. And that I want them to figure out some cover story to ensure the passengers don't mutiny—I can only solve one problem at a time—and all this maneuvering must happen before we sail out of US territorial waters.

I bet you think that's three miles from shore. Thankfully, US waters extend into the Gulf of Mexico twelve miles. Captain CC will still need to slow the ship way down. I tell Ant he needs a cover story for that, too.

Ant gives me the cards, keys, credentials, and ship map I need to get anywhere on the ship, and we part ways. I use the staff entrance to get into the Audacious Club. From the back of the bar, I can see the righteously bearded bearded ladies sitting smashed together in a padded booth. Quintana is pointing some kind of weapon at them and has her back to me, so I carefully unzip my ditty bag and slink into the bar and crouch down.

I look at my watch. Soon.

Carefully, very carefully, I place a few items on the bar where I'll reach them from the other side.

On cue, the captain calls Quintana and gets into an argument with her to give me some time and cover. They seem to be talking about Havana logistics and cigars.

I put on my swim goggles and slip out from behind the bar. I vault in the air, yelling "YahOOOO!" Just before I land on Quintana, one of the bearded ladies points and yells, "Incoming!"

Hey, bearded lady, whose side are you on?

Tear gas shoots out of the Mountain Dew can—two seconds too late, if you ask me—and Quintana turns and pulls the trigger on her taser. I go down on the floor and my muscles seize up.

Quintana coughs and stares at me from just a few inches away. "You? What are you doing here? Holy hell, you're a faking fraud." She might've said some other f-word, but I can't tell with all the wheezing. My muscles won't move. Quintana freaks out. She's going to blow up the ship. She's going to kill the bearded ladies. She's going to kill me. Blah, blah, blah.

The Bearded Lady Barbershop Quartet coughs and sings "Bring Back Those Good Old Days," presumably to calm down Quintana, but it's a godsend because it gives me a few seconds to get my muscles working.

Dora was right; the bearded ladies are very good.

I stand and grab my tranquilizer gun, but I'm still wobbly and uncoordinated and shoot one of the bearded ladies by mistake. I hit Quintana on the second try. She curses as she's falling into unconsciousness. Some crazy shit about my black mamba being eaten by a Cuban python and that I'm not wearing panties.

I zip-tie Quintana just in case I gave her the iguana dose tranquilizer and tell the bearded ladies I'm sorry I tranquilized one of them. I'm not really sorry on account that I hit the one who ruined my plan to jump Quintana.

The Bearded Lady Barbershop Triplet pick up their unconscious friend and head out of the Audacious Club singing "The Lion Sleeps Tonight." It doesn't sound quite right with only three harmony parts.

I call Ant on the ship's phone and tell him I've apprehended Quintana and the captain can return to Galveston. Ant informs me we're almost there because the captain has been moving backward for some time.

He says going backward for several miles is part of the *Fugitive on Board* drill that Captain CC told the passengers they'd get the privilege to see.

"There's no Fugitive on Board drill. Look out the window, Xena, there's Starbucks."

And he was right. I'd been having so much fun being tased that I hadn't noticed the ship slow, stop, and go backward. "Tell the captain she's got a lovely touch at the wheel."

"Tell her yourself. She's heading your way to discuss your ejection off the ship."

"Ejection?" I ask.

"You're not on the ship's manifest. That's a problem."

I step outside the Audacious Club, take off my goggles, and look down at the shopping promenade five decks below. Passengers dance and sing along to the Billy Preston tune "Will It Go Round in Circles." People in yellow leotards hand out lime-green shooters.

Someone taps on my shoulder. "Xena Cali, you're amazing. Here's your golden key to the *Twisted Ambition.* With it, you can sail anytime for free. Drinks are extra, of course."

I smile. "Captain CC, I'm honored."

She nods. "I need to get you off this ship now." The captain then leads me into the elevator.

"But what about my ditty bag?" I ask.

"We'll give it to the local cop who's taking Flores off the ship." She puts a special key in the elevator, twists it, and the elevator drops fast. The door opens. She leads me to an opening where I see the water below. It's closer to the water than the opening where I climbed in. The ship has docked.

Captain CC puts a life preserver on me and points. "I believe that's a friend of yours?"

I see Ned Quinn in his red boat. "That's Ned."

"Great. Go in feet first, stiff as a board, hands at your side. Hurts less. Again, thanks so much. Keep in touch."

Captain CC shoves me off the *Twisted Ambition* so fast I don't have time to react.

Who does that?

I plunge into the water not quite right and scream underwater. The water tastes like gas, so I press my mouth and eyes closed. The ship channel isn't optimal swimming water, if you know what I mean.

Ned drives over and heaves me onboard. "Xena, Xena, Xena, welcome aboard. Is that a black mamba? What happened to your panties?"

I find Ethan beside the paddy wagon that is taking Quintana to the GPD. I grab my phone out of my ditty bag and see I missed a text from Sparky. It's a picture of his bedsheets and the words Q SHOT ME THANKS FOR PIES written with a Sharpie marker.

Epilogue

Ethan charged Quintana with attempted murder and several counts related to intentionally infesting Galveston with invasive green iguanas. Rodent's murder investigation remains open. The forensic accountant Ethan had hired found the Lizard Liquidators' Texas and Grand Cayman bank accounts and confirmed that the company had been sending most of its money to the Blue Iguana Foundation. Ethan's FBI counterpart got a freeze on the assets of both organizations pending their conviction in the unlawful use of invasive species charges. They'd be required to pay the State of Texas for costs associated with capturing, killing, or controlling said invasive species, including their progeny. The foundation would be wiped out, in other words.

The endangered Grand Cayman blue iguana enjoyed a huge win when Prince Charles and Camilla Parker Bowles visited the island. Camilla fell in love with blue iguanas because their laid-back style reminded her of Chuck. She created a new foundation to support the lizard's conservation. British children across that country begged their parents for stuffed blue iguanas, and the media buzz sparked interest from Hollywood to produce an animated film set in Grand Cayman. Chickens will narrate the story.

I read that on Facebook; I know you were wondering.

I may have convinced Ethan to get a tattoo; I'll let you know.

Ned Quinn's research on the movements of green iguanas on the island won him a ten-year grant from the National Invasive Species Council, which is a part of the Department of the Interior. He converted half of his lab space to test natural contraceptives for female iguanas. His most successful intervention involved playing ragtime music through loudspeakers. Iguanas can't stand ragtime, apparently. Nor did Ned's neighbors, which is why his research will continue.

Ultima Penelope Roger was in the news for the seven-figure advance she received to write her memoir, tentatively titled *Method Writer*. In it, she'll take readers behind the scenes to show them how she recruits, performs with, and then writes about her trysts with sex models. The book is expected to break sales records. Show don't tell, indeed.

Skeeter became the *de facto* iguana expert on the island, opened a new branch of Southwest Exterminators and Wildlife Trapping, and promoted his son Andy to Executive Vice President. Andy and Sasha have been seen downing tequila shots at the Poop Deck.

Sparky made a full recovery and is dating his nurse, Aviana. I invited Sparky, Aviana, Dora, and Beauregard over to my house for dinner. It was my first adult dinner party and very fun. I catered from BLVD Seafood, of course. I'm no dummy! The two couples talked for far too long about how to set me up with a nice man. I vetoed *most* of their nominations. The dinner party served as a graduation of sorts, too. We held our wine glasses high and toasted Dale Carnegie in heaven—or wherever he is—and smiled.

The slimy ex-execs from Granny's Home accepted my deal for a truce. I sent them enough evidence to ensure their compliance. I have more, but you already assumed that.

I spent a long weekend in Houston, where I took Gregory and his wife, Lynn, to dinner at their favorite Japanese restaurant to celebrate his retirement and kick off their new life driving in an RV around the country. I then helped the new owner of his spy shop, Agatha Reacher (aka Hiba Olsen,) get set up for a fabulous grand reopening. Agatha and I signed a partnership deal and look forward to working together in the future. We both registered for next year's Houston Marathon and will train together when possible.

Steve Heart interviewed Basil Umber, a member of the Texas Invasive Plant and Pest Council, who summed up the state of the green iguana invasion on the island by saying we must face facts, we're in control mode (past eradication, containment, and management), and will be for the foreseeable future. Basil said islanders will need to find their new normal of what life looks like *with* the green iguana.

Sasha was promoted to Reporter-2 and given the city beat. That was code for batshit crazy stories best told by perky young voices who look good on Facebook, Instagram, and YouTube live streams. She'd told me that this was her dream job. I fixed her up with a minimalist ditty bag that'd help if she encountered any creeps on her new beat.

And I survived turning forty. Sort of. No one except Agatha knew I had a birthday, and I still say I'm thirty-something. That's perfectly normal, right? Agatha took me for a spa weekend in New Mexico. I loved the high desert environment and didn't want to come home. I know I'll be returning to the Land of Enchantment.

In four months, actually. Inspired my Agatha's epic dog-sled experience, I'll be spending a month in New Mexico. That's four weeks of hiking, camping, and living a quiet and reflective life. I might even meet a few new people with whom I can practice and hone my new peopling skills.

Right now, I'm parked under a tree in the Galveston Island State Park waiting for a friend. A large iguana plops down from the tree to sit on my warm car hood. I hold a big yellow hibiscus flower out my window.

Hello, Doug.

Request for Reviews

Reviews are the most powerful tools in my arsenal when it comes to getting attention for my books. As an indie author, I don't have the financial or marketing muscle of a New York publisher. Honest reviews of my books help bring them to the attention of other readers. If you've enjoyed this book, I'd be very grateful if you could spend five minutes leaving a review on the book's retail page or Goodreads.com.

Thank you very much.

Reader Newsletter and Free Book

Building a relationship with my readers is very important to me and one of the best things about being a writer. I occasionally send e-newsletters with details on upcoming book releases, humorous essays, and other news. If you sign up for my mailing list, you will also receive a free copy of the Spy Shop Mysteries prequel novella, *Ghost Rat.*

You can sign up at: www.lisahaneberg.com

Acknowledgements

Thanks to my big sister Monica, for being my eager and creative partner-in-research for matters concerning cruise ships and Grand Cayman blue iguanas. Thanks to my husband Bill, for encouraging my quirky side, even when doing so meant discussing iguana poop longer than seemed appropriate.

Thanks to Royal Caribbean Cruise Director Jeffrey Arpin for helping me better understand how things work onboard normal cruise ships. Although the *Twisted Ambition* is far from ordinary, your input helped me make my fantasy vessel marginally plausible.

Thanks to editors Jim Spivey and Jennifer Barricklow. I treasure your partnership and love the way you let my weirdness flow onto the pages while keeping the boo-boos off them.

Thanks to Stuart Bache and team for creating an amazing cover for this book and the others in the Spy Shop Mystery series. This cover, in particular, makes me fuchsia happy.

Thanks to the late, great Dale Carnegie, for teaching me, Xena, and billions of professionals how to people better. How cool was it that I worked your classic, "How to Win Friends and Influence People," into a murder mystery? Super cool, and thinking about it makes me smile.

Thanks to the Midsouth Writers – Adrielle, Dianne, Jen, Judy, Krista, Nancy, and Nell – for your support, encouragement, and helpful input. You're the best critique group I've ever had. I'd say I'm thankful that you're all so interested in my goofy stories, but that might be a bit of a head hop. You sure seem that way to me, and I feel lucky to be a member of this group.

Finally, thanks to the city of Galveston, Texas, for being enigmatic, gritty, fun, scary, smart, ridiculous, and so many other adjectives all rolled into one. I couldn't think of a better real setting for this fictional mystery series. I'm proud to call Galveston my favorite place to contemplate murder.

About the Author

Lisa Haneberg is the author of the Spy Shop Mysteries and over a dozen nonfiction books. She earned an MFA degree from Goddard College and is an active member of Sisters in Crime. Before writing crime fiction, Lisa was a human resources professional, specializing in internal investigations, for over 25 years. She lives with her husband and dog Hazel in Lexington, Kentucky. Her online home is at www.lisahaneberg.com. You can connect with Lisa on Twitter at @lisahaneberg, on Facebook at http://www.facebook.com/mysteryandmirth and you can send her an email at lisa@lisahaneberg.com.

Books in the Spy Shop Mysteries

Ghost Rat Series prequel novella

Toxic Octopus Book 1

Dead Pelican Book 2

Stiff Lizard Book 3

Books 4-7 in the series will be coming soon.